DARK MURDERS

LOUIE NUNZIATO

EDITED BY
TROY LAMBERT

TRIGGER WARNING

The following book is in the dark horror genre. As a result, it contains graphic content, adult language, sex, violence, and some depictions of rape. If you are triggered by this type of content, this book may not be for you.

If you are in an abusive situation, don't feel safe at home, or feel in danger from an individual, whether they are a member of your family, an acquaintance, or someone you work with, please seek help. Contact your local authorities, or call the National Domestic Abuse Hotline at 800-799-7233.

This is a work of fiction, and any resemblance of any character or person herein with an actual person is purely coincidental.

ONE
THE WAREHOUSE

S arah Kelly looked around her new home. Boxes sat in the corner, waiting to be unpacked. Her husband Michael had insisted on two things: that his military awards hang somewhere in the front room and her painting, the one she created for him after their honeymoon, be placed over the mantle above a good-sized fireplace in the front room of their quaint home.

At twenty-one, she felt lucky to have her own home and a great husband at such a young age. A foot taller than her, he towered over her 5'1" frame, something he often teased her about.

"You have to hand it to short people. Because they can't reach it anyway," he'd say with his infectious laugh.

They'd met when she played outside her childhood home at six.

"I'm Sarah. Do you live around here?" she asked shyly.

"Yeah, I live four houses that way," he said, pointing up the street. "I'm Michael."

"Would you like to play sometime? I don't have any brothers or sisters."

"Maybe, sometime. I don't have anyone around here to play with, either. I'm an only child, too." They'd become friends. He cared for and protected her as if she were his little sister.

On the playground, her in second grade and him in fourth grade, Michael told her, "One day, when I'm grown up, I want to marry a girl just like you." Sarah smiled.

They played ball in the backyard and explored the woods behind their homes together. After Sarah's parents got to know him and his family better, they trusted the kids to go on bike rides alone. Sarah felt like Michael was her protector, being older than her and a boy.

She still remembered the first day she told him she loved him. She was sixteen. He had just graduated high school. "Michael, we've been good friends for like ten years now. I just wanted to tell you... um...that I...I think I'm falling in love with you."

"Oh, Sarah! I've felt the same way about you for a long time. I was afraid to say anything because I didn't want to ruin our friendship. I love you, Sarah."

"I love you too. I was afraid to tell you for the same reason." They hugged and kissed. They announced their engagement several months after Sarah turned twenty.

Michael worked as a forest ranger. While his regular hours were set, he often worked a lot of overtime. The gorgeous sunset reminded her that he was due home anytime. She felt lucky to have a man who took care of her so well, a great provider and lover. Sarah couldn't think of anything he wouldn't do for her.

She gazed out the window as a slight breeze moved the leaves on the trees in a rhythmic, mesmerizing pattern that accented the beautiful orange and purple rays that shone through from behind. Her attention returned to the replay on television.

She heard Pastor Joe say, "The Bible tells us that we're all sinners and have fallen short of the glory of God and his kingdom. No one on earth can say they have never sinned. God tells us if you are guilty of one sin, you are guilty of them all. If you steal a pen from work or tell a lie, God considers you just as guilty as if you murdered someone."

A noise outside distracted her. "What was that?" She heard

another thump. She got up to investigate. She stood on her tiptoes to look out the peephole, but it was too high. Michael promised to install another one a bit lower as soon as possible. Opening the front door causally, she looked outside. Everything looked normal. She left the screen door locked and turned away. *It's probably one of the neighborhood cats getting into stuff again,* she thought.

She heard something behind her and spun around. The sliding glass door leading to the backyard stood open. She was sure she'd closed and locked it. She walked over, slid it shut, and engaged the lock. She dropped an old broom handle into the track that fit perfectly so the slider couldn't be opened even if it was unlocked. When she turned around, she came face to face with a man dressed all in black, black shoes, black pants, a black hoodie, and black leather gloves. The hoodie covered most of his face, the drawstrings pulled tight. He held a black leather bag in his hand that looked like an old doctor's bag.

Sarah screamed. Her heart pounded in her chest.

"Who the hell are you?" she asked, trying to keep her composure as she glanced around for anything she could use as a weapon. Too bad she'd just dropped the broom handle in the slider's track. She couldn't escape that way.

The figure didn't answer. He set the bag down on the floor. Sarah froze. With the man between her and the front door, he had her trapped.

"Get out of my house!" she screamed as the blood rushed from her face. "My husband will be home any minute!"

A small bottle and rag appeared in his hand. When he removed the lid, chloroform's faint, sweet odor instantly entered her nostrils. She pushed at him and ran around the couch to the front door. If she could get the screen door unlocked and get outside…

She felt herself yanked back by her long hair and thrown to the living room floor. Her head made a loud thud, and she saw stars. She wished she'd already put down the area rug. She attempted to sit up. She had to escape. Michael should be home any minute to rescue her.

The man put his foot in the middle of her chest and pushed her back down hard.

He tipped the bottle onto the rag and held her down with his foot. He leaned over and held it over her mouth and nose. She struggled and tried to push it away, but he was too strong.

"Don't fight it. It's okay. Shhhh... Sleep baby," an oddly familiar voice said softly in her ear. She still tried to push his hands away from her face, but it was no use. There was no air for her, only the mind-numbing chemical. Her body went limp, her struggles stopped, and her arms fell to her sides. Everything faded to black.

HE PICKED up Sarah's phone, but it was locked. He tried some simple codes people often use: 1,2,3,4 and 1,1,1,1, then 0,0,0,0. They didn't work, but he remembered his research and tried her birthday. No luck. Their wedding anniversary. That did the trick. He read some of her texts to and from her girlfriends.

"Ah, perfect," he said, choosing the name of a frequent texter who appeared to be her best friend. He found Michael's number and texted him with Sarah's phone.

"I'm spending the night at Laci's. She's having some serious problems.

I'll tell you about it when you get home tomorrow. I love you! Sarah XOXO"

Digging through Sarah's purse, he found her car keys. He put her cell phone in his pocket.

He pulled a syringe from his bag and inserted the needle into her thigh, giving her a hefty dose of tranquilizer.

He picked up the petite woman, threw her over his shoulder in a fireman's carry, picked up his black bag, and headed out the door to the garage. He dropped her into the back seat, tossed his leather bag on the floorboard, and closed the door. He slid behind the wheel, opened the garage door, and backed out.

Something didn't look right about the house. He looked left and right and pulled back in, hoping her husband was later than usual. It wouldn't be good for him to show up now. He returned inside and quickly turned on a table lamp and the porch light. He turned off the television and closed the blinds.

"That'll look more normal when hubby comes home."

He took a quick glance at the gauges as he backed out and noticed the gas tank was full. He drove three miles north until he saw a good place to toss her cell phone and sent one final text to her husband with a smile.

"*Love you, honey. Sweet dreams. See you tomorrow night!*" He added three heart emojis.

By the time the phone was tracked, it would initially take the investigation in the wrong direction. That would buy him all the time he needed.

Making a U-turn, he drove down an old country road almost thirty miles south to a dilapidated warehouse outside the city. It sat in the middle of a cracked, abandoned paved parking lot that had been empty for years. He drove slowly around the foundations of the buildings long ago torn down, weeds poking stubbornly through the cracks, and around a lone tumbleweed making its way lazily across the area.

He opened the roll-up door and drove in. Old wooden pallets, some moving blankets, and other junk littered the floor, and several sets of mostly empty shelves. As he pulled further in, the headlights revealed a couple of the moving blankets he had laid there earlier that evening. He parked with the lights shining them. He laid Sarah's still limp form on the blankets and stripped off almost all her clothes.

Sarah still wore a pair of lacy panties. Strips of muted light from the last of the sunset filtered in through cracks and small holes in the ceiling and metal sides of the warehouse. The sound of rats scurrying over the metal shelves echoed through the large building. He pulled a piece of duct tape off the roll and pressed it over her mouth in case she woke before he was finished.

He rubbed the crotch of her panties, then grabbed them with both hands and ripped them off with a single, rapid tug, a skill he'd developed over years of trial and error. Genetically extremely strong, and working out regularly helped make this endeavor possible. He turned her over, zip-tied her arms behind her, and flipped her onto her back again. He reached into his pocket and retrieved a condom. He'd kept his pubic area clean-shaven since he was a teenager. No need to leave evidence that would lead to his identity.

As he penetrated her, she woke, recognizing what was happening to her. Muffled screams failed to penetrate the duct tape. He punched her in the side, knocking the wind out of her, hearing at least one rib crack.

When she could breathe again, she tried to scream again. He slapped her hard. "Shut the fuck up, bitch, or I'll knock your ass out again." He didn't want to do that. Her muffled screams turned him on. It wasn't like there was anyone nearby to hear her.

She stopped, staring at him with wide eyes. He quickly yanked the tape off her mouth.

"Please, leave me alone," she begged. "Please don't kill me."

He put his hands around her throat, and she struggled for air. He moved in and out of her as she struggled. Once she lost consciousness, he let go in more ways than one. Her head fell back and struck the floor as he had a massive orgasm.

He finished and took a plastic bag from his pocket and wrapped the condom and his now-soiled gloves inside. He put on a new pair.

Once gloved again, he pulled her right leg up against the passenger side tire. He pulled a gas mask out of his bag and put it on. He got in the driver's seat and slowly drove the car forward, stopping with the right front tire on top of her ankle, pinning her in place. He left the engine running, got out, walked around the front of the car, and watched her for several minutes as the warehouse filled with exhaust fumes.

Sarah's eyes opened. She coughed and choked with every breath. The man stood over her, knowing how ominous he looked with the gas mask on his face. The sound of the engine echoed off the walls, and her choking made it impossible for her to scream.

Once she passed out, he stepped outside and waited a while to ensure she was dead. He went back to check and found the warehouse filled with exhaust fumes. He got down on his knees and put his ear to her chest. Nothing. She was dead.

Before he left, he ensured all the warehouse doors were closed.

He walked down to the bus stop, keeping his hood tight around his face, the leather bag in hand. He caught the next bus that passed and sat in the back, just another down-on-his-luck rider on his way to nowhere. He got off close to where he had parked his truck behind a closed store, two blocks from Sarah's home. He got in, started the old but reliable engine, and headed to his home, far from there.

TWO
NO MORE BABIES

The following evening when Sarah's husband, Michael, arrived home, there was still no sign of his wife, and he hadn't heard from her the entire day.

"Where the hell is she? She said she'd be home today. It doesn't look like she ever came home."

After looking through the house and calling out several times, his worry increased. He called his wife's cell phone. It went straight to voicemail every time.

"Where the hell is Laci's number, dammit!" He searched his own phone and found the number of one of her friends.

"Hi Brenda, it's Michael. Have you heard from Sarah?"

"Not lately. She's not home?"

"No, she left sometime yesterday. I got a text saying she was staying at Laci's house. Do you have her number by chance? I can't find it."

"Yeah, I'll text it to you."

"Thanks, Brenda. Let me know if you hear from her. This isn't like her."

"Sure thing, Michael. I'm sure she's fine. Have her call me when you see her."

Michael called Laci's number. "Hi Laci, this is Michael Kelly. Is Sarah with you?"

"No, I'm in Ohio. I've been here all week. I won't be back until next week. What's up?"

"I don't know. I thought Sarah was with you. She texted me that she was going to your place. Have you heard from her?"

"No, she knew I'd be gone this week. What's going on?"

"She's missing."

"Last time I talked to her, she seemed fine. Have you called her other friends?"

"Just Brenda. I'll try a few more."

After exhausting all his contacts with Sarah's friends, Michael called 911.

"911, what's your emergency?"

"My wife's been gone since yesterday afternoon." She's not where she told me she'd be, and her friends haven't heard from her."

After more questions, the 911 operator said, "I'll have officers there as soon as possible."

Michael nervously paced. "Did she leave me? All her clothes are still here. Why doesn't she answer her damned phone? Where the hell are the cops?" He looked around the house aimlessly to see if he could find any clue as to where she might be.

Michael turned on the television to distract himself, finding the channel tuned to that religious channel Sarah liked to watch. He changed it. Flipping through the channels, he looked for anything to occupy his mind. The news caught Michael's attention. A bold headline across the bottom of the screen made him shiver:

"Serial Killer Claims 4th Victim"

"Two hunters came across the naked body of a young lady that has been identified as eighteen-year-old Jessica Owens, missing for almost a week. She was tied up, sexually assaulted, and brutally beaten. Her throat was cut so deep that police say she was almost decapitated.

The police believe the serial killer the media has dubbed The Dark Killer to be responsible for this latest brutal murder as well. Police say they have evidence that leads them to believe these women are all victims of the same person, even though each victim was killed in a different manner."

The view shifted to a man in a plain, cheap suit with a microphone shoved in his face. The name underneath read Captain Connor. "We can't share all the details with the public, as this is an ongoing investigation. Rest assured, we have our top investigators on this case. We're confident we'll bring this killer to justice soon."

The camera returned to the studio.

"If you have any information about these murders, you are urged to call your local law enforcement or Silent Witness. There's a twenty-five-thousand-dollar reward for information leading to the arrest and conviction of the killer. You can remain anonymous and still be eligible for the reward. This is Carrie Rivers reporting for Channel 10 news."

Seconds later, there was a loud knock. "Police." Startled, Michael opened the door to a uniformed officer and a detective wearing a similar cheap suit to the one he'd just seen on television.

"Come in," Michael said, realizing he was still wearing his uniform. He'd been so distraught he hadn't bothered to change.

"I'm Detective David Scott, and this is Officer Gary Kent."

"I'm Michael Kelly. Thanks for coming."

"How long has your wife been missing?"

"She was gone when I got home yesterday. I didn't worry because she texted me that she'd be staying at her best friend's house last night."

"Did you notice anything unusual?"

"No. Everything looked normal. When I got home today, everything was exactly the same as when I left for work this morning.

All her clothes and her purse are still here. The only things missing are her car and cell phone."

"Have you contacted her friend?"

"Yes. When she still wasn't home tonight, I called around and discovered that her best friend, Laci, was out of town, and Sarah knew it. None of her friends or family have heard from her."

"I assumed you tried her phone?"

"Many times. It just goes to voicemail. I left several messages and texted her several times with no reply."

"Did you two have a fight or argument? Maybe she was too scared to tell you that she was leaving. Maybe she just needed a break," the detective said, watching Michael carefully.

"No, everything has been fine between us. She would never leave without her purse," Michael felt the tears he'd been fighting coming, and he choked back a sob.

"We'll start an investigation and put out a BOLO on her car. Did you check with your neighbors to see if they saw anything unusual?"

"No." Michael kicked himself. He should have done that right away.

"Don't worry about it. We'll question your neighbors. Do we have your permission to search your home?"

"Please do, detective. You can do anything that might help." Michael could no longer hold back the tears. Already fearing the worst, he cried openly. "Do you think that serial killer got her?"

"It's too soon to tell," the detective said. "We'll do our best, I promise."

The detective left. The officer stayed with him and tried to make awkward small talk. Within twenty minutes, the CSI team arrived to dust for fingerprints and look for evidence.

A few officers joined the first one. Through the front window, Michael could see them going door to door.

"Mind if we take this just in case?" another tech asked, picking up Sarah's laptop. He could see smudges where it had been dusted for prints.

"Sure, anything that might help."

"Do you have a recent photo we can have as well?"

"Yeah, let me find one." He searched his phone and found a selfie they'd taken the week before in front of their church.

It had been one of his rare Sundays off. They'd been able to attend together.

"Can I text this to you?" he asked one of the techs.

"Sure." She gave him a number.

A few seconds later, it was done. Sending that photo felt too final.

"Can you come with us to the station?" a new officer asked. "We just have a few questions."

"Sure, I'll follow you."

"How about you ride with us? The officer offered. "We can drop you back here when we're done."

A short time later, Michael found himself in a simple room with a table, a few chairs, and nothing else except a video camera in the corner. A detective, complete with the cheap suit, this one gray and well-worn, walked into the interview room. "Hi, Michael. Sorry to put you through this, but you know it's standard procedure to ask you a few more questions." Michael recognized his old friend, Detective Ronald Stone.

"We need your fingerprints." Michael numbly submitted to the procedure.

Michael suddenly felt confused. Did they suspect him for some reason? It didn't take long to realize that was indeed the case when they asked for a sample of his DNA.

SUNDAY MORNING, Pastor Joseph Romano was in the arena waiting to start his sermon at 11:00 a.m. Pastor Joe, as his congregation called him, was a gruff-looking man aged beyond his years. He was 5' 8", if a bit overweight at 210 pounds, but he was built stocky and muscular. He was forty-nine years old, but he could have passed for sixty.

Wisps of thinning salt and pepper hair covered parts of his head in puffs that made him look older than he was. Long strands of hair were combed over the top, completing the look. He covered his gruffness with an infectious smile and quick wit. Most people who knew him would say he was kind and generous, so he heard. The arena was packed as usual. He looked out from backstage.

"Lots of money out there," he said to himself. "Let's see if we can get on the evening news again."

The opening music, his show's theme song, began, and his cue to walk out to the pulpit.

"Welcome to all God's people who braved this beautiful Phoenix, Arizona winter to be here this morning," he laughed. "If you're new to Phoenix and love this weather, just wait until mid-summer." Everyone in the arena laughed. "I have an important message today. I'm sure this will make the news because most people don't understand. Those people need to read and understand their Bible.

God tells us that there'll come a day when God's chosen people must stop having babies. Only one hundred forty-four thousand of God's people will be saved from the rapture, the time when Satan will be released from hell to rule the Earth for the next thousand years.

God promised his chosen people that he would take them away on the wings of a giant bird. When this was written, they had no idea what an airplane was. How could they have known man would invent a flying machine with wings like a giant bird?"

Nervous laughter told him the audience was still with him.

"I'm here this morning to tell the world this time has come! If we don't obey this command, humankind will be extinct before the end of a thousand years, and Satan will win the battle for our souls. We're running out of space to grow food, space for animals to live, and space for people. Every year, the world becomes more polluted. Soon, we will run out of clean air to breathe. We kill off the forests and other vegetation, making the problem worse.

Many families are having four, six, and eight babies and more. Let's say a family has four babies, and each of these four babies grows up and has four babies. Those sixteen people have four more babies each, and so on. Can you see how fast humans can reproduce and overwhelm the planet?"

He heard murmurs but didn't care if they agreed with him. They were still following his words and talking. As long as people talked about him and his views, they would come, watch, and give.

"For every baby you have over four, the numbers increase exponentially. With billions of people having billions of babies, we'll soon have no food, clean water, animals, clean air to breathe, and no place to live on the planet! We need to stop before it's too late. By the time global warming becomes a serious factor, there may not be anyone left to care.

Look around at what's happening in this world, in this country, in our very neighborhoods—robbery, rape, and murder of many innocent people. A serial killer in the news in our home state is taking good people's lives and destroying families. The only good that could be taken from this is fewer people are left to have more babies. If everyone were to stop having so many babies, these heinous crimes would at least be less prevalent."

The first half of his sermon was about why people need to stop procreating, and he knew it struck a nerve. The rest was dedicated to getting them to send more money for God's end-time work. Pastor Joe was right about the media. It began that afternoon on the news. Many people thought his sermon made sense, but many were outraged and thought he was crazy. More people than ever wanted to tune in or attend his sermons to see what he might say next.

The sponsors were worried about what might happen once the novelty of his message wore off. They also wondered if they wanted their businesses associated with what they considered insanity, but as long as he had viewers, he would find sponsors. The network worried about this, too.

Pastor Joe had always been known to be on the fringe. He would tell his congregation, "I'll tell you things other preachers are afraid to tell you. They don't want to scare you, but sometimes we must be scared. If people don't change how they live, nothing in the future will change for the better. But there's still time for change. We not only have to change but also make the right changes. That's why God made me your prophet, so I can tell you what changes to make before it's too late."

THREE
COLLATERAL DAMAGE

"Detective Stone here," he answered the phone.

"An anonymous call came in to 911 reporting smoke coming from an abandoned warehouse on 169th Street and South Valley Lane. Officers are on the way, along with the fire department. Can you go check it out on your way back in?"

"Yeah, I guess." Detective Stone was frustrated anyway. The investigation into the so-called 'Dark Murders' wasn't going anywhere. On top of it all, he hated that name. Who the hell came up with The Dark Killer as a nickname? These guys all want to be recognized and leave a legacy, and the media had given the killer exactly what he wanted.

Detective Stone knew the area. Several times, law enforcement had been called to that location about people selling and using drugs.

He followed a patrol car and a fire engine to the warehouse. When they arrived at the warehouse and opened the door, a cloud of exhaust fumes nearly knocked them over. One officer ran around and opened the big roll-up door to let some fresh air in, and a larger cloud of smoke from the car exhaust poured out.

Just inside the door, a car sat still running. Stone watched as an officer reached in and turned off the engine with a handkerchief over his face. The officer waived him over.

Stone smelled the exhaust. As the gray smoke dissipated, he saw a woman's nude body on moving blankets in front of the car. He recognized the bloated face as that of Sarah Kelly, the latest missing woman in the area, the front tire was on top of her ankle.

"I think we may have found another Dark victim," the officer said.

"Don't call him that!" Stone snapped. "Seal off this scene, and no one breathes a word to the media."

He made a quick call to Detective Scott, his partner.

"Be right there," came the curt response.

Soon, the area was filled with crime scene techs and patrol officers.

"Be careful with any evidence you find," Detective Scott hollered. He turned to Detective Stone. "We need a break here."

"They all slip up at some point," Stone said. He was determined to catch this killer. His kid sister was raped and murdered the day of her high school graduation over twenty years earlier, and she was one of the reasons he'd become a cop in the first place.

"But how many more lives will it take?" crime scene specialist Nicole Carson asked.

"God, Nicky, don't be so negative," Nicole's assistant, Cindy, said. "We'll catch this motherfucker. We usually do."

"Hopefully sooner than later," Nicole said. "I found some hairs in the car that are a different color than the victim's. They still have the follicles attached. I'll send them out for DNA."

Stone knew Nicole was good at her job. She'd been working crime scenes for twelve years. She was a large-chested, sassy redhead who stood five foot nine. Officers joked about her good looks but not to her face. Cindy was a stark contrast at five foot two, blonde, and a little overweight with small breasts, a pretty face, and a much more positive personality.

"Gather all the evidence you can," Stone said. "Photograph

everything. I want a report on my desk ASAP."

Nicole gave him a knowing look. "Will do."

A few hours later, the report was incomplete, but Stone and Scott stood facing a small task force of detectives and uniformed officers.

"This is what we have to go on so far: three hairs and a tiny piece of black leather found under one of the fingernails of a victim. As far as we can tell, all the victims had glue residue on their faces from duct tape, including the latest victim.

A piece of duct tape was found near the women in each case. We didn't find fingerprints or DNA on any of the tape. However, when we match them end to end, it appears they all came from the same roll."

"My bet is the same will hold true for Sarah Kelly," Detective Scott said.

"Right. We know the techs found identical black fibers on each victim's clothing. They're working to track down the fabric these fibers came from, but it appears to be a common, cheap polyester blend."

Detective Scott took over. "The FBI profiler I spoke with thinks this person has probably done other serial killings in the past. Serial killers usually kill their victims in a similar manner. This one so far has killed each victim differently. The profiler thinks this can be a combination of other M.O.'s he may have used.

One thing they all had in common was how the victims' panties were ripped off. Toxicology says all of these young ladies had been drugged with chloroform, tranquilizer, or both. Every victim is left wearing only one earring. He's probably talking one as a trophy. When we find the matching earrings, we'll have the killer.

Each victim had an upside-down pentagram drawn with a red marker on the palm of their left hand. The pentagram drawing, the earrings, the panties being ripped off, and the fibers are not known to the public. This information doesn't leave this room.

We're still interviewing the latest victim's family members and friends, but more interviews will be done, and some of you will be assigned to those. Sarah Kelly's car was towed from the warehouse. CSI is going through it to see if they can find anything else." Stone pointed at the first picture on a bulletin board.

"To review, victim number one was twenty-six-year-old Terri Applebee, a housewife stabbed twenty-six times after being brutally raped almost a year ago. Her black thong panties were ripped off and tossed aside. We found a plastic poncho covered in blood among her clothes, but unfortunately, we only found her DNA.

With so many stab wounds, it could be a crime of passion, even if it appears to be the work of our serial killer. We believe the killer may have known her because of the overkill. We've made a list of other possible suspects and have been interviewing them."

"You think the other murders might be a cover to disguise the actual victim?" Officer Kent asked.

"Possibly. Wouldn't be the first time."

"She had twenty-six stab wounds, and she was twenty-six-years-old. Is that a coincidence?" Nicole asked. "It definitely seems like a crime of passion."

"We have no way of knowing yet," Scott said.

"Victims number two and three were Kristina Adams and Missy Adams," Stone continued. "The thirty-year-old single mom was drugged, tied up and brutally raped and shot in the head once with a .38. Nine-year-old Missy Adams was naked from the waist down. She had been strangled. The ligature was still around her neck. Mother and daughter were found together in an alley. Both were missing one earring. Both their panties had been ripped off, tied together, and tossed aside."

Stone surveyed the room and continued. "Kristina Adams probably wasn't shot right away. Forensics show she was most likely shot from at least three feet away. The angle of the shot looked like the killer was probably on his knees as he straddled Missy's body. Missy's neck was broken. Whoever this is killed a fucking nine-year-old girl! Clearly, this killer has no conscience, and this son-of-a-bitch needs to be caught, dammit!"

Detective Scott picked up where Stone left off. "We don't believe Missy ever regained consciousness. She probably never knew what happened to her or her mother.

Victim number four was eighteen-year-old Jessica Owens. She was about to graduate from high school. This 4.0 student had already earned a full scholarship to college. She was beaten and raped before being strangled to death. Once again, we found her panties ripped off and hung from her rearview mirror."

Stone regained his composure and continued. "The woman we believe is his fifth victim was twenty-one-year-old Sarah Kelly. She was abducted from her home, beaten, and raped in the old warehouse off Valley Lane. Then she was left in the warehouse with her car running, the right front tire parked on her ankle. She apparently died of carbon monoxide poisoning. We'll have verification from the autopsy soon. Her ripped-up panties were hung from her rearview mirror.

Her husband, Michael Kelly, is a forest ranger. I'd known Sarah since she was a kid. She was one of the sweetest people I've known. This one got too close to home, people. I want this asshole caught now more than ever."

Detective David Scott added, "We found a homeless couple that had been sleeping in the back corner of the warehouse. They were both deceased from apparent carbon monoxide poisoning, not to mention dozens of dead rats. We questioned several of the homeless in the area, but no one admitted to seeing anything. I have a feeling a lady who goes by the name Michelle saw something but was afraid to talk. I gave her my number. Hopefully, she'll call. If not, I'll circle back around and question her alone."

Late that evening, Stone's phone rang as he prepared to leave for the day. "Stone here."

"Detective, it looks like we may have another Dark murder. You need to get to the scene right away. We have witnesses."

"Text me the location, and we're on our way." Seconds later, he got a text with the location.

"Let's go, Scott. We got another one."

"Another serial killing?"

"I think so. This time, someone saw something."

"WE WERE PLAYING IN THE WOODS," one boy told Stone. "We heard a woman scream, so we ran to see what was going on."

"When we got close, we heard a loud 'no' and then a thud," the other boy said. "We hid and waited until we heard someone leave. We saw someone running but couldn't tell what he looked like. He was dressed in all black and wearing a hoodie. When we walked around this tree," he pointed, "we saw a naked lady."

The lady's body was now covered with a sheet so the boys wouldn't have to see her again.

"Caroline, grab your camera and come with me." Caroline was a forensics specialist from Phoenix who'd arrived the day before to go over the evidence they had so far in the case. She was another of Nicole's partners in crime...well, crime solving. When she studied crime scene investigation, Caroline was one of her instructors.

"Where are these cops from?" Stone asked.

"They've been coming from all around to help, detective. They know you're in charge," Sergeant Jones told him. Sergeant Jones was temporarily taking Captain Connor's place while he was on vacation. "You have quite a reputation around these parts. You have a different way of getting things done."

"Yeah, but I get them done at the end of the day."

"That you do. Just go easy on these guys. Don't forget most of them are here working on their own time."

"No worries. I appreciate it. Let's see what we're working with."

"We waited for you, Detective Stone," Sergeant Jones said. "We've been canvassing the area for any evidence the suspect may have left behind."

"By the way, no need to be so formal. Call me Stone. Everyone calls me…" Stone stopped mid-sentence as a tech pulled back the sheet covering the body. Caroline's camera shutter clicked. The scene in front of him was gruesome, the worst thing he'd ever seen in all his years as a cop and even as a Marine.

A naked young lady lay with her ankles and wrists tied to four wooden stakes in the ground. Above her chest was a giant piece of tree trunk with ropes wrapped around pulleys in the tree. The ground looked like someone just dropped an enormous log on a pumpkin. Instead of pumpkin guts and seeds, there was splattered brain and shards of skull spread all over the ground and the top of her torso.

There was a circle of rocks around the crime scene. Inside the circle was a pentagram made from sticks.

Stone turned away for a minute, put his hand over his mouth, and gagged. It looked like she'd been beaten and raped. They found her ripped-up panties hanging from a nearby tree branch, apparently tossed there.

"No doubt someone came out here and set this up in advance. That piece of tree trunk looks to be four feet long and almost two feet in diameter," Stone said.

A helicopter circled above them, searching the woods. After pictures of the scene and measurements of distances and footprints were finished, the officers searched the scene under Stone's supervision, placing little yellow numbered triangles everywhere there might be evidence.

"Shit, we need shovels to clean all this up. What about the log?" Caroline asked. "There's clearly evidence on it. Could one man hoist that much weight by himself with those pulleys?"

"Hard to say," one officer answered off-handedly.

"Stone, why don't you pull on that rope? See if you can lift it." Stone pulled on the rope and, with significant effort, got the log up high enough for a couple of officers to swing it out from over the body.

"I guess one person could lift it with this setup," Caroline said.

"Let's get what we can pick up now and get it back to the lab...the morgue or wherever the hell all these pieces go. We need to find out who this is. Check the reports of missing women in the area. Get her DNA and fingerprints, if possible," Stone said.

"On it, sir," Caroline said.

"We need to get a chainsaw out here to cut out just what we need from the log or a truck to carry it out of here whole. Find out who sells those pulleys. When the chainsaw arrives, make sure they know to cut that branch off carefully."

"Yes, sir," another officer answered.

"And measure that log before it gets cut."

"I found her ears, only one with an earring," Caroline said. "I'll send out a couple of lab techs to collect DNA samples from the families of any missing women."

"I'm going to drive by that warehouse to see if I can get Michelle alone to find what she may have seen," Detective Scott said. "I'll let you know what I find out, Stone."

When he arrived at the warehouse, he saw a lone figure scurry behind a dumpster. Detective Scott got out of his car and called, "Michelle, are you here?" he asked, walking around the dumpster.

"I already told you I didn't see anything," Michelle said.

"You know you saw something," Scott said, pulling a twenty from his pocket.

"Okay, okay, but I didn't see much. I saw a short, heavy-set man. He was completely covered with a black hoodie and gloves. He was carrying a black leather bag. He walked to the bus stop around nine o'clock. That's all I know."

"If you see this man again, please call me immediately. My number's on this card."

"I will, detective. A couple of my friends died in that warehouse."

Detective Scott called over his radio. "We need to find out what bus was near the warehouse around nine the night Sarah Kelly was murdered. We need to know where it was going and if it has a security camera. We need to interview the bus driver."

FOUR
WHO'S DARK?

The killer spent a lot of time down in his office in the basement of his home. Sometimes he spent the night there. It was his private place where he could find solitude. No one else was allowed down there. There was a locked doorknob and a double-keyed deadbolt on the door at the top of the stairs. At the bottom of the staircase was another locked door, also with a double-keyed deadbolt.

His family was usually in bed, asleep while he was down in his office working. He had a refrigerator and a microwave there. He also had a bathroom with a shower. He even had a small fireplace that shared a chimney with the one upstairs. This was a good way to destroy evidence. If a pair of gloves or a hoodie may have gotten some blood or other evidence on them, he would burn them.

The most important feature for his cause, and his favorite part of his basement office was a secret door to a tunnel that emerged in an old abandoned detached garage fifty yards from the house. The garage appeared to be a relic left over from a previous time. His newish house had an attached three-car garage on the other side.

He had accidentally found the secret door and tunnel shortly after he and his family moved in. He noticed one of the blocks in the wall he leaned on seemed a little loose. It barely moved. He found another block that moved. After playing with the blocks of the wall for over a month, he found that if he moved six of them in a certain order, the wall opened to reveal the tunnel. Otherwise, you'd never know there was a doorway there. He put lock on the door leading into the detached garage.

He installed a wall safe in the dirt tunnel and covered it up. The tunnel was a perfect place to keep his leather bag. He dug into the side of the tunnel a little at a time, trying to dig a secret underground room, one he could call his own. Their property was near the top of a hill. A door on the backside of the garage opened to a small level area, then a pretty steep slope. He could carry four buckets of dirt at a time out the back door and dump them down the hill. He did most of his digging in the middle of the night.

He had no precise plans for the room. He knew he'd find a use for it one day and he would be happy he'd made the effort. He dug out the doorway area the first, a rectangular hole two and a half feet wide by five and a half feet tall. He dug three feet into the wall the first night. He planned to make the inside at least high enough so he could stand up comfortably.

In the detached garage sat an old truck that he told his wife he was going to fix up one day. The paint looked like it was the original, what was left of it. The truck had several dings and small dents. The upholstery wasn't in the best shape. The engine could use some cleaning and painting to make it look good, but it ran well which was all that mattered. He told everyone to stay out because he didn't want anyone to see it until it was done. The real reason was he used it when he went on his private missions.

"WELL, I guess your dad was up late last night. He must still be asleep in his office," the killer's wife Lisa told their children.

"Can't we eat breakfast without him?" fourteen-year-old Alexa asked. "I'm hungry."

"Yeah, me too," her thirteen-year-old brother Scotty said.

"You're always hungry, Scotty," Alexa laughed.

"Well, I'm hungry, too," Lisa said. "Who wants scrambled eggs?"

Both kids raised their hands. "Can we have bacon, too?" Scotty asked.

"And English muffins and hash browns?" Alexa asked.

"All right you guys, I'll make it all for us," their mother said. "It sounds good to me, too."

Alexa and Scotty finished eating and went to their rooms to play. The killer walked up from the basement, as Lisa washed the dishes. He looked disheveled, tired and grumpy. "Good morning, honey. How'd you sleep?" she asked.

"Not great. I was wrestling with a personal demon all night. That's why I slept downstairs. I didn't want to keep you awake."

"Is that how you got those scratches on your arms, wrestling with a demon?"

He stumbled over his words, and Lisa just stared until he found them. "I was looking for firewood."

She knew better then to press him for an answer when he was grumpy. "It's okay, we'll talk later. I saved breakfast for you. There's a plate in the microwave. We were too hungry to wait for you because we didn't know when you'd be coming upstairs."

"I don't want any fucking breakfast now," he said, and moved to go up the stairs.

"Hey honey, uh..."

"I'm sorry, baby. I know you work hard. I'm just tired. I don't want to eat now. Maybe I'll eat it in a little while."

"You hear that sick bastard killed another woman yesterday?"

"That sick bastard is still a child of God," he said.

"Indeed, he is. Just honey, please try to watch your language, especially when the kids are around, okay?"

"I will," he said, then stormed upstairs to their bedroom.

The killer slept most of the day. That evening, he got up for dinner with his family. They watched TV together until everyone was ready for bed.

"Goodnight everyone," the killer said. "Make sure you take your sleeping pill," he reminded Lisa.

———————

AFTER LISA WAS ASLEEP, he decided to go for a drive in his old truck. As he drove aimlessly down several dark roads, he saw a truck pulled over to the side of the road. The hood was up, and a woman stood staring at the engine.

There had been no traffic. No one was around. There wasn't any cell service either, so she probably couldn't call anyone. He got out of the truck carefully, sure to show his hands.

"Hey there," he said. "Anything I could do to help?"

The woman was startled at first but seemed to be comforted by the sight of a slightly overweight, short, middle-aged man.

"Maybe. I'm not sure what happened. My truck began running rough, then it sputtered to a stop. I barely coasted off the road and ended up here. I know it's not out of gas. I just filled the tank this afternoon. I have no idea what to do."

"Let me take a look" he said as he pulled the hoodie off his head.

"Hey, aren't you Pastor Joe?"

She recognized him. Good.

"Yes, I am. Please, call me Joe."

"I'm Valerie. Nice to meet you," she said, holding out her hand. "I'm so glad you stopped. I couldn't get a signal to call anyone. There's a crazy serial killer out there and being out here all alone made me nervous."

He shook her hand and said, "Let me take a look," as he took another look around. There weren't any lights or buildings for miles. He looked under the hood. "I bet this is your problem. A wire's worked its way lose. I'll reattach it and we'll see if that fixes it. Let me get a couple of tools out of my truck."

Joe walked back to his truck and fetched a pair of pliers and a wire stripper. He slipped a small bottle in his pocket, walked back to Valerie's truck and reached under the hood.

Valerie got in. "Pastor, I'm getting married next month. Would you like an invite?"

"I'd like that." Once the wire was reattached, Joe said, "Give it a try now."

The engine fired up. "Woo-hoo," she shouted. "Thank you. What do I owe you?"

"You don't owe me anything. Just turn the engine off for a minute so I can make sure it won't come off again. And come out here and look at this."

She turned the engine off and got out. "What am I supposed to be looking at?" He was still bent under the hood. "I don't see anything."

"Over there, see?"

As she turned away to look Joe wrapped his arms around her from behind and pressed a chloroform-soaked rag against her face. She struggled, but he held her arms down at her sides with his other arm. She kicked him in the shin several times and finally broke free of his hold. She took off running and screaming. Joe ran after her. He caught her by her hair as she ran. He pulled her to the ground by her hair and jumped on top of her. Once again, he held the rag over her face as she struggled. He finally felt her relax and go a limp.

Joe zip-tied her hands behind her back and placed her naked, except for her white panties, on the tiny back seat of her truck. A piece of duct tape went over her mouth.

He then moved his truck to a pull out he'd seen a little way back. Even if a curious sheriff drove by and checked it out, the truck wasn't registered to him, at least not to the name he was using at the moment.

He walked back to the lady's truck and slid behind the wheel. He checked the registration. Valerie Kantrel. He drove it back the way he'd come, then followed a dirt track into the forest, well off the main road.

She sat up. "What...where...?"

"You woke up just in time." Joe attempted to climb in the narrow jump seat on top of Valerie. She wildly kicked at him, but he was able to grab her ankles. He held them tightly as he climbed in.

"Listen, if you want to live you'll do as I say, okay?" She didn't answer.

He smacked her face hard and asked her again, "Do you want to fucking live or not?" Valerie looked up at him and nodded.

He got back out of the truck so he could rip her panties off. He unzipped his pants, put a condom on and rubbed some lubricant on it. As he entered her, he could tell she was trying to scream under the duct tape. That and her writhing struggles turned him on. He put both his hands around her neck and squeezed hard as he thrusted in and out of her harder and faster. When he could tell she was on the edge of passing out he let go of her neck and pulled the tape off her mouth.

She gasped. Once she was more lucid, she begged, "Please don't kill me. Get off me!"

He stayed silent and just looked at her, so she changed tactics.

"Stop! Help!" she screamed.

He put his hands back around her neck and squeezed. When he felt an orgasm coming soon, he stopped and removed his hands again.

"Don't do this. Please don't kill me, Pastor Joe," she cried.

He pulled her ripped up panties from the center armrest where he'd tossed them and shoved them into her mouth. Pushing them with her tongue, she tried to spit them out turning her head from side to side. Joe used his index and middle finger to shove them all the way down her throat. She gagged violently.

He held his gloved fingers down her throat as he reached a huge orgasm. He laid on top of her like this until he was certain she was dead. He had another orgasm before he pulled out of her. He pulled off one of her earrings and put it in his pocket.

Pulling her body out of the back seat, he sat her up in the driver's seat and closed the door. In front of truck was a massive drop off. Reaching in through the open driver's window, Joe turned on the engine and put the truck in gear. It made it to the bottom of the ravine with a loud crash. Soon, he heard a loud explosion as her truck burst into flames.

The almost full gas tank exploded into a giant fireball that fed the intensity of the fire. He walked over and looked down. The brush around the truck was burning. Several close by trees had already caught fire. Joe got back in his truck and headed home wondering if the police would blame her murder on the one the news called The Dark Killer.

He had thirteen murders planned as this serial killer. He would have to watch the news to see if this one would count so he'd know how many more murders he needed to pin on his DARK persona before moving on to another one. He knew he would definitely kill more than thirteen women all together. The specific number was one of his demented games.

FIVE
LISA

When Joe met Lisa, he was on a business trip to New York City from Chicago, where he lived. It was a Friday afternoon, and he walked into a restaurant behind her. She wore a short, tight dress with a pound of hair spray in her big blonde hair. She sat at the table beside his.

"Hello there, pretty lady," he said.

"Hi, how are you?" she asked in a high-pitched nasally tone.

"I'm well, thank you. Are you here by yourself?"

"Yeah, I finally got my own car. My parents would be pissed if they knew I drove to New York by myself without telling anyone. I'm from across the river in Jersey."

"I could tell. You sound like a Jersey Shore girl. You live with your parents?"

"Yeah, I just turned eighteen. I'll graduate from high school next month."

"We're both eating alone. Would you like to sit together so we can talk while we eat?"

"It does get boring eating alone," she said as she moved to his table. "I'm Lisa."

"I'm John."

They chatted while they ate. They made plans to meet again the following weekend. His original plan had been to kill her that day. He couldn't explain why but put it off for another week. He insisted on paying for both their meals. He wanted to gain her trust. He had big plans for her.

The following weekend, Joe stood in front of the restaurant waiting for her.

I bet she doesn't even show. I should have killed her while I had the chance, he thought.

Someone walked up behind him, reached around, and put her hands over his eyes. "Guess who?"

"Lisa, I didn't think you'd really come," he said, turning around.

"I always keep my word, Johnny," she smiled.

He was holding a bag of fast food. "I thought we could eat in my car if you'd like to go for a ride."

"Sure, sounds fun. Where are we going?"

"It's a surprise. I think you'll like it." He handed her the bag. "Let's eat."

They both had a burger, fries, and a soft drink as they drove. When they finished eating, he pulled into an alley in a quiet neighborhood and parked. This is where he planned to drug her and then go to a more secluded spot. Before he turned off the engine, she knelt on the front seat. She leaned in and kissed him passionately while her hands caressed his chest.

She stopped and said, "I'm sorry. I don't know what came over me. Believe it or not, I'm still a virgin, and you're almost old enough to be my father. I've never done anything like this before. I feel so attracted to you."

"I'm attracted to you, too," he said. "Maybe we have a special connection."

He realized, for the first time, he didn't want to hurt her. He felt like he wanted to love her. He never wanted to have a relationship with anyone before. He had never felt love before, except for his puppy when he was nine.

She was a youngster to him. He was seventeen years older than her but wanted to spend time with her. He made out with her and then drove her back to her car. She made him feel like a teenager, or at least what he thought a teenager might feel like if he had a normal upbringing in a loving family, something he never experienced.

"I feel lucky to have met you. I feel safe and happy when we're together. I've never trusted anyone like I already trust you," Lisa said.

"I feel the same," he said, actually meaning it.

"Can we meet again next weekend?" she asked.

"I would like that. I feel happy and peaceful when I'm with you." He kissed her. "I'll see you next week. In case you can get away before then, give me a call," he said, handing her his cell phone number.

A month after she turned eighteen, they started dating. Three months later, Lisa found out she was over two months pregnant. They decided to get married. Lisa found out his name was Joseph Romano the day before the wedding. He told her John Peterson was an alias he used so his followers wouldn't mob him. Young and naïve, she bought the lie.

Lisa finally got away from her overbearing, controlling parents, free from more beatings and sexual abuse from her drunken father and ridicule from her mother.

"I can't wait until they find out I'm married," she said.

"JOEY, where were you last night? I woke up, and you were gone."

"I went down to my office for a while."

That evening, Lisa led Joe toward the stairs. "We should get to bed early if you know what I mean," she said, winking.

As soon as they got to the master bedroom, she went into the bathroom. She came out wearing nothing but a pair of lacy, pink panties. She knew he had an obsession with them.

He made out with her while she helped undress him. He threw her down on the bed and climbed on top of her. While still kissing her, he caressed her breast with one hand while his other hand rubbed the crotch of her panties. Soon, she pushed him off her.

She stood up and slowly slid her panties off her hips, sliding them down her legs. As they reached her feet, she kicked them up into the air. They landed on his face. Joe chuckled as he pushed them off onto the bed. She bent over and took his penis in her mouth, then climbed on top of him. She kissed him, her tongue dancing in and out of his mouth. She sat up and guided his hardness into her wet pussy, slowly sitting all the way down on it. They both let out a loud moan. She rode him hard and fast.

She leaned over and kissed him, nibbling on his lips and sucking on his tongue. She was so turned on that all she wanted was to feel him cum inside her. They both reached orgasm together without changing positions again. They fell asleep in each other's arms.

SIX

NAILED

L isa made breakfast on Thursday morning. The sound of the news report reached the kitchen from the living room, and she listened with half an ear.

"Twenty-two-year-old Valerie Kantrel was reported missing four days ago by her family after she didn't show up at home after leaving her boyfriend, Jack Divan's house the night before. Police questioned Jack, but he had an airtight alibi. He was with his family and friends all night, and Valerie left early.

She was driving a black older model Ford F-150 pickup truck, Arizona vanity plate VALSTRK. If you have any information about her whereabouts or you've seen this truck, please call your local police. This is Carrie Rivers reporting for Channel 10 news."

Joe arrived at the breakfast table with Scotty and Alexa. "Nice to see you up to eat breakfast with us this morning, Joey," Lisa smiled as she put a pile of country fries on his plate with his eggs. "Is there anything else I can get you?"

"This is plenty. It's nice to spend a little time together before the kids leave for school."

"Did you hear there was a forest fire? They have it under control already. Luckily, they caught it early. They say it only burned about seven thousand acres."

"That's pretty fast. Did they say what caused it?"

"Yeah, I guess someone drove off the road and crashed. They said the truck hit a tree and caught fire."

"I wonder what happened. Maybe they were drunk or on drugs. See, kids, this is only one of the reasons you shouldn't drink and drive or do drugs. If you drink when you're older, have someone sober to drive you even if you have to pay for a ride. Your life is worth way more than that," Joe said.

"I don't know why people go to the bar to drink. I'd rather drink at home if I drank alcohol," Alexa said. "It's cheaper, and you have a comfy bed nearby."

"At the bar, you can pick up drunk chicks," Scotty said. Joe and Lisa both stared at him. "Well, that's what they do on television." Everyone laughed.

"Okay, guys, enough talk. Get going. You don't want to miss the school bus," Lisa said. "I hope you guys have a great day. See you this afternoon."

"Come give Dad a hug," Joe said. "I love you guys. Behave yourselves."

"Goodbye, Mom and Dad," Scotty said as he left. "Love you, too."

Alexa walked out the front door behind Scotty. Lisa stood at the door and watched them until they got on the school bus.

Joe went down to his office to work on a sermon.

When he came back upstairs for lunch, Lisa said, "The news just gave an update about the crash that started the fire. They think it was a murder. They found the woman's body in the front seat of her truck, naked. They couldn't tell much because of the intense fire, but they're still investigating. They think it might have been that Valerie girl who went missing. I have some errands to run today, but I'll be home in time to make dinner."

Once Lisa left for the day, Joe headed down to his office. He loaded up his truck with supplies he might need and drove down the highway toward Phoenix. The traffic on this late Wednesday morning was extremely light. He saw a car on the side of the road with its hood up and a lady standing there, looking helpless. He pulled over and got out of his truck.

"Hello there. Can I help you?"

"Thank you so much for stopping," she said. "My car stopped running, and I don't know why. I think it has gas, but I could be wrong."

"I'm Pastor Joe," he said, pulling his hoodie back.

"I'm Heidi Glick," she said, holding out her hand. "The gas gage is broken. I'm going to feel stupid if I'm just out again."

Joe shook her hand and said, "It's nice to meet you."

"It's nice to meet you, pastor. I watch you all the time. I tried calling for help but forgot to charge my cell phone. My boyfriend says I'm an airhead."

"How old are you, Heidi?" he asked as he looked under the hood of her car.

"I'm twenty-five. My boyfriend and I are trying to have our first baby. We live together already. I only wanted four kids, but he wanted eight, so we agreed to compromise on six. This is Brad," she said, showing him a picture. "Isn't he handsome?"

"Yeah, he's a good-looking guy." He closed her hood and said, "Hop in my truck, and I'll take you to get some gas so we can check that before we call a tow truck. Let me put this stuff in the back so you can sit up front."

As he put his bag on the back seat, he pulled a needle out of it. She sat down on the passenger side and put her seatbelt on. Joe took the first exit and pulled onto a quiet street.

"Why are you stopping here?"

"I want to show you something."

He grabbed her by her hair and held a chloroform-soaked rag over her face. With his other hand, he held both her wrists. She struggled and kicked but couldn't get away. She finally faded into unconsciousness. He grabbed her arm, applied a quick tourniquet, and stuck the needle in her vein.

He pulled onto the freeway, heading back towards Canyon City. After driving ten miles, he pulled off the highway and headed down a dirt road toward a construction site. A new strip mall was being built. The first company that worked on it got into financial trouble and sold the contract to the Clarkson Construction Company to finish it. They hadn't started work yet, and Joe had been out there just two days ago. He had a plan. He pulled around the backside of the building and parked. He unbuckled Heidi's seatbelt and walked around to the other side to lift her out.

The block outside walls of the shopping center were already completed. Some of the framing of the inside walls had been roughed in. He carried her inside and took her top off to reveal a lacy black bra. He took that off, too. Then he zip-tied her hands together above her head around a two-by-four stud. He unzipped her shorts and pulled them off, leaving her wearing only lacy black panties that matched her bra. As he got down between her legs to rip them off her, she regained consciousness.

"Wha...what the hell are you doing, pastor?" she stammered groggily.

"You said you listen to me all the time. Don't you know you're not supposed to have any babies, never mind six? I'm trying to save humanity," he said as he rubbed the crotch of her panties. "It won't do you any good to scream. We're out in the middle of nowhere. No one will hear." Grabbing the crotch and waistband of her panties, he ripped them off.

She let out a gasp. "What the hell are you going to do, pastor?" she asked, terrified.

"Honey, on the news and all over social media, they're calling me The Dark Killer."

"No! Please don't kill me. Oh my God, please," she cried.

"That's what God put me here to do. I have to stop as many baby makers as I can."

"No! Oh my God, please," she begged. "I changed my mind. We won't have any babies ever, Joey. I swear!"

He smacked her face hard. "No one ever calls me Joey except my wife."

Heidi cried, "Stop, pastor! No!"

"You should have gassed up your car and charged your cell phone," he said, smacking her face again. He backed up and put on a condom. Her screams and protests only turned him on more. He entered her quickly and moved in and out in a steady rhythm.

As he was about to cum, he grabbed both of her nipples and squeezed and twisted them as hard as he could. She screamed at the top of her lungs, and he finished explosively.

A gas-powered compressor was in the corner of the room with a framing nail gun attached. He fired up the compressor and grabbed the nail gun. He walked over to Heidi and put it against her head.

She screamed again, "NO!"

He pulled the trigger and shot a nail into her left temple, piercing her brain. He put the nail gun on her right temple and fired again. He fired three more nails into the top of her head. Laying her ripped-up panties on her forehead, he shot another nail to hold them in place right between her eyes.

"You won't be making six babies now," he said, taking off one of her earrings and putting it in his pocket. He found her driver's license in her purse. He memorized her address in Phoenix, thinking of a plan for the future.

SEVEN
THE GUN

J oe had acquired theatrical prosthetics and makeup to add to his disguise when he would go out in public on some of his missions. He would speak in a deep, fake voice when he spoke to anyone.

Pastor Joe stopped at one of his favorite pubs Friday evening wearing his black hoodie and leather gloves. It was more crowded than usual. He pulled his hoodie over his head and walked in.

"What's happening here tonight?" he asked a patron.

"A birthday party. See that drunk girl over there? It's her twenty-first. Looks like she's taking advantage of it."

"Yeah, she looks totally bombed already."

There were probably twenty people surrounding her. They all looked wasted. The banner over the back of the bar read: 'Happy 21st Birthday, Karen!'

As he approached the crowd, one of the girls headed back towards the bathrooms. "There goes the newest legal lady, Karen Wilson," one of her friends hollered out. All her friends held up their glasses as if toasting her. Karen turned around and held her glass up, too, then staggered towards the bathroom. She moved slowly, holding on to the backs of chairs as she walked past to keep from falling.

The bathrooms were in the back behind the bar. Joe quickly pushed through the crowd and went around the other side of the bar to get to the bathrooms before the drunken birthday girl. He made it there with seconds to spare.

"Hi Karen, happy birthday!" he said.

"Thank you, sweetie. Do I know me?" Karen slurred, then laughed. "Uh...you. Do you know me...or me know you? Whatever the fuck." Karen laughed and said, "You know what the fuck I mean, don't you?"

"Sure, you know me, and I know you. You're just too drunk to remember." They both laughed as she swayed. Holding out his hand, he said, "Let me hold your drink while you use the restroom."

"Thanks, sweetie." She handed him her drink and quickly kissed him on the cheek. She almost fell as she turned around to head into the bathroom. Joe grabbed her from behind to hold her up. She finally made it through the door.

Once she was inside, he pulled a vial out of his pocket, poured the liquid into the last of her drink, and swished it around. Karen stumbled out, fell right into his arms, and giggled. He held her close, then kissed her. She kissed him back. She tasted good.

He handed her the drink, and she downed it.

A young man walked up and asked, "Karin, are you alright?"

With all she drank, the drug hit her fast. "I think I just need some fresh air. I'm dizzy."

He took her by the arm and laughed, "That's why I'm here. To take care of the drunk."

By now, he practically had to carry her. Joe took her other arm. "Let me help you get her outside."

They got her out the back door. A young lady stuck her head out the door. "Hey Chuck, you gotta come see this."

"Go, I'll keep an eye on her," Joe said, never looking up. Chuck headed back inside.

It wasn't quite nine o'clock. The sun had already set. Joe's truck was parked in the alley near the back door. He opened the door, helped her into the passenger seat, reached in, and buckled her seatbelt. She laid back on the seat and passed out. They drove quickly out of the alley. In his rearview mirror, he saw the back door open as he left.

"They're looking for you, girl," he told his unconscious victim.

He pulled his truck into the Anderson's driveway as their garage door opened. He knew the Andersons were on vacation overseas. They left a car parked in the driveway. He unlocked the car with a Slim-Jim and pulled the garage remote off the visor three earlier.

He opened the passenger door and unbuckled Karen's seat belt. "Karen, wake up," he said, gently smacking her face. "Come on, baby, let's get you inside."

He picked her up, turned on a light, hit the switch with his elbow, and carried her through the large kitchen and living room. He made his way down the hall to the master bedroom with a four-poster bed. She swayed and fell to the floor as she slipped from his grasp. He picked her up and tossed her onto the bed.

He had prepared for this. There were leather arm and leg bondage restraints tied to the bedposts. He sat her on the bed and took her top and bra off. He pushed her back and removed her shoes and jeans. Then he rubbed the crotch of her silky yellow panties, preparing himself for what was to come.

Pulling her body to the middle of the bed, he strapped her arms and legs down. He took a syringe from his bag and shot a tranquilizer into her vein. In case she woke up before he returned, he put a piece of duct tape over her mouth and left her there.

"Sweet dreams, baby," he said as he left.

JOE ARRIVED home just in time to get through the tunnel and back upstairs to tuck everyone in.

He hugged the kids and sent them to their rooms, almost rushing them.

He kissed Lisa and said, "Goodnight, baby. I love you. Sleep well." He climbed into bed and waited for her to fall asleep. He was anxious to get back to the Anderson's house.

Once he was sure Lisa was asleep, Joe prepared to head back to see Karen. Walking through the tunnel, he stopped by where he had been digging since he found the tunnel. The doorway was still two and a half feet wide and five and a half feet high but only one foot thick now.

The room's floor was half a foot lower than the bottom of the doorway. The ceiling was a foot higher, making it seven feet high. He had dug the room eight feet deep and eleven feet wide so far. He planned to finish at eight feet deep and sixteen feet wide.

"Progress." Progress was good and mattered, even if he wasn't sure exactly what he would use the space for.

Joe left home and returned to the Anderson's house around eleven. Karen was still semi-unconscious, tied to the bed. Joe pulled the tape off her mouth. She groaned and mumbled incoherently. He broke open some smelling salts and waived them under her nose. She coughed and shook her head back and forth as she came to.

"Hi there, cutie. Comfy?" Joe slid down between her legs, grabbed her panties, and ripped them off with a hard tug. He pulled his penis out and put a condom on, then climbed on top of her and worked it inside. She was so drunk and drugged she had no idea what was happening. She was just glad she was getting laid for her birthday.

"I love fucking pretty, young ladies."

"Who are you?" Karen asked.

"You probably recognize my voice," Joe said as he pulled off his hoodie. He didn't have any prosthetics or makeup on now.

"Oh my God, you're Pastor Joe."

"Does it turn you on knowing a world-famous pastor is screwing you?"

"No! Oh, shit." Karen's head was spinning. Between the drug and all the alcohol she drank earlier, she had trouble thinking straight. "Why am I tied down? Where are we?"

"You're in the Anderson's bed. They're on vacation in Africa."

"What happened to my birthday party?" she cried.

"The party's over. Tonight, you die."

"What? Please let me go, pastor! What about God and heaven? Pastor Joe, please don't kill me. I promise I'll never tell anyone anything. I probably won't even remember."

"Fuck that pastor shit. I'm Joe. Pastor is the title I use to get people to send me lots of their hard-earned money. All you stupid people believe that God nonsense. There's no such thing as God or the fucking devil. All that shit was made up because people were scared of dying. It's all crap."

"How can you say that? I thought…"

"It's just a job, you stupid little bitch," he said, slapping her hard. As Joe was close to climax, he reached to his bag on the bed and pulled out a clear plastic bag and duct tape. He placed the plastic bag over her head. Then he wrapped the duct tape around her neck several times to hold the bag airtight over her head.

Karen's breath became fast and hard. She tried to scream but could only get a little sound out. The bag got tighter over her head as her lungs struggled to find oxygen. The bag sucked into her open mouth. She struggled harder than ever to breathe as Joe reached orgasm while he stared into her eyes and watched her die. The bag had become so tight it became part of her face, the look of terror frozen there, her eyes open wide.

He took her ripped panties and hung them on one of the bedposts. "A little extra treat for the Andersons." He took the bondage restraints off and put them in his bag. He drew a pentagram on the palm of her left hand with a red marker. He checked the scene to ensure he hadn't left any evidence behind, took her left earring, and drove home.

When Joe got home, he re-entered his office through the secret entrance. *I should say something God-like in my next sermon about all these murders. We're all going to die. What does it matter how and when? Once you're dead, all your problems are gone. So, dying is a good thing, right?* he thought.

In the morning, Lisa asked Joe, "Did you go out last night?"

"No, why do you ask?"

Lisa sniffed the air and looked at him suspiciously. "I smell perfume. Why do you smell like perfume, Joey?"

"Oh," Joe laughed. "I found an old magazine in the basement. There was one of those perfume cards in it. I rubbed one me to see if it still worked."

"Well, you better shower and get your magazine girlfriend off you." Lisa wasn't sure she believed him but kept it to herself. *First, the hairs on my pillow, now this perfume thing. Am I being over-suspicious, or is something not right?* she wondered.

The network ran a Father's Day special this Sunday instead of his sermon, so he had the weekend off. Before going to bed, he decided to dig out his secret room a little more. By the time he finished, the inside of the room was wider by two feet, and it was 2:00 a.m. He had enough time to get five hours of sleep.

The entire family sat at the breakfast table. Lisa set out a feast. There were scrambled eggs, French toast, bacon, sausage links, hash brown potatoes, biscuits and gravy, orange juice, apple juice, milk, and coffee.

"What's with all this?" Joe asked.

Lisa walked up to him and sniffed him. She was satisfied at the moment that he didn't smell like another woman.

"I guess I got carried away. You know I go crazy cooking when I'm worried."

"What are you worried about?"

"Not in front of the k-i-d-s."

Scotty and Alexa laughed. Alexa said, "Mom, We're teenagers. Do you think we don't know how to spell kids? Heck, even Scotty can spell kids."

Lisa did silly things like that to distract the children from whatever the bad thing was so they wouldn't worry. Instead of wondering what she was worried about, they laughed.

Lisa whispered in Joe's ear, "All these murders. I'm not only scared for me but the kids…"

"We're the safest family in town. God protects us. I would never let anything happen to my children," Joe said out loud.

"Okay, enough talking and more eating," Lisa said. They ate silently for a couple of minutes. The atmosphere felt tense. Lisa finally looked at him and asked, "Why are you like this lately? Are you feeling alright, Joey?"

He saw the worried look on Lisa's face. "I'm fine, Lisa."

After breakfast, Joe announced he was going to his office again.

"Again, Joey. Why don't you move in down there? You hardly spend time with family anymore," Lisa complained.

"I just want to work a little on a project. I won't be long, I promise."

"Fine, honey. I have cleaning to do, anyway."

Joe locked the door behind him. Leaning back in his chair, he thought about how much Lisa added to his life. She was the one who helped get him a slot on a local cable religious channel. She met an executive producer of the station and convinced him to come to one of Joe's three Sunday sermons. He was impressed and hired him to give his sermons in an arena and televise them on his local cable channel.

After about three months, a local primetime TV station picked up his show. After another two months, a major network syndicated his show across the entire nation, and eventually, it went worldwide.

Joe and his church now made hundreds of millions of dollars each year. He finally realized his goal of becoming wealthy from other people's fear. He used a lot of the money for himself and his family, but he reported it all as personal income to the IRS. He saw too many televangelists go to prison for using the tax-free church money for their own purposes and not reporting it. He had plenty of money to share with them.

Lisa was about an inch shorter than Joe. She never wore heels because Joe was self-conscious about his height. In fact, he'd wear shoes with tall heels and lifts that made him look over two inches taller. Whenever he left the house for his special work, he'd wear regular flat shoes as part of his disguise to help him look shorter than usual.

Lisa took a sleeping pill every evening. He'd encouraged this, telling her she needed to get a lot of good sleep to look good when they were out together. He wanted to make sure she didn't wake up he was out doing business she would disapprove of. She could be his alibi if he ever needed one.

"A .38 CALIBER revolver was found in a dumpster," Officer Kent said. "That old couple that were robbed and shot in the head last week were killed with a .38. We ran ballistics on it. The two slugs we recovered from the couple were a match."

"About time we have something solid to work with," Stone said.

"There's more, sir. The gun had three empty casings, but only two bullets were found. As it was the same caliber as the second Dark victim, Kristina Adams, we checked the gun against that bullet, too—another match. We found a partial fingerprint on some of the shells. Not enough to identify them, but maybe they can find some DNA on them."

"We may have DNA on the Dark murders," Stone said. "It looks like that asshole may also be responsible for that old couple. Not his M.O., but who knows? He's done a lot of things the typical serial killer doesn't. Tell Nicole Carson we need to have this gun traced immediately. Tell her it's a possible lead on the serial killer case."

EIGHT
CAREFUL LITTLE GIRL

It was Sunday morning, Father's Day. Joe woke up and rolled over to say good morning to Lisa, but she wasn't there. He found himself in bed alone.

He called out, "Lisa, where are you, baby?"

He heard the kids out in the hall whispering. "I think Dad's awake now. Go tell mom it's time." He lay there for several minutes.

He finally asked, "Are you guys out there spying on me? I hear you."

The bedroom door opened. Lisa was in front of the kids with a tray of food. "Happy Father's Day," they all said.

"It's your turn for breakfast in bed," Lisa said.

"Thank you, guys. You didn't have to do that, but I appreciate it."

"The kids wanted to make breakfast for you, but I wanted to treat you. They did help me a lot," Lisa said as she set the tray in front of him. "French toast with my homemade blueberry sauce, a mushroom and spinach omelet with extra crispy hash browns, coffee, and apple juice. Anything else you need, Joey?"

"Yes. I need the kids to leave the room for a minute so I can get up, pee, and put some pants on," he laughed. "Other than that, the breakfast looks and smells amazing. I hope I can eat it all."

The kids laughed as they stepped into the hall. Joe got up and went to the bathroom. When he came back out, he was wearing his boxers and a robe.

"Kids, you can come back in."

Alexa and Scotty returned to the bedroom, hugged him, and said Happy Father's Day again. Joe sat on the bed to eat.

"This is awesome! You three did a wonderful job." He winked at Lisa because he knew she did most, if not all, the work.

"What would you like to do today, Joey?" Lisa asked.

"I would like a peaceful day with family. Nothing special. That would mean a lot to me."

Joe finished breakfast. Lisa and the kids took the plates and tray back downstairs. Joe got into the shower and turned the water temperature as hot as he could stand. He stood there with his eyes closed and let the hot water beat down on his face. It felt good. He turned around, rubbed the water out of his eyes, and opened them with a start. Lisa was naked in the shower, right behind him.

"Does big daddy need help soaping up on his special day?" she asked as she squirted body wash into her hand.

"Big daddy always needs your help, baby."

He put his arms around her and pulled her close to kiss her. While they kissed, Lisa washed his back, all the way down to his butt, where she lingered a little longer. She ran her hands back up to the middle of his back. She worked from the center of his back out and around the sides, then pushed her hands between their bodies and soaped up his chest.

Lisa reached between his legs, soaping up his inner thighs and balls and then his now semi-erect penis. She pushed him away and stepped out of the shower.

"If I missed any spots, you could finish, okay Joey?"

"What the hell? Where do you think you're going, woman?"

"I said I was here to soap you up. It was a bit of a preview of what's coming tonight. The kids are expecting me to come right back down," she said as she dried herself off. "Think about that all day."

"Okay, I'm going to hold you to that, you little prick tease."

"Don't worry about that unless you're not up for the challenge tonight."

"Oh, I'll be up for anything you got."

While he finished bathing, he thought about what he wanted to do for Father's Day. Joe dried himself off, got dressed, and headed downstairs.

"I know what I want to do today," he said. He smacked Lisa's butt as he walked past her. "How about a snack food day while we watch the first three Star Wars movies?"

"That would be awesome," Scotty said.

"Yeah, it would," Alexa agreed. "We've talked about doing that for a long time."

"Sounds fun," Lisa said. She busied herself getting snacks from the cupboard. "Later, I'll make a bunch of taquitos for lunch. We can order pizza and wings for dinner."

"Sounds perfect," Joe said.

They settled in on the couch and started the first episode. After their pizza and wings and the third episode, Lisa said, "I have a little surprise for you, Joey. I baked one of your favorites while you were in your office last night." She carried a homemade blueberry pie into the living room, set it on the coffee table, and served up four slices. "I gave you an extra-large slice, Joey."

"Thank you, honey. I could eat your blueberry pie every day and never tire of it."

After dessert, everyone headed up to bed a little early. Scotty went to his room to play video games. Alexa went into her room to call one of her friends.

Once in their bedroom, Lisa kissed Joe. He pulled away and asked, "Don't I need to get soaped back up again? You soaped me up for the preview."

Lisa laughed, saying, "Shut up and take those pants off, mister."

They undressed and made out like teenagers. Lisa held his penis and felt it growing in her hand. She got down on her knees and quickly put it in her mouth.

After several minutes, he pulled her up and laid her down on the bed. He got on his knees beside the bed and returned the favor.

He got up as she slid to the middle of the bed. He climbed on top and slowly made love to her. She quickly grabbed the pillow out from under her head and pressed it over her face to muffle her screams of pleasure.

After about fifteen minutes, she pushed him off and rolled over on top of him, guiding him back inside her. She bent over, stuck her tongue in his mouth, and kissed him as she rode him. It was only a few minutes until Lisa reached orgasm. Joe came with her, both moaning loudly in ecstasy.

She lay down beside him and said, "I love you so much, Joey."

He hugged her tightly and said, "I love you."

There was no room for thoughts of murder, just sweet love with his wife. He felt very close to her as she cuddled up to him, and they drifted off to sleep, happy and satisfied.

When they woke, Lisa rolled on top of him and kissed him. "Good morning, sweetheart. Last night was so awesome."

"Yes, it was," Joe replied.

Lisa finally rolled off him and got out of bed. "I need to make breakfast so I can get the kids off to school. I have a long day ahead."

"I need to shower and shave," Joe said. "I don't have all that much to do. I promised Mark I'd help him out at the mission today. The sooner I leave, the sooner I'll be back."

Joe ran downstairs, grabbed a quick breakfast snack, and then showered. Afterward, he went down to his office to dig out a little more of his secret room. He emptied four five-gallon buckets full of dirt five times before he figured he better get going.

Before he went out, he took another quick shower in his office bathroom and changed out of his now-dirty clothes. When he was ready, he grabbed another quick bite and headed down to the Charity

Mission in Phoenix to help set up a special event for people experiencing homelessness. It was only about an hour's drive each way, so he should have plenty of time to hunt for a new victim.

When he arrived in Phoenix, Joe drove around before heading to the mission. He saw a little girl walking to school all by herself. He pulled over and said, "Hi."

"Hi, Pastor Joe," she said with a smile.

"You know there are bad people that hurt little girls. It would be best if you didn't walk to school by yourself. Hop in, and I'll drive you the rest of the way."

She got into his car. "Thank you, pastor. I usually walk with my friends, but I got a late start today. I'm Kathy."

"You sure are a pretty young lady. How old are you, Kathy?"

"I'm eleven."

As Joe approached her elementary school, he told her, "Be careful out there. Have fun, okay?"

"Okay, thanks for the ride." As she exited his car, a group of her friends arrived. As they walked away, Joe overheard them talking.

"Did you see who gave me a ride? That was Pastor Joe!" Kathy said excitedly.

"Wow, no way. Lucky you," he heard. He smiled at the thought and drove away.

When Joe arrived at the mission, Anita, Mark's wife, was in the kitchen. Joe peeked his head into the back to say hi.

"Hi, Joe. How's everything?" she asked.

"Not bad. What are you up to?"

"Straightening up. Seems like nothing ever gets put back where it belongs. Have you seen Mark yet?"

"Yeah, he was mopping the floor when I came in."

"Great, one less thing I thought I'd have to do."

Joe walked up behind Mark. Mark turned around, startled. "I didn't even hear you come in, Joe. How you doing?"

"Pretty darn good. What can I do to help? I need to work hard enough to earn a beer."

"I'm about finished mopping, so we can start setting up tables and chairs."

A truck pulled up with donated food from a local grocery store. Joe helped them unload the food and get it on the shelves and in the walk-in refrigerator. Once the truck was unloaded, they worked together to set up the tables and chairs.

When they finished, Anita came out with three beers. "You boys thirsty?"

They sat down at one of the tables, drank beer, and chatted about the old times.

NINE
STONE & CINDY

L ab Tech Cindy walked into the room. "We identified our Jane Doe from the woods. We cross-matched her DNA with recent missing person reports. Her name actually was Jane. Her last name was Hill. She was only eighteen. Her family came down from Six Peaks to visit friends when she disappeared."

"Good work. Has the family been informed yet?" Stone asked.

"No sir, you're the first I've told," Cindy replied.

"Son-of-a-bitch, this is one part I hate. I want to take a female officer with me," Stone said. "Having a woman there can sometimes help comfort a little bit."

"We can call one in from the field. Or if you want, I can come with you. I need a break from the lab," Cindy said.

"If all the female officers are busy and you don't mind, I guess you can come."

"I'll grab the address," Cindy said. "They've already gone back to their home in Six Peaks. They had to get back to their jobs."

Stone and Cindy left to inform the Hill family of the terrible news. "Damn it, Cindy, this is the worst part of the whole fucking job for me. And the horrific way she went. I had never seen anything like that before, and I sure hope I never do again," he said, his voice cracking a little.

"She just graduated from high school. Dammit, Stone, we'll get this sicko."

"Yeah, we will. I hope we can get him before he hurts anyone else."

After the long drive, Stone and Cindy walked slowly up to the door of the Hill's residence. Neither of them looked forward to this encounter. Stone rang the doorbell.

A couple in their mid-forties answered the door together. "Hello," the woman said nervously. "Is this about Jane?" Tears already welled up in her eyes.

Stone cleared his throat. "Mr. and Mrs. Hill, I'm Detective Ronald Stone, and this is my lab assistant, Cindy Williams. May we come in and talk?"

"I'm Freddy Hill. Come in and have a seat." They all sat down in the living room.

"I'm Judy, Jane's mother," the woman said.

"I remember you. I took your DNA sample," Cindy said.

"I suppose this is about Jane. Is she alive?"

"I'm so sorry, this is the worst news I have to give anyone. Your daughter is no longer with us. We found her body in the woods," Stone said.

"How did it happen, detective?" Tears ran down Judy's face.

"I'll tell you she didn't suffer," Stone felt a lump in his throat and couldn't say more.

Cindy jumped in, "It happened so quickly she didn't feel anything."

"Who would do such a thing to my baby?" Judy sniffed. "Was it that Dark killer?"

Stone composed himself a bit. "We believe it was."

"Are you absolutely sure it's her?" Judy asked.

"Unfortunately, yes. We identified her through DNA."

"She was ready to start college in Flagstaff. She was so happy there with her roommates. She came with us to visit some old friends. She was going out with a couple of them, but she never made it to meet them. They called asking for her hours after we thought she was already with them." Freddy sobbed into his hands. "Can we see her?"

"I don't think that's a good idea," Stone said.

"We really need to know. We can handle it. We have to find out some time," Judy said.

Stone choked back another lump and said, "Her body...uh, doesn't have a head."

"Oh my God! He cut her head off?"

"Not exactly. She was tied down to stakes in the ground, and a piece of tree trunk was dropped on her. Her head was completely smashed. There's nothing left of it."

Cindy stood, walked over to the couch, and sat between them. She put her arms around both.

"We hurt now, but Jane is no longer hurting. We have some counseling services we offer for victims and their families. Do you have family or friends who can come help you?"

Judy said, "We have family out of state I'm sure will fly in. We have many friends here that come as soon as we call them," Judy sniffed. Stone handed her a clean handkerchief. "Thank you, detective."

"Here's some paperwork about the counseling Cindy told you about. Would you like us to stay here with you until someone else arrives?" Stone asked.

"No, thank you," Judy said. "We need a little time to ourselves first."

He handed them each one of his business cards. "My personal cell phone number is on that card. Anytime, night or day, if you think of something that might help or if you need anything, even if it's just a shoulder, feel free to call."

They got up and walked to the front door. Judy held out Stone's hanky she had wiped her tears with.

"You keep that," Stone said. The Hills thanked them and closed the door as they left. As they walked away, Stone said, "It doesn't get more real than this."

"This has got to be the low point of my career so far," Cindy said as she struggled not to cry. "I've never done anything like this before."

"This your first time delivering bad news to a victim's family?" he asked.

"Yes, sir, and you're right. It sucks." Cindy cried as they got into the car. "I knew it wouldn't be easy, but I didn't think it would feel this bad."

"This was one hell of a case to start you out with," the hardened detective said. "I'm sorry there wasn't someone else to come."

"There had to be a first time. Maybe the next one won't be quite as bad."

"Unfortunately, it doesn't work like that." Stone held his arms out to Cindy.

They hugged as she cried on his shoulder. Still in his embrace, she pulled her head back off his shoulder, looked him in the eye, and said, "Thank you, Ron." She kissed him on the lips. They looked at each other and started making out, tongues dancing in the air and darting into each other's mouths. Cindy rubbed his leg.

He slid his hand up her leg. She spread her legs a little to let his hand make its way between them. He felt her grab and squeeze him through his pants. Suddenly, she pulled back and pushed Stone away.

"Oh God! I'm sorry, Ron. I don't know what got into me," she said awkwardly.

"I'm sorry too, Cindy. I don't know what got into me either," he said. "I think we just got caught up in the emotion of the moment. I'm a married man, separated at the moment. My wife's staying with her sister."

"How come?" Cindy asked.

"She's pissed because I'm hardly ever home lately. She says I love this job more than her. I told her it's not like that. She said when I decide what's more important, I can reach her at her sister's house."

"Sorry to hear that, Ron. She'll be back once this case is over. You love each other."

They drove back to the station in silence. They both vowed never to tell anyone what happened.

Captain Gary Connors entered the room with a few cheers. "How was your vacation, Captain?" Detective Scott asked.

"It was awesome. None of you dickheads were there," the captain laughed. "It was too short as usual, although I kinda missed work. Now that I'm back, I miss my vacation."

"We don't have the greatest welcome for you," Detective Scott said.

"We're up to eight murders on the Dark case that we know of. Technically, we are attributing ten murders to him if we count the homeless couple in the back of the warehouse. We found who that gun is registered to," Stone said.

"A couple of officers are at the owner's home now, questioning him, but it was reported stolen three months ago. We have a statement from the neighbor across the street who saw two guys carrying stuff out of the house. He called 911. When they saw he spotted them, they sped off. He said they looked like they had gang tattoos."

"Shit, keep me updated," Stone said. "Have someone pull that theft report and see if anything else was missed or if there's something we could use to catch Dark. We need to talk to that neighbor and get some sketches of the tattoos. With those, we should be able to figure out which gang stole the gun.

Even with the ballistics evidence, I'm still unsure if we're on Dark's track. Most of these gangbangers are basically kids. They're not usually good at leaving no evidence. They usually kill each other or people when they rob them. Why would they kill random people?"

"They wouldn't," Connors said.

"Just in case, see if we can find any gang connection with any of the victims," Stone said.

TEN
MR. CLEAN

Several days later, Joe went for a drive in his old pickup to search for an easy victim. A new neighborhood was almost finished, and some of the houses were already bought and occupied. There were still houses that weren't occupied yet, and some were still under construction.

He parked his truck on a side street just outside the completed part of the neighborhood and went for a walk to check things out. He carried his bag with him. He had a plan. He just needed to find the right victim.

A car with dark tinted windows pulled up to the stop sign as he stood on the corner, waiting to cross the street. The front windows were rolled down. He recognized the young lady as eighteen-year-old Tara Franklyn. Joe and Lisa were casual friends of her parents. The last time he saw her was at a barbeque at their home, where Tara had performed a song for them. Tara was a skilled pianist and sang with perfect pitch. He walked up to the passenger window.

"Hello, Tara."

"Hi, pastor. How are you?"

"I'm okay, except my car broke down. Can I pay you for a ride? It would be best if you weren't late for school. I don't need to go far."

"Sure, hop in. I finally got my own wheels. I love to drive my little car," Tara said.

Joe got into the back seat, opened his bag, and set it beside him. He thought *this is perfect.* The dark tint kept anyone from seeing him in her back seat.

"Where can I drive you?" Tara asked.

"Drive straight ahead a few blocks, and I'll tell you where to turn, okay?"

Tara drove up the street, past the turn toward her school.

"My parents were just talking about inviting your family over again."

There were a couple more streets with houses they passed. They quickly left the neighborhood. Tara stopped the car. "Where are we going? We're almost out of paved road. I don't see anything up ahead."

He looked around. There was no one in sight. "See that little side street there? Just pull in there and let me out." As Tara put the car in park, he already had a chloroform-soaked rag. He reached around to her face from behind. She screamed and grabbed his wrist but couldn't pull his hand away from her face.

Tara opened her door. When she tried to jump out, her seatbelt held her. He held onto her with his other hand. Soon, she was unconscious from the chloroform. He put his bag on the floorboard, exited the car, opened the driver's door, unbuckled Tara's seatbelt, and pulled her out. He laid her on the back seat, got behind the wheel, and drove her car further down the dirt road into a wooded area.

He parked where there was a small area of grass between the trees, got out, carried her, and laid her on the ground, placing duct tape over her mouth. He stripped her naked, except for her panties. Then he rolled her on her stomach and zip-tied her arms behind her back.

Tara came to as he ripped her panties off. She tried to scream, but the duct tape held most of the sound in. He pulled out his penis, donned a condom, and climbed on top of her.

"If you scream, I'll hurt you bad," he said as he pulled the tape off Tara's mouth.

"Stop!" she screamed.

He smacked her face. "If you scream again, I'll kill you. Behave, and I'll let you live."

"Please don't hurt me," Tara begged.

"Do what I want, and I'll let you live, I promise."

After his orgasm, he pulled a piece of rope out and wrapped it around her neck.

"What the hell are you doing? Stop! What more do you want?"

"Time to die, Tara."

"No! You promised! Please don't kill me!" Her voice trailed off. "You promised."

"Guess what? I fucking lied," he said as he pulled the rope around her neck. She struggled, but he held her down with all his weight. As she ran out of breath, the struggling stopped. He continued strangling her until he was sure she was dead. He took her left earring. He checked to make sure he didn't leave any evidence behind.

He put his hoodie back over his head, drove Tara's car back to the edge of the new neighborhood, and parked it on a side street where they hadn't started construction yet. He grabbed his bag and walked down the sidewalk two blocks to where he parked his truck. The kids were all in school now, and no one was in sight.

———

AFTER SCHOOL, some kids walked home together. One suggested they take a shortcut to smoke some weed before going home. He lit a joint as they walked through the woods and passed it around. After they all had a hit, they stopped dead in their tracks. There was the dead, naked body of a classmate. Horrified, they called 911. When the police arrived on the scene, they discovered Tara's body.

"ALEXA, Scotty, I need to talk to you," Joe hollered at his kids. "Come to my bedroom." Alexa walked in, followed by Scotty. "Close the door. Do you guys know what next month is?" he asked.

"It's your wedding anniversary," Alexa said.

"Yep, on the last Friday of the month. Don't tell your mom, but I got a present for the whole family. We're all going on a cruise to Alaska."

"We've never been there," Alexa said. "We've never been on a cruise ship."

"On the Sunday that the cruise leaves, we'll all go together down to Phoenix. We'll head to the airport right after my sermon and fly to Seattle."

"Wow, I can't wait," Scotty said excitedly. "How long will we be gone?"

"We'll get back the following Sunday morning. We'll get back to Phoenix just in time for my sermon."

"That sounds awesome, Daddy," Alexa said.

"Remember, not a word to anyone about the cruise. I wanted to let you know ahead of time if you want to get online and see what you can do on the cruise ship. Okay, guys, get washed up for dinner. It should be ready any time now."

The bedroom door swung open. "What's this, a secret meeting without Mom? What are you three plotting?"

Alexa laughed, "Dad was just talking to us. Scotty pushed the door closed."

"I don't know why. Just habit, I guess," Scotty said.

"I came to tell you guys that dinner's ready. Wash up and come down. We have some dessert after dinner if you're not too full."

"When it comes to dessert, I don't think I could ever be too full.

Maybe some of us were born with an extra stomach just for desserts," Joe laughed.

When Joe got out of the shower the following day, he looked at himself in the mirror and thought, "*Hell, I look like crap. I should lose some weight and fix myself up.*" He got dressed, then looked again. *This comb-over looks ridiculous,* he thought. *I think I'll shave it all off. I wonder what Lisa would think if I looked like Mr. Clean?*

He got a pair of scissors and cut the hair he had left as close to the scalp as possible. "Now to shave it." He felt nervous. Leaning over the bathroom sink, he splashed water on his head and covered it with shaving cream.

Holding the razor just above his head, he moved slowly at first. It was too late to change his mind, so he just went for it, stroke after stroke with the razor, until nothing was left on his head but skin. He rinsed his head and dried it.

"*I don't look half bad,* he thought. *I hope Lisa likes it.*" He peeked out of the bathroom door. No one was there. He ran across the bedroom to grab a hat.

"Joey, coffee's ready," Lisa called.

"I'm coming, honey." Joe walked down the stairs with his hat on.

"Why the hat today, Joey? I thought we'd be casual. Oh shit! What did you do?" Lisa asked. "Don't tell me."

Joe smiled, took off his hat, and watched the expression on her face.

"Oh my God, Joey! Do the kids know?"

"Not yet. What do you think? Be honest."

"At first, I thought, what the hell did you do? But you look much better like this. It would be best if you had done it years ago. You look younger. That combover was kind of bad."

"No, it was *very* bad." They both laughed and hugged.

"Can I touch it?"

"Baby, you can touch it anytime you want."

Lisa ran both her hands over his head. "It feels soft and smooth. I love it, Joey."

"I'm glad you do. I was nervous. I finally said screw it and just went for it."

"I'm glad. You look sexier. I didn't know that was possible," Lisa winked.

"I know I'm that not so sexy anymore, but I'll be better soon. I'm going to start eating less desserts. I want to lose a little weight. You deserve your old Joey back. You're just as beautiful as the day we met."

"You may not look the way you did when we met, but you're still sexy to me and sexier with your shaved head. I never thought I'd like that."

"DAD!" Alexa hollered as she ran down the stairs. "Wow, I can't believe you did something so cool! Scotty, get down here. You've got to see this."

"See what?" Scotty asked. "What the heck! Dad's bald. It looks awesome! I love it."

"You're going to get quite a reaction when you step out on stage," Lisa said.

"I bet. They'll get used to it. I like it better. It'll be a lot easier to care for and cheaper. No shampoo or conditioner."

"But more sunscreen, shaving cream, and razor blades," Alexa said. "Sunday, you should wear a hat, then take it off at the pulpit. They'll show you up close on the video screens."

"Sounds like a good idea." Joe smiled and rubbed his head.

ELEVEN
AMANDA

The next day, Joe told Lisa he needed to do some charity work. There was a stretch of an old country highway almost nobody used anymore. He pulled way off to the side of the highway to see how many people, if any, would pass by. The brush on the side of the road mostly hid his car from view. He sat there a good part of the day, and only one car passed at 2:45. A girl was driving alone.

For a couple of days, he went out to the spot around 2:30 and watched. Every day, the girl drove by at almost precisely the same time. Joe needed another kill soon. It had already been over a month since his last one.

After lunch, Joe told Lisa he was going down to his office. When he got down there, he changed his clothes and shoes and put on his killing disguise. He grabbed his black bag and left through the tunnel to get his truck.

He drove down the highway until he reached a spot he'd chosen days before. There were the remnants of what looked like it used to be a dirt road heading toward a small, wooded area about a quarter mile off the main road. He stopped and lifted the hood to make it look like he was broken down.

When he saw the woman coming, he stepped out and waved his arms with his cell phone in one hand. She pulled over and stopped in front of his truck but locked her door before she rolled down her window just enough to talk to him. She was clearly nervous.

"Hi, I'm Pastor Joe," he said, removing his hood.

"Oh my God, pastor, you shaved your head! It looks good. I'm Amanda," she said as she rolled her window all the way down.

"Nice to meet you, Amanda. My truck broke down, and there isn't cell phone coverage out here. I was so glad to see you coming. You're the first person I've seen for hours. I thought about walking."

"That sucks. Would you like a ride?"

"Are you old enough to drive? You look like you're twelve."

Amanda laughed. "I turned eighteen three months ago. Everyone always thinks I'm a lot younger. I was always the smallest one in my class at school."

"I see," Joe said. "I like that you colored your blonde hair purple. Those wild colors seem sexy and kind of naughty to me. Anyway, you look cute."

"Thank you, pastor. Hop in. I'll give you a ride."

"Okay, let me get my bag and lock my truck. I'll be right back." He had a rag and a small bottle of chloroform on the top of his bag. He poured the chloroform onto the rag, leaving it in the bag. Joe locked all the doors and closed the hood. He looked around. There was nobody in sight.

He walked to the driver's side of her car and said, "I'm just going to throw my bag in the back seat." He leaned in, tossed the bag onto the passenger side, and sat down right behind Amanda. He grabbed the pre-soaked rag from his bag, reached around from behind, and held it over her mouth and nose. He held onto her with his free hand. "Shhh, don't fight it. Just relax. Sleep," he said softly as she struggled against his hand. She opened her door, but the seatbelt held her. Her struggles weakened, and soon, she was unconscious.

He got out of the back seat, unbuckled her seat belt, and then slid her onto the passenger seat. He turned her car off the main road and drove slowly down the very uneven and bumpy former road. When he got to the trees, he found a nice spot that couldn't be seen from the main road, although that probably didn't matter.

Joe got out and walked around the other side of her car. When he opened her door, she fell halfway out. He pushed her back up on the seat, slid it as far back as it would go, and laid it back. Then he climbed in and pulled her body forward so he could zip-tie her arms behind her back. She was a tiny lady, which helped him maneuver in the confined space.

Joe pulled a sharp knife out of his bag, slid it under her t-shirt, and sliced it open up the middle. He pulled the fabric aside and discovered she wasn't wearing a bra. He marveled at her small but firm breasts. He unbuckled her belt and pulled her shorts down to her ankles. Her purple panties matched her hair.

He grabbed her panties and pulled them down to her ankles, too.

"What a beautiful sight."

He pulled his penis out and put a condom on. He rubbed his penis on her crotch.

After several minutes, Amanda began to regain consciousness. "Wha...what's happening, pa...pastor," she stammered. "Where are we? I feel...I feel weird."

"It's okay, Amanda, we're here for God." He stroked her young face.

Amanda became more coherent. "Why...why am I tied up, pastor?"

"Didn't your mother ever teach you about stranger danger? You should never pick up someone on the side of the road. I know you'll never do that again. I'm doing this for my mother...I mean for God. I'm doing it for God." Joe stopped himself. *Why did that slip out?*

He put his hand on her firm, clean-shaven crotch and rubbed it, paying special attention to her clitoris. She let out a moan of pleasure in the middle of the pain. He slowly inserted his middle finger inside. She gasped, and he pulled his finger out of her little hole.

He lubed up his condom-clad penis. "I bet you've never had a dick this big inside your tiny pussy," he said, pushing it inside.

She cried, "No, stop."

"Damn, little lady, your pussy feels so good. I wish I could take it home with me."

"Please don't kill me," she sobbed.

"If I could, I'd take you home and keep you as my sex slave," he said.

"It hurts! It's too damned big," she cried.

"Shut up, you fucking little bitch." Her tears soaked her face and her chest. He rubbed the moisture around on her chest and over her hard, little nipples. He grabbed both nipples simultaneously with his thumbs and forefingers and squeezed and twisted.

Joe felt he was close to orgasm. He stopped and pulled out. He didn't want to cum yet. It felt too good. When the urge of his pending orgasm finally subsided, he started again.

"Keep me as your sex slave. Don't you want to keep my sweet little pussy?" she asked.

"I would love that. I don't know where I'd keep you."

Her fear turned to anger, then bargaining. Joe liked it. "Take me with you. Keep me drugged. Whatever you want, just don't kill me. I'll do whatever you want. I'll treat you good. I swear."

"You tempt me, but it would be too risky. I love my wife and kids."

"Nobody will be looking for me."

Joe stopped moving, his penis still inside her. "Don't move, Amanda. I don't want to cum yet, and I'm about to if you move."

"I don't want you to cum too quickly, either. I'm finally used to that huge cock. I can make you feel so good. Please let me be your sex slave, pastor."

"Dammit, girl, shut up. I almost came listening to you. Now I have to wait longer. And call me Joe."

The orgasm sensation finally passed again. Joe continued to screw her at a slow, steady pace. He thought about how he could keep her as a slave without getting caught. It could be risky, but the idea excited him. Amanda was now actively pushing back against him.

"Doesn't this feel awesome, Joe? Whenever you want it and however you want. If you untie my arms, I'll show you just how good I can make you feel."

Joe thought about it. He was intrigued by her behavior. No other woman had ever reacted to him this way. "Okay," he said. He pulled her forward, grabbed his knife, and carefully cut her arms loose.

She reached down and grabbed Joe's cock. "Oh damn, it's bigger than I thought." She rubbed it back and forth. She put it between her legs and rubbed it on herself, moaning. Soon, she guided it back inside her. She reached around and grabbed Joe's ass, and pulled him into her as she thrust her hips up to meet his. She fucked him hard for several minutes. He'd never had a victim do anything like this before.

"You make me feel so good. I'm in love with your little pussy. I love your whole little body. You're going to spend the rest of your life with me."

"The rest of my life sounds good. Find a place to keep me, and I'll be yours forever."

"I already have a place to keep you. We'll be there soon."

"I can't take it anymore," Amanda said as she grabbed his buttocks and forced him to screw her harder and faster. "Fucking pound me, master! God, I'm CUMMING!" she yelled.

Joe couldn't hold back. He shot an extremely intense load into the condom inside her teenage crotch. "Damn girl, you're my best victim ever."

"I told you I could make you feel good. You sure made me feel great. I don't wanna call you Joe anymore. I'll call you master. I want to be your slave. It's strange, but I feel a strong connection with you."

Joe got out of her car and removed his condom. He cleaned his still semi-hard penis off with a handkerchief. He felt the connection, too. He put on another condom.

"Want to do it standing up?" she asked.

Amanda got out of the car. He expected her to run. Instead, she took her cut-up shirt off and threw it on the ground. She kicked her shoes off and finished undressing.

"Come give it to me, master," she begged, leaning against the roof of her car with her hands, spreading her legs and pushing out her rear. Joe entered her from behind.

She said over and over in rhythm to his strokes, "Fuck me, master. Fuck me, master." She must have said it at least ten more times.

"Sorry, Amanda," Joe said as he was about to cum again. "I don't want to, but I have to do this," he said. He pulled an old phone wire out of his pocket. "I love you, Amanda," he said as he wrapped the wire around her neck and pulled it tight.

She screamed, "MASTER!" The wire was too tight for her to get out another word as it dug into her neck. Joe's orgasm seemed to last for a very long time as he strangled her.

"I told you we'd be together for the rest of your life," Joe said as her body slowly slid down the side of her car.

TWELVE
SECRET ROOM

J oe let go. Amanda fell to the ground. Her body just lay there, not moving. He could tell she was no longer breathing. Joe panicked. He changed his mind. He didn't want her dead. He felt a connection with her like he hadn't felt since he met Lisa. He got on his knees and put his ear to her chest. He heard her heartbeat. He gave her mouth-to-mouth. She coughed and gasped. Her eyes opened.

"What happened?" she asked, looking confused.

"I was going to kill you, but I changed my mind almost too late. You were unconscious and not breathing. I gave you mouth-to-mouth. I thought of a place I could keep you that might work. I can't let you go home. It would destroy my family and myself. If I let you live, it has to be on my terms."

"Oh God, Joe. Thank you for not killing me. I'm scared, but I'll be your slave like I said."

He loved her young body and her eagerness.

"I know we just met. I can't explain it, but I feel like I love you."

"I love you for not killing me, master," she sniffled.

Joe held her close and wiped away her tears. "Get dressed, and I'll take you to your new home."

She got up and got dressed. She put her shirt on backward so the cut was in the back. They got back into Amanda's car, and he drove it up to the road to where his truck was parked.

"I'm going to drug you. You'll wake up in your new room."

Amanda laid down in the back seat of his truck at his request. "Just relax, honey. This shot will make you sleep. You'll be in your new home before you know it."

"Goodnight, master," she said as he injected her. "I'll see you in a little while."

When he arrived home, he parked his truck in the detached garage and entered his basement to get things ready. He had finished digging out the room and put up four sheets of plywood for the ceiling. He joined them using 2 X 4s and dug groves in the ceiling so they wouldn't show. He held it all up with 4 X 4 beams in the corners of the room and along each wall. He also put a beam in the center on the corners of the plywood.

Two rugs covered the entire dirt floor. He'd moved a futon into the room and added three pillows and two blankets from his office on it for her. He'd also fashioned a locking stainless-steel door over the entrance. He welded stainless-steel panels to cover the one-foot-thick wall's inside and to help support it. The doorframe was held in place by more stainless steel panels.

While she remained in the truck, he put two five-gallon buckets and a roll of toilet paper in the room, one in case she had to use the bathroom at night, the other for garbage.

Joe also ran a wire through the dirt wall closest to the nearest power source. He finally patched it into the electricity in the basement and installed an outlet in the room along with a power strip. He put a digital alarm clock and a TV radio combo in the room and plugged them in.

He returned to his truck and carried Amanda through the tunnel to her new home. He laid her down on the futon and waited beside her until the drug wore off. When she finally came to, she looked at Joe, smiled, and quietly said, "Thank you, master."

"You're welcome. Later tonight, I'll go to the store and buy you a flushing camp toilet. There's a bucket and a roll of toilet paper for right now. I have a bathroom with a shower you can use whenever I'm down here. Let me know what you'd like when I go shopping. Do you need to use the bathroom now?"

"Yes, I do," she said.

"You probably can't walk well yet. I'll carry you." When they got there, he sat her down on the toilet, walked out, and closed the door. "Let me know when you're done," he said. When she finished, he carried her back to what was now her home.

"I'll be back in a little while when you're more coherent so you can take a shower." He stepped out, closed, and locked the steel door.

"Ok, master, thank you," Amanda said from the other side. Joe loved her attitude even if she wasn't sincere.

Joe took a quick shower himself, then went upstairs and spent some time with Lisa and the kids. After a while, Joe told her, "I'm going back to my office for a little bit, but I'll be back up before dinner. I don't have much work left to do."

"Ok, Joey. Don't be too long."

Joe went into the kitchen and grabbed himself a snack. He wanted to give Amanda something to hold her over, and he also grabbed several sports drinks.

Back in her room, he sat down on the edge of the futon. Amanda sat up, clearly feeling better. She ate a sandwich and a granola bar. "Thank you, master."

"You don't have to call me that all the time. I wish I could let you go."

"I understand why you can't. If I were in your shoes, I wouldn't let me go, either."

"I wish I wasn't in this situation. I love you. I know we just met. I can't explain it. It was the same thing years ago when I met my wife, Lisa. I planned to rape and murder her, but I just knew I loved her and couldn't. She was the only person I'd ever loved until I met you."

"Did you almost kill Lisa, too?"

"No, I never went there with her. I felt like I *had* to kill you. I was afraid I might lose my family and life if I didn't."

"I was sure you were going to kill me."

"Everyone thinks I'm losing my mind. Now *I* think I am. Who the hell keeps a sex slave in the basement of their family home?"

"Maybe this is a good thing. Maybe you're changing for the better. You were going to kill me, but you saved me."

"I did, didn't I? I gave you an alarm clock. I don't know if you'll ever need it, but at least you'll know what time it is and the day and date."

"Thanks, Joe."

"I better get upstairs. I'll be back down after Lisa's asleep. Is there anything you need before I go?"

"No, thank you. I'm okay for now. I had something to eat and drink, and I have my bucket," she laughed. "I'm still pretty tired. I'll probably just sleep. This futon is more comfortable than my bed at home."

He put a couple of wooden tray tables in the room and gave her a deck of cards.

"That's a portable radio and TV combo I used to take camping. I can run a line in here for a digital antenna for you later. It also has a light you can use. It has brand new batteries in it in case the power goes out. I'll see you later with dinner. Then I'll go shopping for you." Joe kissed Amanda, locked the door, and headed back upstairs.

After he ate dinner, Joe cuddled with Lisa on the couch. He felt extra close to her. That night, when he had sex with Lisa, he thought about his day with Amanda.

After Lisa fell asleep, Joe grabbed some leftovers from dinner and headed downstairs.

"Do you drink alcohol?" he asked.

"Yes, sometimes. I love wine coolers."

Joe left her to eat while he went shopping.

He returned with the camp toilet and a small refrigerator. He picked up a bunch of different drinks, including two twelve-packs of wine coolers for her. He bought her snacks along with some heartier food items.

He bought her some new clothes and a dozen pairs of panties so she would have something to change into. He added a box of tampons and some hand lotion.

He also picked up a couple of plastic stackable three-drawer storage containers. It was like she had a six-drawer dresser to keep her things organized. She told him she liked the shampoo and conditioner he had in the shower so that they could share that.

"Do you drink coffee?" he asked.

"Yes, I usually have a cup or two in the morning."

He left the room and came back with a coffee maker he wasn't using, along with a can of coffee grounds, a package of coffee filters, and three gallons of water.

"I'll wash your clothes for you whenever I have the house to myself, and I'll get you more clothes when I can. Goodnight, Amanda. I love you. I'll see you tomorrow."

He hoped the whole situation didn't blow up in his face.

Joe had sex with Amanda most nights for the next few weeks once Lisa was asleep. They had long talks, played cards, and watched TV together. Amanda was happy. She liked how well Joe treated her.

THIRTEEN
ABUSED

T he next several weeks passed quickly. On Friday morning, Joe rolled over in bed and kissed Lisa.

"Happy anniversary, my love," he said. "I love you."

"Happy anniversary, Joey. I love you, too."

"I'm sure the kids have something planned for us. We'll get their present tonight. I have a present I want you to open now. Hold on a minute."

"Kids, come to our bedroom," he yelled. Both ran down the hall, still in their pajamas.

"We all wanted to be here when I give you this present. It's for the whole family, but I think you've dreamed about this for a while."

"Stop teasing and give it to me," Lisa said, grabbing the envelope from his hand.

Everybody watched to see her reaction. She opened the envelope and peeked in. "Aaaahhh," Lisa screamed. "I saw a plane ticket!"

Joe and the kids laughed. "You don't even know where the flight goes."

She peeked cautiously inside the envelope again.

"No," Joe said. "Pull everything out of the envelope."

Lisa reached in and pulled out the plane tickets. She looked at them. It took her a minute to realize where they were going. "My dream is to spend a week in Seattle?" she asked with a puzzled look.

"Huh..." he sighed. "Is there anything else in there?"

The kids giggled.

"Oh...what in the world is this?" Lisa asked excitedly.

Joe and both kids shouted simultaneously, "We're going on a cruise to Alaska!"

"Not only that, but we'll be in the Captain's Suite. There's free room service, a ton of restaurants and bars, stores, a game room for the kids, laser tag, and a lot more. They have live shows and music, and we'll have unlimited WIFI," Joe said.

"What!" Scotty exclaimed. "We're going to have WIFI in the middle of the ocean? Can I bring my laptop?"

"You sure can," Joe said.

After the kids left the room to get ready for the day, Lisa said, "I plan to take you out to your favorite restaurant in Prescott for breakfast or maybe brunch by the time we get ready and make the drive. There's some crumb cake on the kitchen counter to hold us over." Lisa leaned over and kissed him. "I'll make coffee."

"Sounds good."

"Scotty, Alexa, we're going to brunch," mom said.

"Where are we going?" Scotty asked.

"Prescott," Dad said. "We don't ask mom anything until she's finished her first cup of coffee. She can be a little grouchy otherwise."

"A *little* grouchy?" Alexa commented.

"Mom doesn't always get ready too quickly. Most women don't."

"I heard that," Lisa said. "I'm too happy to be grouchy." Ten minutes later, she came out dressed and ready to go. "Let's go, guys. Mommy's hungry."

"Damn woman, you *can* get ready quickly."

"Don't get used to it. Give me plane and cruise tickets every day, and I'll always be ready quickly," Lisa laughed.

After brunch, they got some drinks to go and drove to Lynx Lake.

"It's beautiful here. Look at the people fishing from the shore," Lisa said. A few people fished from small boats, too. Scotty spotted something else.

"Paddleboats. Can we ride them?" Scotty begged.

"It's up to your mom if she wants to paddle her ass across the lake."

"Sounds like fun," Lisa said.

"Okay, the paddleboats hold two people each. How do you want to split up?"

"I want to paddle with you, Daddy," Alexa said, putting her arm around him.

"I'll take Scotty," Mom said. "Come on, son, you're on my team."

They played on the lake in the paddleboats for the next hour. After the paddleboats, Joe said, "Let's see who can skip a stone across the lake the best, then we'll head home."

"Your dad and I used to do this when we were younger," Lisa explained. "Let's see who can skip a stone the furthest and get the most skips."

They spent half an hour skipping stones. Scotty and Alexa picked up the art quickly. When they finished, Scotty had the longest distance skip, and Alexa had the most skips of one rock. It had been a fun family day.

"This day, even without the cruise tickets, was great, Joey. Thank you and the kids so much. I love you all."

"Starting tomorrow, we'll need to figure out what we need to take on vacation so we can be organized," Joe said.

"Guys, we haven't given you our present yet," Alexa said.

"And we bought it with our own money," Scotty said.

"You already gave me the best gift. It was a wonderful day," Lisa said.

Once they were home, Scotty said, "We hope you like our present. It's one gift from the two of us. We're not good at picking out gifts unless they're for us," Scotty said.

"I'm sure we'll love it," Lisa said as she unwrapped it. "Oh honey,

I love it! Where did you guys find this wind chime? You must have had it custom-made with all our names."

"We made it," Alexa said. "Scotty had the idea. We know you like wind chimes. We came up with the design together, and both carved all our names into the different chimes." A mixture of metal and bamboo rods gave the chime a unique look and sound.

"This is awesome, you guys," Joe said. "You two did quite a professional-looking job."

Mom pulled Scotty and Alexa to her for a hug. "Thank you so much. It's extra special because you two made it. It's going on the porch, so everyone who comes over will see it."

"This *is* very special," Dad said. "You could sell custom wind chimes like this online."

Everyone slept in late the following morning.

In preparation for the cruise, Joe took his computers out of his office and locked them up. "Amanda, I'm sorry to have to leave you all alone after only several weeks. You should have plenty of food and drink. I stocked up the refrigerator, and there's a bunch of microwave meals in my freezer." He showed her how the latch worked on the hidden door. "I'll leave it unlocked so you'll have full access to the bathroom, fridge, and microwave. I hope you don't get too lonely."

"I'll be fine. I lived alone. I don't have any friends. My mom's in prison for child abuse."

"Your mother abused you?"

"Not directly. My dad abused me when I was nine. He'd molest me a few times a week. She was in the room sometimes. After a while, I no longer cried. I just went numb.

When I was twelve, I finally got the nerve to call CPS. They came out with two police officers to investigate. When they left, they took me with them. As we got to the car, we heard a gunshot. The officers ran back and found my dad had shot himself in the head.

They went back days later and arrested my mom. I moved in with my aunt. She kicked me out when I was seventeen because she was a drug addict and a bitch. The crappy little house I grew up in was paid off, so I just lived there by myself. I dropped out of school and got a job. I've mostly kept to myself. Then I met you."

"I'm sorry, Amanda."

"That wasn't my car I was driving. It was my aunt's. She didn't know I had it. She probably thinks one of her druggy boyfriends took it. She has like four old cars, and her boyfriends always borrow them without asking. She never cares."

"Maybe that's why I felt something special towards you," Joe said. "When I was three, my abuse began. My dad would pull me out of bed. There was a lot of yelling and hitting when he came home drunk.

"Damn, you were only three?"

"Yeah, I was still three when the yelling and hitting mostly stopped, and his abuse became sexual. My mother watched. She'd tell me to shut up and obey my father. She knew the more he abused me, the less he abused her. I grew to hate my mother even more than my father. She wasn't drunk. She could have rescued me. Sometimes, he'd insist she join in abusing me. I believe she did it out of her own sick desire."

"Oh my God, Joe."

"She wouldn't leave him because she said she loved him, despite how violent he got when he was drunk, which was most nights. I think she was scared because she was so young. She was only fifteen when I was born. My father was thirty. There was a rumor that he got her pregnant for the first time when she was thirteen.

When I turned eight, my uncle gave me a puppy for my birthday. I had her for six months. One night, I hid in my closet, hoping my dad wouldn't find me when he got home. I fell asleep cuddled up with my puppy. In the morning, I was happy to see I was still in the closet but couldn't find my puppy. I asked my mother if she knew where Daisy was.

She screamed, "You're a fucking little asshole! Where were you last night? You pissed your dad off. He got mad at me and it's your fault!" She smacked me in the face.

I asked her again if she knew where Daisy was.

She yelled, "Yeah, she's out back. Go take care of her now, then get ready for school." As I walked past her, she smacked my face so hard that I fell down. I got up and ran out back, still crying from the sting of her hand. I stopped and screamed. Daisy was staring me in the face, hanging by her neck from a tree."

"Holy shit, Joey. Your parents were more fucked up than mine."

"She told me I made her do it, and I was lucky I wasn't hanging from that fucking tree. She said if my uncle asked, I better say Daisy ran away. She told me to take the dog down, put her in a garbage bag, and get it in the trash, and I better not be late for school. I went to my room, lay there, cried for several minutes, then fell asleep.

Mom came into my room, woke me, and screamed, "You missed the school bus! Get your little ass up and do what I told you, or you'll wake up with Daisy on your pillow. You better not be late for school again." I threw Daisy away and ran all the way to school.

My father was killed in a bar fight the day I turned nine. That was the only day I felt happy as a kid. That ended the following night. My mother insisted I sleep in her bed, where my dad slept. I would pretend to be asleep. I knew what she was up to. She continued to abuse me. It disgusted me, but it felt sort of good, too. I was confused.

My mother never remarried. There were different guys spending the night all the time. When one of her boyfriends spent the night, she'd send me to my room to sleep. I kept to myself. My fear turned into hatred and rage. Everyone was evil, and I didn't trust anyone.

When I was almost ten, three thirteen-year-old bullies attacked me on my way home from school. They had me cornered. I took out all my pent-up rage on them. All three of them ended up in the hospital. Rumors circulated around the school. People were intimidated by me after that and left me alone. I had no idea how naturally strong I was.

On the night of my sixteenth birthday, someone strangled my mother to death in the middle of the night. A lot of people suspected me, but they never found any proof. All those men came and went. Any one of them could have killed her.

It's still a cold case. I know who killed her, but I've never told anyone. I was just glad she was gone. I moved in with a friend's family until I graduated high school. Every Sunday, I watched religious shows with them. That's where I got the idea to become a preacher to get people to send me money."

"How could you grow up normal with parents like yours? When did you first kill?"

"It started when I was ten. I was on a family reunion camping trip. My little brat of a cousin annoyed me. Lexi followed me everywhere. I told her to stop following me or else. She asked, "Or else what?" I said, or else this. I pushed her with both hands, not realizing we were by a cliff. When she fell, she landed on the edge. The ground sloped down there, and she slid towards it.

She held out her hands, screaming, "Help!" I watched her slide over the edge. It all happened quickly, but it was like in slow motion to me. I got so turned on I couldn't move. I had my first orgasm ever. I didn't even know what just happened. I just knew it felt good.

I told the family that she was playing too close to the edge. I told her to be careful, but she ignored me, started spinning around, and twirled off the edge before I could grab her. My mother came running over. I looked at her and smiled."

"You were in hell all your life. I feel bad for you, Joe."

"I'd already stopped feeling by then. The only thing I enjoyed was seeing others suffer. All I cared about was myself until I met Lisa. It was the first time I ever felt any positive emotion for anyone. You're the second one I've ever cared about. Both you and Lisa had been abused. Maybe I could sense it somehow."

"No one has ever made me feel this special before. Thank you for treating me so good."

"You're special to me. You told me before that nobody would be looking for you. What about your job? Won't they miss you?"

"No, people come and go all the time there. They pay daily in cash, so if I'm not there, someone else will do my part. Hell, they don't even know my real name."

"We have so much in common. Lisa didn't learn about my latest identity as Joseph Romano until the day before we married. She thought my name was John Peterson. I told her I used this alias so my followers wouldn't mob me."

"Wow, that's quite a story. Would you mind if I call you Joey?"

"The only one who ever calls me Joey is Lisa, but I would love it if you did too."

"Thank you, Joey. I've never felt this close to anyone. You can call me Mandy if you want."

"Would you like to have sex before I leave, Mandy?"

"I'd like that."

Joe unbuttoned his pants. Amanda grabbed his hands.

"That's my job."

She opened his pants while kissing him. As they had sex, Amanda screamed loudly with pleasure. She quickly put her hand over her mouth.

In between gasps of ecstasy, she said, "I hope your wife didn't hear."

"The basement is soundproof."

He felt an orgasm welling up. He could tell she was close, too. As she came, Joe couldn't hold back anymore. They collapsed on the futon, out of breath and dripping with sweat.

"We'll be gone for a week. I'm sure going to miss you while I'm on vacation."

"I'll miss you, too," she said. She laid her head on his shoulder and held his hand. They both dozed off.

They woke up early and lay there cuddling. After a while, Amanda looked at the clock and said, "Oh shit. It's morning, and you're still down here with me. How will you explain not being in bed with Lisa?"

"She won't be up for a while. I can be in bed with her before she wakes up. Even if I wasn't, she knows I fall asleep down here sometimes when I've been working. I made sure you have everything you'll need while we're gone."

"You'd have a better time if you took me instead."

"You'll be there in my thoughts every day. If you need anything else, make a list, and I'll go shopping when I get back."

"If you want, you can go by my house sometime and pick up some stuff. I was the only one living there, so the house is empty. I don't have a lot, but having some personal things would be nice. I like sleeping with my stuffed animals."

"I can do that when we get back. Make me a list of things you'd like from there. I'll get all I can."

"I'll look forward to it."

Joe kissed her and said, "I won't get to see you again before we leave. I guess this is goodbye for now."

"Goodbye, Joey. Have a safe trip."

Before heading upstairs, Joe printed out a letter he planned to mail from Alaska. He wore thin cotton gloves so he wouldn't get fingerprints on the paper or the self-sealing envelope. He put the envelope into a larger one and took it with him.

FOURTEEN
CRUISE

Sunday morning when Pastor Joe walked out onto the stage, he wore a floppy hat pulled down over his head. As he walked up to the podium, he took it off and waved to the crowd with it. There was surprised laughter and thunderous applause. When the applause died, he asked, "Do you like my new look?" There was another roar of applause.

His sermon was about family, love, and loyalty. He offered a strict command to stop procreating. The sight of his shaved head received mixed reactions. Most people thought he looked better with the clean-shaven look. Pastor Joe would make the news again. This time, he wouldn't be around to see it.

After the sermon, Joe was met backstage by one of the producers. He was informed the network would be running a special next Sunday. The Romanos headed to the airport.

"We're going to be flying first-class. The seats are large and spread out. We have a couple of private bathrooms. We get special service, good food and drink, and free movies."

This was the third time Alexa and Scotty had flown, but their first time in first-class. Joe and Lisa walked through the curtains, followed by the kids, who were in awe.

Arriving in Seattle, they took a shuttle to the dock. Once they entered the check-in area, Lisa said, "Jeez, look at those lines. It's going to take an hour to get through."

Joe smiled, "See that sign there that says Express VIP Check-in? That's where we go."

"Joey, you thought of everything."

"Why do we have to put our stuff on that conveyor belt?" Scotty asked.

"That shrinks it so more luggage can fit on the ship," Alexa said.

"No way! That's cool."

Lisa, Joe, and Alexa laughed. "Son, that x-rays the bags to make sure no one brings weapons or anything else they shouldn't bring onboard," Joe said.

Once they made it onboard, they were in awe at the beautiful atrium with a three-story high chandelier. The floors, the stairs, and the columns were Italian marble.

"Let's find our stateroom. Then we can check out the ship," Joe said.

"We have a few hours before we leave port," Lisa said.

The rest of their luggage was by the door when they got to their Captain's Suite. When they opened the door, they were stunned. "It's a frickin house!" Lisa said. "And look at the size of that balcony! It starts in front and wraps around the side, too."

"We'll have plenty of time in the cabin. Let's get out and check out the ship," Joe said.

"When we get back, we'll unpack and get organized so we'll be ready for sail away," Lisa said.

Joe said, "We're going to the top deck first. You can check out the racetrack, laser tag, the rock-climbing wall, and the water slides. Next deck down, you can look down over two swimming pools, four hot tubs, and two bars.

"It's almost time to sail away. We have a great balcony to watch from or stay out on the deck. Which one does everyone want?" Joe asked.

"Balcony," everyone said.

After they were away from the dock, everyone remained on the balcony. They stared, mesmerized by waves as far as you could see.

After a while, Lisa said, "Let's get washed up for dinner. Dress nice, please. It's a nice dining room. We don't have a port tomorrow. You kids can play, swim, and drive race cars."

"Our first port in Alaska is Ketchikan," Alexa said. "It's known as The Salmon Capital of the World. It's best known for the Creek Street boardwalk. Back in the gold rush days, this was the home of brothels. They turned one into a museum."

"Someone's been doing their homework," Joe said. "Who wants to go to a brothel with Daddy?" Joe laughed.

Lisa nudged him with her elbow. "Joey!" she laughed.

"How about video games first, then race cars?" Alexa asked.

"Race cars should come after lunch," Scotty said. "It'll be warmer then."

"Remember, we have a whole week here to play," Lisa said. "And don't make yourselves sick by overeating. It's easy to do on a cruise ship."

"You guys hurry up. Daddy's ready for some food," he said, patting his belly.

"We'll be eating in one of the main dining rooms. Please be on your best behavior," Lisa said. "We'll be seated with other people who probably know who your dad is. Set a good example." They headed to the elevators to go down to dinner.

The Romanos were seated with another family of four from Tucson, Jerry and Vicky Newhart, and their two teens. They were in their late thirties.

"It's nice to meet you and your family, pastor," Vicky said. "Kevin is fifteen, and Makayla is thirteen. We call her Micki."

"It's nice to meet you, too," Joe said. "Scotty's thirteen, and Makayla is fourteen."

"Nice to meet you. I'm his wife, Lisa."

"How are you dealing with the negative publicity you get from the media?" Jerry asked.

"If you don't follow what others believe, then you're a crazy person. I shaved my head, and everyone went nuts with their comments."

"Why did you shave it?" Jerry asked.

"I thought it was about time to quit trying to hold on to something that didn't want to be there anymore. I think it looks better this way and certainly feels better."

"Makes sense," Jerry said. "It does look better. You look younger, too."

Once they finished eating, Joe said, "Now I need to lose some weight. Going on a cruise isn't the best method for that." Right on cue, the waiter came around to take dessert orders.

After dessert, everyone wanted to relax. "The first night, you always eat a little more than you should," Joe said, letting his belt out a notch.

The Romanos and the Newharts sat by the pool in lounge chairs to watch a movie. After the movie, they were ready to go back to their suite. Joe invited the Newharts to drop by for a drink, and they accepted.

"You think we'll all fit in your cabin, Joe?" Vicky asked. "The cabins aren't bad, but they're a bit small for eight people."

"We don't have a cabin," Lisa said. "We have a frickin' apartment."

They walked up the hallway. "Are we going to the front of the ship?" Jerry asked.

"The front of the ship as far as the cabins go." When they arrived, Joe unlocked the door and held it open for everyone. The Newharts stood looking around. "Come check out the balcony," Joe said.

"Wow, this is awesome!" Jerry exclaimed. "I could live here."

"Anybody wanna play video games?" Scotty asked. "We brought some."

"No way, man!" Kevin exclaimed. "That's so cool."

The kids headed back inside. The adults relaxed on the patio. They looked at the ocean, sipped on wine, and talked.

"Looks like the kids are getting along well. Don't they make cute couples?" Vicky asked.

"They sure do," Lisa said.

Would anyone notice if I pushed someone over the side of our balcony in the middle of the night? Joe thought, then stopped himself. Now wasn't the time.

They drank more wine and talked. Jerry and Vicky both yawned at the same time.

"I see how it is. We bore you," Joe said. "Fine, just go back to your cabin and sleep."

"I think we'll do that," Jerry laughed. He finished his drink. "Kids, we're leaving now."

After thanking them, the family left.

"They sure seem like a nice family, don't they, Joey?" Lisa asked.

"I must admit, it felt like we were with old friends we hadn't seen in a while, catching up on what we'd missed. The kids sure had fun."

Joe didn't know why but felt good about hanging with the Newharts. He never wanted friends before except for the couple that ran the Charity Mission in Phoenix.

The next morning began their first sea day. Alexa and Scotty slept while Lisa and Joe both took a shower.

"Where would everyone like to eat breakfast? One of the formal dining rooms or the buffet?"

"The buffet," the kids answered.

They walked to the buffet and got their food. "That looks like a good table by the window," Joe said. "We'll have a great view."

As they set their trays down, they heard someone say, "Hey there, strangers. Long time no see."

Turning around to see who it was, Lisa said, "Look, Joey, the Newharts are right behind us. Should we pull the tables together?"

"I have a better idea," Vicky said. "Why don't the four kids sit at one table and the four adults at the other?"

"We need to hang out with more families to learn all the tricks," Joe said. "You four kids can sit together, and the adults will sit over here."

"Cool, thanks, Daddy," Alexa grinned.

After breakfast, the kids went down to the arcade. Jerry and Vicky went their own way. Joe and Lisa strolled around the ship.

After lunch, the adults met up and watched their kids drive the racecars without telling them. The kids saw them and waved as they came around the track on their second lap. When they were finished racing, the kids ran to them.

"That was so much fun!" Scotty said excitedly.

"Yeah, even though I let Scotty win," Alexa said.

You didn't let me win," Scotty said. "You just wanted to hang back with Kevin."

"If you guys want to go swimming, we're all going to sit by the pool, listen to the band, and drink," Joe said.

"We'll go get our swimsuits and be right back," Alexa said.

"Ok, hurry back, but don't run," Lisa said.

"Can we go get ours, too?" Kevin asked. Jerry looked at Vicky.

"Ok, ahead. Come straight back." Jerry said. "Stay together."

After an afternoon of swimming and drinking, it was time to get changed for dinner. Everyone ate less than the night before. After dinner, the kids wanted to play laser tag. The adults sat in the lounge and listened to a lady play piano and sing while they relaxed and drank.

"Are you guys going on an excursion tomorrow?" Jerry asked.

"No, we're going to walk around a little on our own, check out the boardwalk and the brothel. We've never been to a brothel together as a family," Joe laughed.

"Joe, you're not like any minister I've known. You're just like a regular cool guy."

"That's me, just a regular Joe."

"Vicky and I had a great time hanging out with you. Too bad we live so far apart."

"It's only a three-hour drive from our place to Tucson. I drive around the state all the time. That is if you wouldn't mind us coming down to visit sometime," Joe said.

"That would be great," Jerry said.

Lisa and Joe called it an early night, relaxing in their suite with drinks and snacks. They were scheduled to dock in Ketchikan at 7:00 a.m. They ordered breakfast from room service the night before to be there at six.

In the morning, everyone got up and dressed early. "We're going down to get off the ship when we're finished eating," Joe said.

It was a lovely sunny day. The temperature was already in the mid-50s, and the high was forecast to be sixty-nine.

"I thought it would be colder here," Lisa said.

They strolled down the boardwalk, checking out the little shops. Dolly's House was a well-known brothel in town back in the 19th century. It was turned into a brothel museum, showing authentic items from the gold rush days. There were secret places where they hid alcohol during prohibition. There were a lot of old pictures of the prostitutes that worked there. There were outfits they considered sexy back in those days.

"We're eating lunch here today," Joe said. For lunch, they had the best salmon they'd ever tasted.

They had to return to the ship by 2:00 p.m., so they headed back after lunch. The rest of the day on the ship, the adults had a relaxing afternoon.

"We can sleep in tomorrow," Joe said. "We get to Juneau right after lunch. We're going on an excursion to see the Mendenhall Glacier tomorrow, then a whale-watching boat."

At lunch, Joe, Lisa, and the kids went to the buffet and headed to disembark. While standing in line to board the shuttle, they ran into the Newharts.

"I guess someone thinks we need to hang out more," Jerry said.

"I guess so. But I think that's a good thing." Joe leaned in and whispered, "Much better than being stuck hanging with some old snooty people."

Jerry whispered, "You got that right. The first night they seated you with us, we thought you would be our snooty people."

They walked down a path through the rainforest to get to the glacier. Their guide pointed out the different indigenous plants.

I bet Amanda would love this, Joe thought. *I wonder if she's escaped? Damn, there are lots of places you could hide a body in the rainforest.*

They were almost back to the beginning of the trail. Lisa nudged Joe and whispered, "Look at those two, Joey." Kevin and Alexa were holding hands.

They took a shuttle to get to the whale-watching boat. They saw over a dozen whales.

In the morning, they arrived in Skagway. They stood in line to ride on the White Pass and Yukon Route Railroad. It was an old-fashioned train with two seats facing each other on each side of the train car. The Newharts walked up right behind them. The four adults sat across from each other, as did the four kids.

There were open platforms at the front and rear of each train car where several people could stand outside between the cars. After a while, Alexa and Kevin got up and walked back to stand there. Joe saw them face each other and hold hands.

"Oh my God," Vicky said, glimpsing them too. "Is that boy finally gonna have his first real kiss?" Sure enough, they leaned in towards each other at the same time. Slowly, their lips met in a long, clumsy kiss.

"That was Alexa's first kiss, too," Lisa said. "They'd be so embarrassed if they knew we saw them. When they're a little older, I'll show them the picture I took of it."

The next day was another sea day. The kids found more things to do independently while the adults went to their first art auction and then a Broadway-type show. The Romanos bought two pieces of art.

The Romanos wanted an amazingly detailed painting of Tuscany by Sam Park. They bought another painting the Newharts liked but wouldn't bid on because they didn't have that kind of money to spend on artwork.

"Tomorrow we'll be in Canada," Joe said. "It's an island called Victoria BC. We have an excursion to Butchart Gardens."

Alexa asked, "Are Kevin and his family going there, too?"

"Oh, it's Kevin and his family now," Lisa laughed.

"Yes, I'll be there, and I'm bringing my family." Everyone laughed. "I guess you can't get away from us."

"I don't think we want to get away from you," Alexa said. "I know I don't."

Back on the ship, they walked around and shopped. "We should get everyone a souvenir from the ship. Then we can stop by the Newhart's cabin."

They knocked on the Newhart's cabin door. Jerry answered. "Are you guys lost? Your cabin is several decks up, isn't it, or should I say your vacation villa?"

"We wanted to stop by to give you something, being as this is our last day onboard," Lisa said as they gave them souvenirs.

"There's something we can't give to you yet. You know that Michael Godard painting we bought at the auction?" Joe asked.

"Yeah, the one I loved. I hope we can come see it sometime," Vicky said.

"Well, you couldn't see it at our place. It's paid for and will be shipped to your home. We hope you enjoy it as much as we enjoy giving it to you," Joe said. "Maybe we can come down and see it sometime."

"Oh, no way!" Vicky exclaimed. "I don't know what to say other than thank you very much. I wish we could return the favor."

"You already have," Lisa said. "Now we have another reason to come visit you guys. You'll need to drive to Canyon City to see our Sam Park painting. We need to get going. I think meeting each other may be the only thing the kids remember from this trip. They sure got along great."

"We're going to miss you," Vicky said, giving them both hugs.

"We'll miss you guys, too," Joe said. They exchanged phone numbers and left.

FIFTEEN

WHERE'S AMANDA?

Nicole told Detective Stone, "We got the DNA results on the hairs I found in Sarah Kelly's car. Unfortunately, they belonged to her husband, Michael. Also, the fibers we found on most of the victims match each other. After the statement from homeless Michelle, we tracked them to a specific brand of black hoodies made in China. We've gone over everything with a fine-tooth comb. Let's go over the crime scenes again."

"There might still be something we missed," Caroline said. "There's nothing more we can do here while we wait for lab results."

"Ok, girls, take a couple of uniforms with you and get going," Detective Stone ordered. "Let me know if you find anything."

Captain Connors walked in and said, "After that forest fire was put out, they found Valerie Kantrel's naked body in the front seat of her truck. The truck was at the bottom of a ravine. Looks like someone left the truck running and put it in gear. Normally, they would look for soot in the lungs to see if she was still breathing during the fire to help determine the cause of death. Her truck and body were burnt so badly that her organs were completely cooked from the intense fire. They had to identify her through DNA."

Detective Scott asked, "This isn't a Dark murder?"

"The fire destroyed any possible clues," Captain Connors replied. "The Channel 10 news director received a letter from someone claiming to be our Dark serial killer. The postmark on it was from Alaska. They scanned it and sent it to us in an email." They gathered around the computer screen to read it.

Dear News Director,

I'm the one you call The Dark Killer. The name fits, but not because the killings are at night. I consider it an acronym. To me, **DARK** stands for what I do, Drug, Abduct, Rape, Kill. Maybe the police couldn't tell because of the fire, but Valerie Kantrel was my eighth victim. I ripped her panties off before shoving them down her throat. If you don't believe me, here's a picture of her earring I took.

Sincerely,

DARK

At the bottom of the page was a picture of the earring.

"That earring looks like a match from the picture we got from her parents," Nicole said. "They took a picture of her before she went out the day she was murdered. This has to be him. We never released the information about the panties or the earrings."

Captain Connors called the news director at Channel 10 immediately. "I'm coming over to pick up that letter from DARK. Please don't release all the information in it. That could compromise our case. You can say what the acronym stands for and that Valerie was a victim of the serial killer, nothing more. That's your scoop. Nothing else."

———

THE ROMANOS ARRIVED home from the cruise. Once everyone was finally in bed asleep, Joe headed downstairs to check on Amanda. He unlocked the bottom door and opened it. It was dark and quiet. He wondered if she somehow escaped while he was gone. Both doors leading up to the house were still double-locked.

"Amanda, I'm home," he called out. "Are you here?"

He got no answer. He turned the lights on and looked around. Everything looked normal. He called out for her again. No answer. He looked into the tunnel and called out again. Nothing. He looked in her room. It was dark. He turned on the light and let out a sigh of relief. She was asleep on her futon. He took his clothes off and cuddled up to her.

She woke up and looked at him. "Joey! I missed you," she said, throwing her arms around his neck. She rolled over on top of him and kissed him for the longest time. "I've been so horny thinking about you every day. I love you, Joey."

"I love you, Mandy. I missed you. I thought you might not be here when I got home. I sure would have found a way out in less than a week."

"I planned to, but while you were gone, I realized I had strong feelings for you. I have it made here. You take better care of me than anyone ever has. You may not believe it, but this is better than my life before I met you."

"I'm glad you're happy being here. Would you like to see pictures from our vacation?"

"Sure, that would be fun." They looked at over a hundred pictures on his phone. She saw pictures with Joe's family in them.

"It looks like you had a lot of fun. Lisa's cute. Your kids are precious. Who knows, maybe one day we can go on a vacation together. I wish I were their stepmother."

"I don't see that happening, but who knows the future?"

"When do you think you can get my stuff from my house?"

"I can go later tonight."

"Here's a key to my house and the list of things I would like to have from there when you get a chance. The address is on the top. Do you want to have sex with me, Joey?"

"Not tonight."

She looked disappointed.

"Tonight, I want to make love to you."

Her face lit up. "I would love it if we made love." It turned out to be a quickie. They had missed each other and were so horny that neither of them could hold back. They fell asleep in each other's arms.

Joe's alarm went off at 1:00 a.m. He got dressed and headed out to Amanda's house. He picked up most of her clothes, a couple of books in her room, and the stuffed animals from her bed.

When he got back home, he put Amanda's stuffed animals on the bed with her. After he dropped her things off in her room while she slept, he headed back upstairs to get in bed with Lisa. In the morning, Lisa woke him with a kiss.

After that, most nights that Joe stayed home, he spent much of the night with his new lover after Lisa was asleep. It worked out well for him. His relationship with Amanda didn't take anything away from his relationship with Lisa. If anything, it made their relationship better, even though Joe felt Lisa becoming more suspicious of him.

He loved having sex with them, and he felt in love with both. He didn't just have sex with Amanda. They played cards, watched movies, and shared long conversations.

Wednesday was a lazy day at the Romano house. It felt good. Thursday was a different story. After weeks of being unable to further his cause, doing God's work as he put it, Joe wanted to get out of the house for a while. He just needed to come up with a good excuse. Lisa walked into the living room, where Joe sat on the arm of the couch, looking toward a blank TV screen.

"Joey, those things work better if you turn them on." They both laughed.

"I was just staring off into space, thinking. I didn't realize I was looking at the TV."

"Maybe you need to get out of the house for a while. Go sit in a park and enjoy nature. Take a day for just you, okay?"

I have the perfect excuse: my wife is kicking me out of the house for the day, Joe thought. "Okay, honey. Maybe that's what I need. Get out and clear my head. Anything you need me to take care of while I'm out?"

"No, this is not a day for chores. It's just a Joey day," Lisa said. "Be home in time for dinner, please. Dessert will be served later in the bedroom if you're interested in something sweet and spicy," she smiled coyly.

"Okay, you got it. I'll be in my office for a bit, then I'm out of here. I'll be home for dinner.

I'm looking forward to dessert." Joe couldn't believe how perfect this turned out. His wife actually gave him time to kill someone.

Down in his office, he spent some time with Amanda. "Baby, you can't just stay down here in this hole all the time. I'll find some time to bring you to the garage so we can sit outside the back door. I'll put a couple of chairs behind the garage for us."

"That sounds awesome. Do you have any exciting plans for today? Are you going to kill anyone?"

"I hope so. If not, I hope to at least find someone to stalk."

"I wish I could come with you. I think we'd make a great team. I'll do things with you Lisa would never do."

"Maybe one of these days, baby. I'd enjoy that, too."

"Sounds exciting. Would you let me do some of the killing? That would be so hot to do together," she smiled. "I wouldn't mind if all I got to do was watch, but I'd love to be part of it. I used to fantasize about killing people. I never thought I'd get the opportunity to do it and get away with it."

"I think the day will come when we can go out together. I think we'd make a great team, too." He looked around the basement and gathered anything he might need. He hoped to be able to get the whole job done today. He felt like he needed it. He put his tools in the bed of his truck, and then he went back into the house.

"Lisa, I'm ready to go," Joe called out.

Lisa gave him a hug and kiss. "Don't you worry about anything, you hear, Joey?"

SIXTEEN

CABIN IN THE WOODS

It was late morning, almost lunchtime. Joe stopped at a local diner, sat down, and picked up a menu. "I'm Katie, your waitress. Can I start you off with a drink?"

"I'll have a cup of coffee."

She came right back. "Here's your coffee, honey. Have you decided what you want?"

"I'll take the Heart Attack Omelet with toast and hash browns. Why's it called that?"

Katie laughed. "It's just loaded with everything. The name sure gets people's attention."

Joe took a sip of coffee, reached around, and picked up a newspaper from the table behind him. "Front page of the religious section. People either love or hate me but never stop talking about me. There must be some crazy reason Pastor Joe shaved his head," he said quietly to himself.

"Honey, if you're going to sit there and talk to yourself, I can come keep you company. Not much going on around here right now."

Joe was startled. He didn't realize Katie was back.

"Sure, It'll be nice to have someone to chat with."

"I'll be back as soon as your food is up," Katie smiled.

She brought his omelet out and two pieces of blueberry pie when it was ready. She put the omelet and a slice of pie in front of him. She sat down with the other slice. "I hope you like blueberry pie, honey. It's the only one we have right now."

"Blueberry pie is my favorite. I'm Joe."

"Oh my God, you're that preacher from the television, aren't you?"

"Yeah, that's me. I'm trying to lay low. This is my 'me' day."

"I can sure use a 'me' day sometime. Connie comes in at eleven, but my shift doesn't end until nine tonight. Too long of a day for this old lady."

"Old lady? How old are you, if I may ask?"

"I'm thirty-eight, but this job makes me feel like eighty-eight."

"You're not old. You're just overworked and tired."

"Ain't that the truth! Sometimes, I wish I could just run away, at least for a day."

"Maybe I can help, at least for half a day. When does the lunch crowd thin out?"

"Most customers on Thursdays are gone by one."

"Great, meet me by the back door of the restaurant at 1:30. Tell them you have an emergency or something."

"Honey, I can't afford to miss half a day's pay and tips, even if it isn't much on Thursdays. I get most of my tips from the lunch crowd today, but I still need every cent I can get. This ain't the highest paying job."

"Leave that to me," Joe said, slapping a hundred-dollar bill down on the table. "Keep the change. Will a few more of those cover your pay and tips for the rest of the day?"

"Yes, just the change from the hundred would be more than enough, but Miss Katie Johnson ain't that kind of lady, pastor."

"Don't get me wrong. I wasn't thinking of you as a prostitute. I just thought we could have a nice day keeping each other company as friends. I'm happily married. I just didn't want you to lose money."

"Okay, but just the change is enough."

They chatted while they ate together.

"Pick you up by the back door at 1:30?"

"Uh, I don't know."

"You know you need it. Just get away for one afternoon. I'm a happily married man and a pastor. Consider this as life counseling."

"Okay, fine." She yelled, "Hey Chuck, I'm quitting this job at 1:30 today."

Chuck yelled back, "Ok, see you tomorrow, Katie."

"It could be a whole lot worse. I work with a lot of hungry, homeless people. At least you have a job and a roof over your head."

"True, but I wish I could make enough money and have the time to start a family. I have some friends I hang out with when I'm not working a million hours a week. Eat, sleep, work, that's my whole life. I always wanted to have kids."

"It sounds like you need a way out. I can help you find your peaceful place. Please don't tell anyone who I am. I like to stay under the radar in public."

"Not a problem. No one would believe me anyway. How was your omelet?"

"The omelet was awesome. This blueberry pie was, too."

"I'm glad you liked it. I'll see you out back around 1:30."

"See you soon," Joe said. *She needs to get out of here*, he thought. Joe drove around to look for a spot for his new friendship. It had to be very private for what he had planned.

Years ago, a retiree built three cabins in the woods. They were closed down years ago, shortly after he died. Joe drove up an old forest dirt road that badly needed repair. It looked like they had been abandoned.

He drove about a mile up the road before he came to the first cabin. They were way back in the woods and over a half-mile apart.

As a result, it took over another mile of driving before he reached the third cabin. "This looks perfect. It's over two miles from any road."

The front door was locked, but he had his lockpicks with him and picked the old lock easily. He stashed his black bag in the cabin, retrieving a syringe filled with midazolam from the bag. He noticed small end tables on both sides of the couch, each with a little drawer. He did some quick dusting.

He decided it would be best to leave the syringe in the drawer on the right side of the couch, furthest from the door. He just had to make sure that Katie sat to his left. He found a queen-sized four-poster bed in the bedroom that gave him perfect places to attach restraints. When he had everything set up, he looked at his watch and realized he should head back.

Going back to the diner took less time than he thought. He was almost ten minutes early. He would sit there and wait until 1:30 when he saw Katie taking a trash bag to the dumpster. She spotted him.

"Hi Joe, you're early. I hope you haven't been waiting long."

"I just got here. I know I'm early. I'll wait."

"Give me a minute," she said, taking off her apron as she walked to the back door. "I quit, Chuck. I'm out of here." She grabbed her tip money from her apron pocket and stuck it in the side pocket of her skirt. Then she tossed the apron inside and got into Joe's truck. "This is exciting. I feel like I'm being naughty, skipping out on work. I do need this," she said as Joe pulled out of the parking lot.

"I know you need this," Joe said. "I need this, too. I love to get away from the whole world and go to a place of solitude whenever possible."

"I bet. You're in front of thousands of people all the time. I'd run away, screaming."

"Trust me, I've been tempted more than once. I think you'll love this place. You can't get more secluded." Joe slowly turned onto the dirt road. It was very rough.

"Uh...are you sure we can make it? This isn't much of a road."

"I have four-wheel drive, and this non-road means we'll be left alone. You'll love it to death."

After several minutes, Katie asked, "How far are we going? Looks like we're lost in the middle of the wilderness." She looked concerned.

"Only about two miles. It seems a whole lot further because of how slow we have to drive. Roll down your window and smell the fresh, clean air out here."

"Joe, this is heaven. I wish I never had to leave," Katie sighed.

"Look up ahead, that's the first cabin."

"Is that where we're going?"

"No, mine's the third one. We're almost halfway there."

After a few minutes, she commented, "You sure do like seclusion, don't you? I don't think anyone I know knows this place exists. You could do anything out here, and no one would ever know," she said nervously. He saw her hands shake.

"Never thought about it like that. You're safe with me. You trust me, don't you?"

"Of course, I trust you." After driving a while longer, Katie asked, "Is that the second cabin coming up?"

"Yep. The next one's mine." Several minutes later, he parked in front of the third cabin. "This is my place to get away from everybody. Now it's your place of solitude, too," Joe told her as he exited the truck. He walked in the front door, and she followed.

"You were right, Joe. I do want to spend the rest of my life here."

"That's a comfy couch, and you can see out of three windows sitting there. Kick off your shoes and have a seat." Joe quickly sat down on the right side of the couch. Katie sat down on the left end and kicked off her shoes. "Why are you so far away, baby? I don't bite unless you want me to," he laughed.

"Why did you call me baby?" Katie asked nervously.

"I didn't mean anything by it. You kept calling me honey at the diner. Let's just relax and enjoy the peace for a while."

Katie nervously leaned back. "How long are we going to be out here?"

"We've only been here a few minutes. You wanted to spend your life here."

"Not literally. I don't want to be out here after dark," Katie said in a shaky voice.

Joe reached into the drawer while Katie was looking the other way. He slid over close to her.

"Why are you so far away? Don't you trust me, baby?" She was up against the armrest. She tried to stand, but Joe grabbed her and held her tightly.

"What are you doing? Let go!"

"Shhhh," he said, sticking the needle into her thigh right through her skirt. "Don't fight it, baby. Close your eyes and relax. Enjoy the peace." Joe held onto her for a few minutes as she struggled to escape. He finally let go, and she jumped up off the couch quickly. She ran out the door into the woods. Joe followed her. He sat on the ground beside her and put his arm around her when she fell.

"What did you do? I feel very stra...strange. I can't...can't..." Katie's head fell over onto Joe's shoulder. She was out.

Joe picked her up and carried her back to the cabin and into the bedroom. Sitting her up on the bed, he took off her blouse and bra. He slid his hand between her legs under her skirt and rubbed the crotch of her panties.

He unzipped her skirt, pulled it off, and threw it on the floor. All she had left on were a pair of thigh-high white stockings and white panties. He grabbed the top of the hose on her left leg and pulled it off. He repeated the process for her right leg. He tossed one of the stockings to the head of the bed. He slid her panties off.

He pulled her right arm up and attached the leather bondage restraint to her wrist. He did the same with her right leg. He moved to the other side of the bed and attached her left arm and leg.

Joe opened the leather bag he had stashed there earlier and got out a cold bottle of water. He sat on the edge of the bed while he drank and waited for his conquest to wake.

Katie slowly woke up. She shook her head back and forth to try to clear the fuzziness. "What are you doing, pastor? Let me go."

"I told you you'd spend the rest of your life here. No one comes out here anymore. I don't think anyone knows this place still exists. It's been abandoned for years."

"Why are you doing this, pastor?"

"I'm no pastor, baby. I just play one on TV to get money from all the stupid people that believe heaven and hell are real."

"What are you going to do?"

"You hate your life. You should thank me for taking away all your sadness, pain, and misery. You'll never be overworked again. You'll rest in peace eternally."

Katie screamed, "No! Oh God! Don't kill me!"

"No matter how loud you scream, no one will hear you. There's nobody for miles." Katie cried uncontrollably. He buried his face between her legs. He knew that if they ever did find her out here, they wouldn't find any DNA from him. Any evidence would be long gone. Her body would rot away and be nothing but dried-up old bones.

Katie cried, "Please don't rape me. I was nice to you. I gave you pie."

"Katie, I'm a sick motherfucker." He grabbed his lubed-up penis and entered her.

"Stop, it hurts." She struggled against the restraints.

He grabbed her stocking as he felt a pending orgasm. He lifted her head and put it under her neck, then crisscrossed the ends across her throat. He wound the ends of it around each hand and pulled hard. He came as he pulled it tight. She couldn't breathe, and no blood was getting to her brain. He let out the longest grunt of pleasure.

After he came, he realized the stocking had stretched enough to let her breathe. She started to struggle again. He wrapped it around his hands some more so they would be right by her neck as he pulled. At the same time, he pushed his thumbs into her windpipe. After a few more minutes, he was sure she was dead.

He picked up her skirt and felt inside the pocket. "She won't need this anymore." It was more than he'd given her. He got all her morning and lunchtime tips, too. He didn't need it, but why let it go to waste?

SEVENTEEN
PUPPY LOVE

J oe headed back to Amanda's house in the early evening with another list she made for him. He rounded everything up and put it in a large plastic garbage bag. He carried it to his truck and put it on the back seat. Joe drove home feeling satisfied. He hoped Lisa wanted to have sex tonight so he could relive this day in his mind while screwing her.

When he arrived home, he parked his truck in the detached garage and carried the rest of Amanda's things to her room.

"Hi Mandy, how are you doing?" Joe asked.

"I'm okay, Joey. I guess you're going to spend time with Lisa now," she pouted.

Joe kissed her. "I'll be with you later."

He went back to the garage and walked to the front door. "Lisa, I'm home." With a sigh, he collapsed into his easy chair. Alexa and Scotty sat there watching television. They watched a show for a while when Lisa entered the living room.

"Hi baby, I hope you had a good day," she said.

"I sure did. I hope you did, too."

"Joey, we need to talk about something."

"What's up, Lisa?"

"We should talk in private. Let's go to our bedroom."

"Ok, I'll be there as soon as this show ends."

"How much longer?" Lisa asked in a sultry voice. He didn't seem to notice.

"About five minutes."

"Ok, Joey, I'll be waiting for you up there," she said in the same sultry tone.

Joe walked up the stairs to find the bedroom door closed. He was surprised when he opened it. Lisa was lying on the bed completely naked, other than a pair of sexy panties.

"Damn, I didn't need to watch the last five minutes," Joe said as he undressed. He climbed onto the bed and kissed her.

"The kids are home, so we need to be quiet and make it quick. I still need to make dinner," she said, going back to making out while she rubbed his manhood. She leaned over and took the tip of his erect penis in her mouth.

"Didn't you shower after the last time we had sex, or do you have a girlfriend, Joey?"

"I was in a hurry and didn't shower. Sorry."

She mounted him, pulling the crotch of her panties to the side. Joe was so turned on knowing that Lisa just tasted Katie's pussy on him. They both had intense orgasms within a few minutes.

Lisa cleaned up quickly and went downstairs to start dinner while Joe took a hot shower. Just before he got out, Lisa walked into the bathroom. She took off all her clothes and joined him.

"Again already?"

"No, Joey, I just wanted a minute in here with you before I shower. I have dinner cooking. When you get downstairs, can you watch it for me?" Lisa asked as she rubbed her soaped-up body against him.

"Well, maybe," Joe said as he reached between her legs.

Lisa kissed him and then pushed his hand away. "Joey, we've got to get dinner on the table. Rinse off and get downstairs. My turn in the shower." She stuck her tongue out at him.

"Okay, I probably couldn't rise to the occasion again yet anyway," Joe laughed as he stepped out. He dried off, got dressed, and went downstairs. He checked on dinner, sat down, and watched TV with the kids. He checked on dinner again at commercial.

About fifteen minutes later, Alexa asked, "Where's mom?"

"It was her turn to take a shower. She'll be down soon," Dad said.

"Yes, she will," Joe heard from behind him.

"Lisa, I didn't hear you come downstairs."

"I've been in the kitchen already. Who's hungry?" she asked. "Dinner will be ready in two minutes."

"You know we're all hungry smelling you're cooking," Joe said. "Go wash up, kids."

After dinner, Joe asked, "Who would like us to have the Newharts over next weekend?"

"Seriously, Dad!" Alexa said excitedly. "Kevin's going to be staying here next weekend?"

"Yeah, I was thinking we might even invite Jerry, Vicky, and Makayla, too."

"Can they stay? Please."

"Yes, they're staying the weekend. We have plenty of room. Micki can sleep in your room with you, and Kevin can sleep in Scotty's room. Their parents can use the guest master bedroom. I have no sermon this weekend because they're running an old rerun again this Sunday. Jerry and Vicky have this Monday off, so they'll be here from tomorrow morning until Monday afternoon."

"Alexa loves a boy," Scotty taunted. "Kissy, kiss, mwah."

"You're just jealous, Scotty. You're too scared to kiss Micki," Alexa taunted back.

"Cool it, guys," Mom said. "You both have a case of puppy love."

"Puppy love? What does that mean?" Scotty asked. "And I'm not scared to kiss anyone," he said, sticking his tongue out at Alexa. "I'll even kiss a puppy."

"Puppy is because you're young and cute and love because it's your first infatuation. It's an old expression. It's awesome to see. You'll always be my little puppies."

"Scotty, we're puppies," Alexa laughed.

"Woof-woof," Scotty said, sounding like a dog. Everyone laughed.

"Do you know when they're supposed to arrive in the morning?" Lisa asked. "Should we wait for them to eat breakfast?"

"Jerry told me they will be heading out by 6:00 a.m., so they should be here by around nine or so," Joe said. "I'll call Jerry tonight and let him know not to eat breakfast."

"Great. I'll have breakfast ready," Lisa said. "I can get some stuff ready tonight so we can have sourdough biscuits by morning. I'm looking forward to seeing them."

"I am, too," Joe said. "I've never known another couple that we've ever felt so comfortable with right off the bat, or ever."

"I know, right?"

The next morning, everyone got up early, excited about their company. Lisa made enough food to feed a small army. The house smelled awesome. The odor of bacon filled the air, along with the smell of freshly baked sourdough biscuits. Lisa's homemade sausage gravy added to the heavenly aroma.

When it was close to the Newhart's arrival, Alexa and Scotty sat by the front window.

"He's here!" Alexa shouted. "And Kevin brought his whole family."

Everyone walked out on the front porch. They parked their car, got out, and waved. The Romanos waved back as the kids ran to meet each other. Alexa ran straight into Kevin's arms and hugged him. Micki ran up to Scotty and threw her arms around him. He hugged her back. Jerry and Vicky made their way onto the porch. They all welcomed each other with hugs.

"It's so beautiful up here," Vicky said. "And look at your beautiful home. I love it!"

"Come on in. I hope you're hungry. Lisa made enough food to feed an army or a couple of families with teenagers," Joe said.

The adults walked inside and were smacked in the face by the aromatic smell of breakfast. Joe watched the kids from the front door.

Before they headed inside, Scotty said, "Hey, Alexa, watch this." He pulled Makayla to him and planted a kiss on her lips. "See, I'm not afraid to kiss a pretty girl."

Makayla kissed him. "Now we're even," she said. Joe chuckled as he walked inside.

"It smells like heaven in here," Vicky said.

"Thank you. Alexa, please show the Newharts where the bathrooms are so they can get ready for breakfast. Unless you guys need some of your things now, we can eat breakfast first, then have the kids bring your stuff in."

"I don't think we need anything before breakfast," Jerry said. "Lisa, it smells so divine in here. I can't wait. My mouth's watering."

Everyone finally made it to the table. Alexa and Kevin sat there holding their forks, staring across the table at each other.

"Alexa. Alexa? Earth to Alexa, are you here?" Mom asked.

"Oh, sorry, mom. What's up?"

"How's the food? Don't you like it? How about you, Kevin?"

Alexa and Kevin both laughed. "Sorry, Mrs. Romano. It's all delicious. I just got a little distracted," Kevin said, putting a forkful in his mouth.

"We can see that," she laughed.

After breakfast, Lisa, Alexa, and Scotty cleared the table while Joe and the Newharts returned to the patio. The others joined them shortly.

"Dad, is it okay to show Kevin and Micki around our woods?" Alexa asked.

"It's okay with me if their parents don't mind, but the four of you stay together."

"Ok, Daddy, we will. Is it okay with you, Mr. and Mrs. Newhart?"

"That's fine, but be careful. Don't get hurt or lost or anything else you shouldn't get. Anything to add, dad?" Vicky asked, looking at Jerry.

Jerry shook his head and said, "Have fun, guys." The kids ran off into the woods to play while the adults kicked back on the patio, drinking iced tea and talking.

After a few hours, Lisa called Alexa on her cell phone. "Do you guys want to come eat lunch now?"

"Sure, Mom, we'll be right there."

"Lisa makes the best sandwiches," Joe said. "She even bakes the bread herself."

"That bread smells fantastic," Vicky said.

"Thank you, Vicky. I baked it last night."

"The beginning of the line is where the plates are, obviously. Help yourselves. You kids go get washed up."

Everyone chowed down and ate too much. They sat around out back, talking and eating watermelon.

After about an hour, the kids were ready to go back to the woods to play. "I wish Kevin and Micki could stay here longer," Alexa said. "Maybe we can go down there and visit them next weekend," she said before running off to catch up with the other three.

"I don't have a live show next weekend. They're having a marathon all weekend," Joe said. "You know what I'm thinking? If you guys wouldn't mind, how about we come down to Tucson next weekend? Your kids could spend the week here, and we'll bring them back with us."

"I think that sounds okay," Jerry said, looking at Vicky. "What do you think, honey?"

"Sounds great. I just hope it won't be too much trouble for you guys."

"Don't even think about it. It's no trouble at all. We'd love for them to stay. You have great kids. When we come down there, we can stay at a hotel if you don't have the extra room," Joe said.

"Having enough room for everyone was the only thing I was worried about, so I appreciate that," Vicky said.

"There you go, it's decided," Lisa said. "You guys get to spend some time without any kids around for a change. Enjoy it."

"Your kids can stay with us next weekend. That way, you only need one hotel room and can have a little alone time, too. I know the kids would love that," Vicky said.

"Sounds perfect," Lisa said. "They'll be excited."

When they got back to the patio, Joe called them over. "Alexa, Scotty, would you like Kevin and Micki to stay up here with us this week?"

"Are you serious?" Alexa asked. "Don't mess with me, daddy."

"Then next weekend, we'll go down to Tucson, and the two of you will stay with the Newharts while Mom and I sleep in a motel."

"No way, Dad! You're the best parents ever!" Alexa exclaimed.

"Awesome, Dad!" Scotty said. "This is the best summer ever!"

"There are two sets of best parents ever. We all came up with this plan, not just me and your mom," Joe said.

"You're right, dad. The Newharts are great parents, too," Alexa said.

Jerry said, "I didn't even ask. Is this alright with you and your sister, Kevin?"

"Heck, yeah, Dad!"

"I love it, daddy," Makayla said.

"We're going to have pizza and wings for dinner tonight," Joe said. "I ordered eight extra-large pizzas, two meat lovers', two veggie lovers', two pepperoni, and two cheese with four dozen hot wings," Joe said.

"You ordered eight extra-large pizzas for eight of us?" Vicky asked. "Plus, four dozen wings?"

"We have four teenagers here," Joe said. "Plus, no one hates leftover pizza."

After dinner, Lisa put the leftovers away. "You know, there are only seven slices of leftover pizza. That's less than one pizza and no wings left."

After everyone was asleep, Joe brought some pizza to Amanda.

The smell of freshly brewed coffee and bacon filled the air on Sunday morning. Lisa also made omelets and hash browns.

"This is how you get fat," Joe said. He unbuttoned the top button on his pants and leaned back. "Too much good food. It's about time to teach the boys how to split firewood. It's almost September. It won't be long before we can have a fire in the fireplace."

"We should teach them today," Jerry said. "Give them something to use up some of that teenage energy."

"Great idea, Jerry," Joe said. "Kill two birds with one stone. We can teach them sometime after lunch. Kevin can impress Alexa with his muscles and axe-handling skills."

An hour after they finished eating lunch, Joe and Jerry called their kids over to the woodpile.

"We're going to teach you how to split wood properly without hurting yourselves, hopefully," Joe said.

Joe gave each of the kids a pair of work gloves and a pair of safety glasses. After going over the technique, they decided to have a contest to see who could split the most wood in five minutes. Micki didn't compete. She split a few pieces when they were being taught. She said it was too hard for her to go fast. To everyone's surprise, Scotty, the youngest, split over twice as much wood as the other two. "Looks like I'm a natural."

"It looks like you have a new chore. That'll teach you to do so well." Everyone laughed.

"That's okay," Scotty said. "I like doing it. I don't mind being the new family wood splitter. How much does it pay?"

"You get to sit in front of a warm fire with us this winter, and we'll even let you continue eating our food," Joe said with a hearty laugh. "Don't worry, Scotty, I'll take care of you. It depends on how much wood you split. We go through a lot every winter. It's nice having a fire burning all day whenever we can."

The four kids had fun splitting wood the rest of the afternoon.

"They should sleep well tonight," Lisa said, walking out onto the patio with two cold beers. "Are you boys thirsty?" she asked, handing them the beers. "What can I get you, Vicky?"

"Do you have any of that wine we were drinking earlier? That was good. I think there may be half a bottle left."

"We sure do. We have another full bottle, too. I'll get glasses and the wine," Lisa said. "Hey Joey, want to build a small fire in the pit tonight? We can roast marshmallows and make s'mores if you'd like."

"Sounds good. We can try out some of that split wood."

They made a small fire, roasted marshmallows, and ate s'mores. The evening cooled off enough that the fire felt good.

Sunday morning was a peaceful, lazy day. Good family, friends, food, beer, and pre-season football. Monday morning felt busier. The Newharts slowly got their things together so they could leave for home after lunch. After lunch, they sat on the back patio, drinking iced tea and talking.

At one o'clock, Jerry said, "I think we should hit the road. We'd like to try to get home a little early. It'll be our first night in years, just the two of us. And we're going to run into rush hour traffic."

"We should leave our kids with you for a week sometime," Joe said.

"We'd be happy to repay the favor," Jerry said.

"We all need time away from everyone except each other sometimes," Vicky lamented. "The car is all packed. I can't tell you how much we appreciate you keeping the kids for the rest of the week and all you've done for us. We've had the best time. We already love you guys like family."

"Yes, we do," Jerry agreed. "It's never just the two of us. We'll see you Friday night or Saturday?"

"Well, you guys are family. We'll come down Saturday. You guys have a good Friday night together," Joe said. "I'll text you when we leave the house. We may sleep in a little."

Vicky called Kevin and Micki over. "You guys behave and mind

Mr. and Mrs. Romano. We don't want any bad reports, you hear?" Jerry lectured.

"We're at Pastor Joe's house. We would be too scared to misbehave," Micki said.

"Maybe we should leave you with them so you'd never misbehave," Vicky laughed.

"But wouldn't you miss us?" Micki asked.

"Not at all. We'd come see you on the weekends," Jerry laughed. "I'm kidding. Of course, we'd miss you."

EIGHTEEN
THE DREAM

After the kids and Lisa were asleep, Joe headed down to spend time with Amanda.

The following five days seemed to fly by. Joe and Amanda had sex almost every day, sometimes more than once. Sometimes, the sex was romantic. Sometimes it was hot and heavy rough sex, and sometimes it was simulated violent rape sex. Amanda loved it all. She was the kinkiest woman Joe had ever known.

The Romanos started packing up their car Friday night to avoid doing it all in the morning. Saturday morning, after breakfast, they hit the road about nine o'clock. They headed straight to the Newhart's house for lunch. After lunch, they drove to the motel to check in and unpacked. They relaxed for a while before heading back to the Newhart's.

After a great weekend together, the Romanos headed home Monday morning. The whole ride home, Alexa texted Kevin, and Scotty borrowed Mom's phone to text Micki on Vicky's phone. Neither of the thirteen-year-olds had their own cell phone yet. School would be back in session soon.

Joe hadn't been able to go on the hunt for too long now. His urge to kill grew. It seemed like the more he killed lately, the more he felt he needed it. It was Monday evening already, and Joe was ready for everyone to get to sleep so he could go down and sneak out. Before he left, he spent some time with Amanda. Then he put on his trolling disguise and left. This time, he didn't have a plan.

Joe drove up to Prescott's Whiskey Row. He walked down the sidewalk when he saw two drunken ladies stumble out of a bar. They laughed and leaned on each other so they wouldn't fall.

"Hi girls, I'm Joe. What are your names?"

"I'm Heather, and she's...uh. What the fuck's your name? Oh yeah, she's Spring."

"Damn, Heather. You're *totally* fucked up, girl!" Spring said.

"I think I'm more fucked up than you for a change. That doesn't happen too often."

"You girls want to go to a party?" he asked.

"Sure, but I don't know if we can walk too far," Heather said.

"No worries. I can drive you there."

"We should just walk. Where's the party?" Spring asked.

"It's a couple of miles from here."

"We can't walk that far. We're too drunk," Heather said.

"That's why I'm giving you a ride. At least sit in my truck and share a joint with me."

"Oh yeah, I want to get high," Spring said.

Joe helped them into the back seat of his truck and drove off. "How old are you, Heather?"

"I'm twenty-five. How old are you, Joe?" Heather asked, slurring her words.

"I'm a bit older. How about you, Spring?"

"I'm twenty-seven, right Heather?"

"Yeah, I think so. Where's that joint?" Heather asked.

"It's at the party," Joe said.

After a while, she looked out the window. "Hey, where are we going? Is this party in the woods?"

"The party *is* in the woods, ladies," Joe replied, pulling over in a secluded spot. He got out, opened the back door, and helped Spring get out.

"Where the fuck's the party?"

"I'm going to walk you to it. You can't drive all the way there. Heather, you stay here. I'll walk Spring and then be back for you."

He walked Spring a little into the woods while putting his leather gloves on.

Spring asked, "Where's the fucking party, Joe?"

"It's right here, baby," Joe said, spinning her around and grabbing her by the neck. It felt good to feel her struggle as he squeezed as hard as he could, pushing both his thumbs into her windpipe. Her arms flailed around as she tried to get away.

It didn't take long for Spring to lay on the ground with Joe's hands still around her neck, leaning over her and putting all his weight into pushing his thumbs deeper into her windpipe. Her legs kicked aimlessly for a short time while her hands tried to push him away until they fell limp. He listened for a heartbeat. She was dead.

He left her lying on the ground and went back to get Heather. When he got back to his truck, Heather was asleep. She woke when he opened the door. It took a minute for her to remember what she was doing there.

"Where's Spring? Did she leave already?"

"She's at the party. Come with me." He helped her out of the truck. Heather stumbled and leaned on him. They got to where he'd left Spring's body.

"How come you're sleeping, Spring?" Heather slurred. "Get the fuck up bitch and let's party, woo!" she said, kicking her friend's dead body.

"Here's your party, Heather," Joe said as he choked her with both his hands around her neck until she was unconscious. He laid her face down next to Spring and zip-tied her arms behind her back. He rolled her onto her back. Sliding his hand under Heather's skirt, he rubbed the crotch of her panties.

Joe put on a condom, knelt between Heather's legs, and pushed her little skirt up. Heather regained consciousness as he had his way with her. She was still extremely drunk.

"What the fuck are you doing? Get off me! Spring, help," she slurred.

"Spring's dead. I killed her with my bare hands, the same way I'm going to kill you, bitch."

She tried to struggle, but she was way too drunk. Joe could feel an orgasm coming quickly. He wrapped both his hands around Heather's throat and squeezed as hard as he could, pushing his thumbs deep into her windpipe. He had an incredible orgasm, pressing his thumbs harder and deeper with each ejaculation. Once she was dead, he got off and rolled her over, laying her body face down on top of Spring's.

"Now you two can party together," Joe said as he walked back to his truck.

When Joe got home, he cuddled up to Lisa. He reached between her legs, pushed the crotch of her panties over, and rubbed her clit. He felt her get wet. Slowly, one of his fingers slid inside her. He put a second finger in her and slid them in and out of her sweet mound as it continued to get wetter, and her hips ground back against his hand. He pulled his fingers out and guided his cock inside her. She let out a gasp of pleasure as he slowly screwed her.

Lisa pushed back against Joe's cock and moaned loudly. While he was having sex with Lisa, he fantasized that he raped Spring before killing her, then Heather. They screwed steadily until they both came. Lisa fell back asleep quickly. Joe now felt utterly content. Once Lisa was asleep, Joe woke up and went down to sleep half the night with Amanda.

"I love being your sex slave," Amanda said. "Living here has been the best time of my life. I don't feel scared anymore like I used to. I have a safe place to live. I have good food and drink. I don't even have to wash my own clothes. I was never wild, kinky, and horny all the time before I met you. I bet Lisa isn't wild and kinky like me. I wish she was gone."

"I'm so tired. I just wanted to get a good night's sleep. What the hell? Did I just turn down sex? Better call a doctor," Joe laughed.

"That's okay," she said. "There's always tomorrow."

"I do love you," he said. They fell asleep in each other's arms.

Joe woke up. He tried to sit up on the futon, but he was tied down. Amanda knelt over his head. He looked up and saw Lisa at his feet. "What's going on? (going on...going on)" He felt in a daze, as if he had been drugged. He could hear his own words echoing in his head. "Lisa, (Lisa...Lisa) what are you doing? (doing...doing) Amanda? (Amanda...) What's happening? (happening)"

"You've been a very naughty boy, Joey. Mandy told me everything," Lisa said. "Everything, Joey. You're evil."

"A very naughty boy, Joey," Amanda said. "It's your turn now." She slapped him hard in the face while her other hand was between her legs.

Lisa punched him in the stomach. "How does it feel, Joey?" She leaned over and made out with Amanda. She grabbed both of Joe's nipples, pinched them, and twisted them as hard as possible. "I know you like this. You've done it to so many women, haven't you, Joey?"

He let out a scream of pain. "Stop! Why are you doing this? I love you, Lisa."

"I love you, Lisa? What the fuck about me?" Amanda yelled. "You're a bad man, pastor. It's time to send you back to hell where you came from."

"No, please. I'm sorry. I'll do anything. Please don't kill me," Joe begged.

"It's too late, Joey. You belong in hell. There *is* a God, and it's not you," Lisa said as she wrapped her hands around his neck and strangled him. She was wearing his leather gloves. He struggled, but he was tied down too tight to move.

Amanda kissed him, sticking her tongue down his throat as he gasped for air. She raised her head and laughed. Lisa laughed, too, as he felt life slipping away. Amanda stabbed him over and over with a butcher knife as Lisa continued to strangle him.

Suddenly, Joe sat up on the futon. He felt his chest and belly. There were no stab wounds or blood. He looked around. The only person there with him was Amanda. She was asleep. It was just a bad dream. He shivered, wiped the sweat off his face, lay down, and fell asleep after a few minutes.

At 3:00, his vibrating alarm woke him up so he could spend the rest of the night with Lisa. Joe put his boxers on and headed back up to the master bedroom. Lisa woke up enough to turn over and cuddle up to him as he got settled in. *Maybe there is a God,* he thought. *I have two young, sexy women in the same house in love with me.* With that thought, Joe fell back asleep.

By late September, school was back in session. The leaves on the trees around Canyon City turned beautiful colors. The air was cool and fresh.

Joe came home from running errands. He walked in the front door. "Hello Lisa, I'm home," he shouted.

"I'm in the kitchen, Joey," Lisa shouted back.

Joe thought, *Great! She's making dinner early. I'll have plenty of time for a mission tonight.* "Where are the kids?" he asked as he walked toward the kitchen.

Joe's mouth dropped open when he saw her. She wasn't cooking. She stood there in a short, black, see-through baby doll nightie and black lacy thong panties. She faced the sink.

"They're spending the night at their friend's houses." Lisa slowly turned around. "Like what you see, Joey?" He was speechless. As she walked past him, she grabbed his hand. He followed her up the stairs to the master bedroom. This was reminiscent of the days when they were first married.

"Look at you, sweet little devil," he said as he grabbed her, pushed her down on the bed, and climbed on top to kiss her. She rolled over on top of him, unbuttoned his shirt, and ran her hands over his chest. She reached down between his legs and grabbed him through his pants.

She climbed off him and said, "Stand up, mister. Let's get those pants off." As Joe stood up, Lisa pulled his pants down. He stepped out of them. Lisa fell to her knees and took his manhood in her mouth.

"What's gotten into you, baby?"

"I've wanted to do this many times. There's always a kid here. Can I get back to it now?" Joe nodded as she continued. He closed his eyes and leaned back. It seemed to go on forever.

Lisa stood in front of him, slowly lifted the bottom of her nightie, and slipped it over her head. She moved closer and rubbed her breasts back and forth on his chest. They simultaneously grabbed each other by the back of their heads and came together in a passionate, sensual kiss.

As they kissed, Joe reached down between her legs and rubbed the crotch of her panties. Lisa moaned as Joe pushed her back on the bed. He grabbed her panties and slid them down. It was his turn to get on his knees.

He nibbled, licked, and sucked between her legs for several minutes while she pulled him towards her by the back of his head. When he finished his appetizer, he climbed onto the bed. Lisa climbed on top of him and guided his hardness inside her.

She slowly sat all the way down with a loud moan. She rode him slowly up and down for a few minutes. The motion got faster and harder. She rode him hard for several more minutes. Joe lifted her just enough for him to slip out from under her. She was still on her knees. Joe pushed her down on all fours and entered her from behind. She let out a scream. He flipped her over and climbed on top of her. His tongue found her mouth before his cock found its way back inside her on its own.

Joe couldn't remember anything this good in a long time. It was even better than sex with Amanda. After a few more minutes of making out the whole time they made love, Lisa had a huge orgasm she thought would never end. By the end, Joe reached his own climax. He laid there for several minutes, then rolled off her.

They both rolled on their sides, facing each other, and kissed again. "I've never felt more love than I do right now, Joey. I don't know what happened, but I hope it happens again."

"Me too. I have never felt so good or so close to you. You horny little devil."

Joe lay there and thought about the most incredible sex he could remember. *It wasn't just sex,* he thought. *It was making love.* He closed his eyes and drifted off to sleep.

Joe woke up in the middle of the night and went down to see his other young lady.

"I've been thinking. Could I help come up with the fantasies for your adventures?" Amanda asked. "I would love to help you. I'd feel like I was part of it. It's exciting to me."

"That sounds exciting to me, too. I've never had anyone to share this with."

The next morning, Joe decided to stay home all day to spend time with Lisa.

"Tomorrow, I have to go back down to Phoenix to tie up some loose ends for Saturday's Charity Mission meal," Joe mentioned at dinner.

"That's fine, Joey. I have a bunch of stuff to do tomorrow, too. I get more done when you're not around," Lisa said, winking at him.

"Can I come with you?" Scotty asked.

"I don't think so, Scotty. You have a commitment tomorrow," Mom said.

"What commitment do I have?"

"It's that little thing called school."

"Oh yeah. Can't I miss just one day, Mom? Please!"

Joe saw the look on Lisa's face. He was sure she was about to give in. Not tomorrow of all days. He had plans. "You'd be bored if you came with me tomorrow."

"Fine, maybe next time? It's never just you and me, dad. You know, just the guys."

"You're right, Scotty. We'll have to make up for that, but not tomorrow. I'll let you know when." With that, Joe got up from the table. He kissed Lisa on top of her head. He was off to his recliner to watch TV.

NINETEEN
LOOSE ENDS

⟨⟨⟨⟨⟨⟨⟨⟨⟨⟨⟨⟨ ⟩⟩⟩⟩⟩⟩⟩⟩⟩⟩⟩⟩

After breakfast, the kids got ready for school. Joe was already dressed, ready to start his day. "Alexa, Scotty," he hollered up the stairs. "Have a good day at school. I love you both." He turned to Lisa and said, "I love you. Have a great day. I should be home late afternoon."

It was still early when Joe arrived in Phoenix. He thought back to when he killed Heidi with the nail gun. Knowing her old boyfriend, Brad wanted to have eight kids, still bothered him. He remembered the address from Heidi's driver's license. He drove by Brad's home first thing. He lived in a lower-class neighborhood and hadn't left for work yet.

"Why is it the people who can afford it the least seem to be the ones that want the most kids?" Joe wondered out loud. He looked around and didn't see anyone outside. He put on his leather gloves, walked up to the door in his hoodie, and rang the doorbell. Brad opened the door with a coffee cup in his hand. Joe pulled his hoodie off as the door opened.

"Pastor Joe, what brings you to this part of town?"

"Actually, I came to talk with you, Brad."

"Really? How do you know who I am?"

"I talked with Heidi shortly before she was murdered. May I come in?"

"Sure, pastor. Come in and have a seat." Joe sat on the couch. Brad sat on the other end and set his almost empty coffee cup down on the coffee table. "So, what did Heidi say?"

"Well, one thing she told me is that you want to have eight children."

"At least. I love large families. My new girlfriend said she wouldn't mind having a dozen if I want."

"Do you think it's wise to have so many kids? For one thing, kids are expensive."

"I know they can be, but when the older ones are old enough to get a job, they can help with the bills."

"You have it all figured out. You sure sound excited about it."

"I am. We're going to do it right. She doesn't want to get pregnant until we're married."

"That's good. Can I trouble you for some water, please?"

"Sure thing, pastor. I'll be right back," Brad said as he walked into the kitchen. As soon as he left the living room, Joe pulled a vial from his pocket and poured it into Brad's coffee. Brad came back with a cold bottle of water. "Here you go."

"Thank you. My throat got a little dry."

As he opened it and drank, he watched Brad pick up and down the last of his coffee. He gasped and then froze in place. His arm dropped to the couch as he dropped the empty cup. It bounced on the carpet without breaking. His body slumped over, lifeless, his eyes stared straight ahead.

"I know you feel a tingling and burning in your throat. That's from succinylcholine. It's usually injected, but I had to improvise. You can't move a muscle. You can't even breathe. No more babies. Why can't you young folks understand that?" Joe took another sip of water.

"Ah, that's refreshing. Too bad you can't drink anymore. By the way, I know who killed Heidi. The news calls me **DARK**. Shocking, Pastor Joe is a serial killer. You should have obeyed so I wouldn't have had to kill you, too."

Joe picked up the coffee cup and took it into the kitchen to rinse it out. He made sure there wouldn't be any trace of the succinylcholine left. He drove to the Charity Mission. He parked and walked around to the front. Mark met him at the door.

"How you doing, old man?" Mark asked as he shook Joe's hand.

"Pretty good, older than me, man."

"I'll tell you, Joe, sometimes these days I feel quite old," Mark said.

"How's your wife?"

"Anita's okay, ornery as ever," he laughed. "She said she's looking forward to seeing you and Lisa Saturday."

"What I need help with today is painting. We had some wall repairs done. They still need paint. A couple of the homeless people stopped by unexpectedly to help. They wanted to give back a little. This is James and Shondra."

"Nice to meet you. I'm always glad to help. Give me a paint roller, and I'll get busy."

"Thanks as always," Mark said, handing him a paint roller. With the four of them painting, they finished the twelve-foot-high walls in several hours.

When the painting was done, Joe said, "Thank you for letting us help. And on that note, I almost forgot to give you this." Joe handed Mark a check for ten thousand dollars. "My ministry wants to help keep this mission running. Plus, it's a write-off."

"This will go a long way. I can't thank you enough."

"Well, how about a beer for the road?"

"Sounds good," Mark said, returning to the walk-in refrigerator and grabbing four bottles of beer.

After they finished, Mark said, "Thanks again for helping paint. And Joe, I appreciate the generous donation."

"It's always my pleasure, Mark. I'll see you Saturday," Joe said as he walked to his car.

Joe couldn't wait to get home and share his latest adventure with Amanda. He knew it would excite her. The rest of the week passed somewhat uneventful.

The Romanos climbed into the car on Saturday morning and headed down the mountain. "Do we have any snacks for the road?" Scotty asked.

"You just ate breakfast, Scotty. Don't you ever stop?" Alexa asked.

"Yes, we have snacks. We'd never make it all the way to Phoenix with two teenagers and no snacks," Lisa laughed. "It's a whole hour."

When they got to the Charity Mission, Joe parked in the back. They went in and found all the tables and serving trays were already set up. Joe looked around.

"Wow, not much for us to do until people arrive."

"We had a lot of help from some high school kids last night and this morning. We're blessed to have such a wonderful bunch that will one day lead this country, making it even better than it is now," Mark bragged.

"It wouldn't take much to make it better than it is now," Joe said.

"We also had some help from another family today. They came up from Tucson," Mark said. "You should meet them. They're in the back room."

When they heard them talking, the Newharts walked out of the back.

"Kevin!" Alexa yelled. They all hugged. Kevin and Alexa kissed. So did Scotty and Makayla.

"What are you guys doing here?" Joe asked.

"Kevin said Alexa told him you were volunteering here today," Jerry said. "We weren't busy, so we thought we'd offer help."

"Surprise," Vicky said. "We're spending the night in a hotel so that we can come to your sermon tomorrow."

"Mark, these are the friends we met on our cruise," Lisa said.

"Wow, small world. I'd like the Romanos to help serve. That'll make the people feel so special that even you guys would sacrifice your time. Kevin and Makayla can help serve, too. Jerry and I will walk around the floor to make sure everyone has what they need and pick up used plates and utensils," Mark said. "Vicky, would you mind helping Anita in the kitchen?"

"Not at all," Vicky said. "Anita likes to gossip almost as much as I do."

"Unlock the front doors. Time to feed some hungry people," Mark said.

Joe made sure he got at the end of the line. He had his pants and his coat pockets stuffed with twenty-dollar bills. He handed out the rolls, butter, plastic forks, knives, and napkins. Whenever he picked up a napkin for an adult, he slipped a twenty-dollar bill in the fold. He did this until he ran out of bills. He had Lisa put more twenties in her purse. She got the money out and gave it to him.

Mark noticed what Joe was doing. He walked over. "We prefer just to give them food and drink, Joe. If we give them money, they'll probably just spend it on alcohol or drugs."

"I know that's a possibility. Thing is, I'm doing the right thing trying to help them. If they do the wrong thing with the money, that's between them and God."

"I see your point."

"It's church money, not personal money, and it's only twenty bucks. I figure what better use of church money than to give some to those in need?"

When everyone had their food, the volunteers sat down to eat.

Mark stood up and announced, "There's plenty more food. Feel free to help yourselves to seconds. I don't want anyone to leave hungry."

The next morning, the Newharts checked out of their hotel room and drove to where Pastor Joe's sermon was live, with over fifty thousand people in the arena. Pastor Joe continued to make headlines with his comments.

"Many of you think that I think I'm God. I'll tell you, I am! And so are you. God lives in all of us. He sent me here to do his work and lead the righteous down the correct path. Ask yourself if you're worthy of God's love? Are people still having and planning to have babies after God said the time has come to stop? You must be obedient. You must obey my word. My word is God Almighty's word. So, if you ask me if I'm God, I must answer yes, I am.

Ask the people we served a hot meal to at the Charity Mission here in Phoenix yesterday. Do they think God sent me to them? Do they believe? There will come a time when God will ask each of you to make a sacrifice in your life. If he stood before you today, would you be ready? The end will come sooner than anybody thinks because people don't honestly believe the end will come. It's coming, and if you're not ready, you'll be left behind."

AS LISA WATCHED and listened to Joe speak, she wasn't sure what was happening with him. He had attitudes like this in the past, but this time, it felt different, worse than ever before. She wanted to find out what was really going on with him. She could feel it in her bones that something wasn't right. She knew she had to be careful if she spied on him.

Call it women's intuition, but she felt sure he had cheated on her. She had no proof, but she was determined to find out.

TWENTY
TOWN HALL

"What's wrong with him?" the show's producer asked.

"More people are tuning in than ever to see what comes out of his mouth," a cameraman replied.

"But how long will they tune into this? The station manager and the network aren't going to put up with a crazy man going off the deep end," the producer said.

"I think a lot of them are brainwashed by him. I hope he doesn't start telling people to drink his special punch if you know what I mean," an assistant said.

"Oh God, don't even say that. This can get scary. I hear there's an angry crowd outside the arena carrying signs and yelling. They're protesting things he's been saying. Some are even calling him the Antichrist and have made death threats."

Backstage after the show, Charles Bain, the executive producer, said, "Joe, we need to take you and your family out a secret exit."

"How come?" Joe asked.

"We're afraid someone might get hurt by the crowd outside. We like to caution on the side of safety." The family was ushered down under the arena to the secret exit.

The lot attendant pulled the Romanos's car up to the back door, where they would typically leave the building. Instead of the Romanos, it was undercover police officers with their jackets pulled over their heads. They got in and slowly drove away as the crowd chased them.

As they walked through the lower section of the stadium, Jerry asked, "Do you really believe you're God, Joe."

"Yes, as much as I believe you're God, too. The Bible tells us that God lives in all of us, and we're all a part of God."

"Okay, I understand what you mean," Vicky said. "I guess people are taking it the wrong way."

The Romanos and the Newharts were taken out of the secret exit in a white panel van. After getting the word that the Romanos were taken to safety, the undercover police stopped the car and got out with a badge in one hand and their other hand on their guns, still in their holsters. Four marked police cars drove up the road towards them, lights flashing. Upon seeing no one else was in the car, the crowd quickly dispersed.

All of Joe's regular followers were disturbed by the crowd. They believed all he said.

The Newharts headed back down to Tucson after long goodbyes. The drive home for the Romanos was quiet. No one was sure what to say. Breaking the silence, Dad asked, "How about some music? Hand us a CD you'd like to hear, and we'll put it on. The case is under the passenger seat."

Scotty handed a Shinedown CD to Lisa to put in the stereo. "We figure this isn't too hard for you older people and not too mellow for us."

"You called them older people, and they didn't yell at you," Alexa said. "You're lucky."

"He's not lucky; we *are* older than you little kids back there," Joe taunted. That broke the heavy tension. They all laughed.

"Besides, I like most music. I like rock and metal a lot," Joe said.

Shortly after they got home, the phone rang. Joe answered it.

"Pastor Joe, this is Charles Bain. I just wanted to let you know that the network is running a special next Sunday."

"Ok, so I'll be down the weekend after."

"Well, no. The network wants to run some of your older sermons for maybe two or three weeks, maybe four. I'll get back to you when I have more information."

"Ok, thank you, Mr. Bain. I'll look forward to your call." Joe frowned and hung his head as he ended the call.

All week, Joe waited nervously to hear back from Mr. Bain. He finally called late Thursday morning. "Joe, here's the deal. The network wanted to cancel your live broadcasts. Your followers caught wind of this, and they have been calling, emailing, and sending letters by the tens of thousands. They will play reruns of your older sermons for the next several weekends. A special was already planned for this coming week."

"So, after that, I'm back on, right?"

"Listen, Joe, this is what the network wants. It's a compromise for now. They want you to script a sermon and turn it in for approval. Then..."

"They want me to stand up there and read a sermon to my congregation?"

"Not quite, Joe. Once they approve the script, they'll put it on a teleprompter. They said you can shoot the show from your home if you'd like."

"Wait a minute, Charles, what about my people? I'm not doing this just on camera. I need to have my audience."

"Please think about it, Joe. The choices are in a studio or your home with a script or nothing. They won't budge. They didn't even want to offer you this opportunity. They said they were through with you. I talked them into giving you one more chance. This is it, Joe, don't blow it. I don't think I'll be able to get you any more chances. It'll be at least a month or two before we implement the new format."

"You know the network will lose an awful amount of money if

they pull my show. I have millions of followers worldwide that tune in every week."

"I told them so. That's the only reason they decided to give you another chance. I worked hard to get this. Please don't mess it up."

"Ok, I guess I can try. Less driving for me."

"Thank you, Joe. Good luck. Work on some good sermons. I'll be in touch."

"Lisa, the network wants me to shoot my sermon from a studio or right here in our home, without my congregation," Joe told her after he hung up. "I guess they don't need me for at least a month or two. They'll let me know when they're ready for me to start shooting."

Joe knew Lisa thought it was his fault and he should do what they wanted. He didn't know why he cared about the congregation being there so much if the money was still coming in. He didn't even believe in God. This was all about the money. Still, his pride was hurt. He took the rejection as a personal attack.

"It's not right for them to treat me like this," Joe grumbled.

"Why are they doing this, Joey?" Lisa asked.

"I think they want me to record a sermon before the end of the week before it airs, so they have time to check it out and edit it before the broadcast."

"It doesn't surprise me with what you've been saying, Joey," Lisa said. "There are millions of dollars at stake. If they lose their sponsors, it won't matter how many people watch you. It's their job. With no money, there's no station. At least you still have the show."

"This comes from Satan trying to disrupt God's plan." His pride made him frustrated and angry.

"Joey, these people at the network don't care about God or Satan. They just want to make lots of money. They're probably afraid that sponsors will pull out. You know, that's where they make their money. You have to make nice with them."

"Why should I have to bow to the people I helped make wealthy? Maybe I should start my own network like Ted Turner. My church should have plenty of money for that."

"You have to play the game if you want to get anywhere. They made us wealthy, too. You've been doing this for years. What's the difference now?"

"The rules of the game have changed, and they're scared. They should be more open-minded, Lisa. They want everyone to keep playing the same game. They're going to play it my way, one way or another."

"What the hell are you talking about, Joey? You sound like one of those crazy people." Lisa said, clearly annoyed.

"Never mind. I'm just frustrated," Joe said as he walked away.

FRIDAY MORNING at the Canyon City Police Station, Sergeant Captain Connors called everyone in for the morning briefing.

Detective Stone spoke up. "We need a block watch for the whole damned city."

"Not a bad idea, Stone," Captain Connors said. "We need as many eyes out there as we can get. Let's call an emergency town hall meeting. We can train those who want to help on how to handle different situations. All we need from the public is extra eyes."

"We probably won't be able to get everyone into the town hall building," Stone said. "I wouldn't be surprised if everyone in the whole damned city came out."

"Yeah, maybe we should meet at the high school auditorium," Connors said. "Let's get this set up ASAP."

Monday night was the emergency town hall meeting. As Stone expected, the auditorium was packed. There was standing room only. Everyone was scared, and people wanted to help.

By the end of the night, they had over a hundred people signed up to keep a vigilant eye out in different areas at different times. Being able to be involved helped people feel a little more secure.

TWENTY-ONE
THE GIFT

After lunch the next day, Joe and Lisa went their separate ways to take care of what they planned for the day. Joe drove around looking for victims. The schools let out. Kids and parents were everywhere, but they thinned out quickly as you moved further away from the school.

Turning down the next street, he saw a blonde teenage girl walking ahead of him. He slowly followed her, keeping a good distance back. She turned and walked up to a house. As she held out her key to unlock the door, it opened to reveal her mother.

He drove to another neighborhood, up and down each street, with no luck. He decided to check out one more place. If this one didn't pan out, he would need to come up with another plan for now. As soon as he entered the next neighborhood, he saw a young lady quite a way down the street walking in his direction.

Joe pulled to the side of the road and parked. She strolled slowly down the street. He thought she'd never get to her house, but as she got closer, he saw she was worth the wait. She wore a short denim skirt and a button-down blouse tied in a knot at the bottom, showing off her firm belly. She neared where he was parked before she turned and walked up a sidewalk to a house. He laid his seat back to wait and see if someone else came home and when.

It didn't take as long as he hoped. In less than five minutes, two people who appeared to be her parents arrived. He decided to drive home for now, but he memorized the address and timetable in his mental vault for another day.

Joe arrived home and noticed Lisa's car was gone.

"I beat her home today. I think I'll surprise her when she gets home." He headed for the front door.

"Alexa, Scotty," he hollered out as he walked in. "I could use some help, please."

The kids ran up. "What do you need help with?" Alexa asked.

"I want to surprise your mom when she gets home. Alexa, I'd like you to clean up the kitchen and get the dirty dishes in the dishwasher. Scotty, you can straighten up the living room. Put any dirty dishes in the kitchen first so Alexa can get them in the dishwasher. Anything on the floor, I don't care how or who got it there, just pick it up and put it where it goes. If it's garbage, throw it away."

Alexa asked, "So what are you going to do other than tell us what to do?"

"I'm going to cook dinner, then I'll take a quick shower and put on some nicer clothes. Then I'll come down and finish dinner. Okay, let's get busy."

After he cleaned up and the kids did their chores, Joe made chicken Marsala.

The house looked like a home again. Magazines were nicely laid out on the coffee table. All the dirty clothes made it into the hamper. Joe got them into the washer. The beds were made. The kitchen sink was empty and clean. Joe ran the dishwasher after he finished cooking.

Alexa talked Scotty into helping clean the floors. The house looked and smelled good. It was time to get the clothes into the dryer. When they were clean and dry, all three of them folded the laundry and put it away.

Joe seasoned the chicken again and got out some Brussels sprouts.

"I hate Brussels sprouts," Scotty said. Alexa nodded in agreement.

"You haven't had my Brussels sprouts. Trust me, I think you'll like them," Dad said. "The first thing I do after I clean them is cut them in half. Then I season them and add lots of butter. You have to try them, at least. You can spit it out if you must, but I bet you'll like it."

"I'll try, but I don't guarantee I'll like them," Scotty said.

"They sound good," Alexa said.

"Why don't you guys pick a few wildflowers so we can put them in a vase in the middle of the table?" Joe suggested.

"Let's go, Scotty. I know where there's a bunch." The two took off together to pick wildflowers. When they returned, Joe arranged them in a vase to accent the table while Alexa set it.

When they were finished, the three of them kicked back on the couch and turned on the television while the food simmered. When Lisa got home, she noticed everyone was sitting around and watching TV.

"Busy day, I see." She looked around. "Wow. This place is spotless, and that smell. You even made dinner." She walked into the kitchen. "It's clean in here, too. How special, guys."

"Don't get too used to this, or it won't be special next time, if there is one."

"Good excuse, Joey," Lisa laughed. "It smells scrumptious. I wasn't hungry until now."

"I couldn't have got it all done without my two helpers. They did a great job. Tomorrow, it's my turn to come home late to an awesome meal."

"Well, let's see how awesome yours is first," she laughed. "If it tastes half as good as it smells, you might be doing more cooking around here from now on. I certainly didn't expect this. Now I just need to get you to do laundry and vacuuming."

"Maybe this is the only thing I can cook well. We all enjoyed doing this for you. It was fun seeing your reaction. By the way, Lisa, the laundry is done and put away, and the downstairs is already vacuumed," Joe said. "All that's left is vacuuming upstairs. The kids will do that tomorrow if I don't do it first."

"No, I'll vacuum upstairs in the morning after breakfast while the kids are in school. You guys did so much already. You spoil me like this, I might forget how to do it."

They sat at the kitchen table and ate dinner. Scotty made a face as he tried a Brussels sprout. The look changed to a smile.

"How did you make them taste so good? I love them."

"Me, too," Alexa said.

After dinner, the kids went to their rooms. Joe and Lisa sat in the living room.

"What'd you do today, Joey?"

"First thing, I drove around a little to keep an eye on some of the school kids."

"I thought I saw your car parked near the high school." Lisa knew he sat there and watched, then drove from neighborhood to neighborhood to sit and watch other girls. She had followed him.

"The police want everyone to help keep an eye on the schoolgirls. Just doing my part."

"I hope that's all you're doing." She'd watched him sit and stare at the house until her parents came home. Maybe it was all innocent, but she had a nagging feeling something wasn't right.

The following day, breakfast went quickly, and the kids were off to school. "No time this morning to jump back in bed, but who knows what the night holds," Lisa smiled and winked. "I have a lot to do today, so get out and do your stuff, Joey."

"Fine, just kick me out. I love you, baby. I'll see you tonight."

"I love you, too. Drive carefully, Joey."

"I will." Joe wondered just how much more 'normal' he could get.

Joe drove off to the house where he saw the young lady yesterday. He parked down the street and saw both her parents as they left for work. He waited for a while, and still no schoolgirl yet. After over forty-five minutes, she walked out the front door and headed to school. He could get her in the morning.

Now, he could drive around and look for another victim. He drove to the grocery store to pick up a few things for Lisa, plus several bottles of wine. Once he finished putting the groceries on the floor in the back seat, a cart girl grabbed his cart.

"Thanks a lot, young lady." Looking up, Joe said, "I see they mounted cameras on the light poles."

"You're welcome, pastor. They just got those cameras mounted this morning. They should be hooked up by the end of the day tomorrow."

He looked at her nametag. "Hannah, you're awful young to be working here."

"I'm eighteen. I graduate from high school soon so that I can work full time."

It was early morning on a weekday, so there weren't many people out shopping. There was no school today. The teachers were all in a conference. The parking lot was almost empty. There were very few cars and no other people in the lot.

"Let me show you something I have in the backseat of my car, Hannah." The door was still open. Hannah looked in. Joe stood right behind her.

"Where is it?"

Joe quickly struck her in the head several times with a blackjack he had in his back pocket, knocking her out. He pushed her into the backseat and closed the door; the row of carts she had gathered sat in the middle of the parking lot. Joe looked around and felt reasonably confident no one saw him abduct her. Pulling out of his parking spot, he saw Mrs. Corinth walk out of the store. This was way more risky than he should have taken, but he wanted to do this for Amanda.

The kids are at school. Lisa's gone for the day. I've never taken a victim home. I have tarps I can lay down and wrap her body in, he thought as he drove toward home. He pulled onto a side street and gave Hannah a shot of tranquilizer. He parked in the detached garage. Leaving her in his car, he went in through the tunnel. He laid the tarps down on the floor in Amanda's room.

"I have a gift for you. I'm going to get it out of my car now." Joe handed Amanda a grocery bag and then returned to his car. Joe carried Hannah through the tunnel to Amanda's room and laid her on a tarp. Amanda helped him take off her clothes.

"This is an awesome gift, Joey!" she said excitedly.

He rolled Hannah over so he could zip-tie her arms behind her back. Rolling her back over, Amanda covered her mouth with duct tape. Joe chained Hannah's ankle to the beam in the center of the room.

"She was the cart girl at the store."

He returned and parked the car in the regular garage, carried in the groceries, and put them away. He headed back to Amanda's room. Hannah just started to come around. He noticed Amanda was already naked.

"Hi, how are you doing, sweetie?" Hannah looked up at him with a puzzled look. Joe knelt by her head. "I know someone will get you pregnant one of these days. We can't let that happen." Hannah struggled and tried to scream, but the tape held it in.

"Hannah, if you want me to take the duct tape off your mouth, you better be quiet. This place is soundproof. I just don't want to hear it. Will you be quiet if I take the tape off?"

Hannah nodded yes. Joe pulled the tape off.

"Why are you doing this? Let me go."

"You're at my home. You're the only one besides Mandy and me that has ever been in this room. Mandy is also eighteen and happy to be my sex slave."

"What? I'm confused. You want me to be a sex slave?"

Amanda climbed on top of Hannah and kissed her. Hannah turned her head from side to side, trying to avoid Amanda's mouth and tongue. She sucked on Hannah's neck while she slipped her hand inside Hannah's panties. "I can't wait to watch my master fuck you. He has a giant cock." Amanda kissed her again, then got off her. Joe's cock was already semi-hard in his pants. "I want to watch you fuck her good."

"Not yet, Mandy."

"Where am I?" Hannah cried.

"You are in the home of the one they call **DARK**."

"What? Why?"

"I had to make sure that you never have any babies. They also call me Pastor Joe."

"Pastor Joe? Please let me go."

"I'm not a pastor. God, Satan, heaven and hell don't exist. I preach to make lots of money. It also makes a great cover for a serial killer, don't you think? My wife and kids have no idea who I really am or that I have a sex slave I kidnapped, living right below our home."

"Please let me go. I swear, I'll never tell anyone."

"After my wife falls asleep, I'll be back. Keep an eye on her for me, Mandy."

"Yes, master. May I play with her while you're gone?"

"You're going to rape me while your wife and kids are home?"

"Maybe his new wife doesn't mind," Amanda said.

"Yes, Mandy, do anything you want to her. Just don't kill her." Joe pulled out a syringe. "You're going to sleep while I spend time with my family. Mandy will take care of that little honey pot for me until I get back."

"Oh my God! Please!" Hannah screamed.

"You were told to shut the fuck up," Amanda yelled, smacking her face hard.

Joe loved seeing it. He pushed the needle into Hannah's thigh.

"She'll be out soon. If she wakes up and gets loud, you can duct tape her mouth again or just kick her ass." Joe gave Amanda a passionate kiss while Hannah lay there and watched as the tranquilizer kicked in.

"My new wife, Amanda?"

"You never know what the future holds, Joey."

TWENTY-TWO
SUPERGLUE

Upstairs, Joe grabbed a beer from the fridge, sat in his recliner, and turned on the TV. Lisa came home twenty minutes later. Joe kissed her. "I hope you had a good day."

"It was great! I went to this one shoe store, and I found the cutest shoes. I looked at the price tag. They wanted over seven hundred dollars. Can you believe that? Over seven hundred dollars for one pair of shoes! But then I went to this store down the street and saw a pair of shoes that looked almost exactly the same for forty dollars, so I told them about..." And she droned on and on while all Joe could think about was Hannah and Amanda downstairs. The situation turned him on so much. "...and I finally decided to get these. What do you think? Joey, are you listening to me?"

"I'm sorry. I had something I couldn't get out of my head. I do like those shoes. They're very nice, and you got such a good deal, too. Great job."

Joe rolled his eyes as she walked out of the room. She got on his nerves. He wondered if Amanda was right, and it was time for a change.

Soon after dinner, Lisa said, "It's been a long day today. I'm going to bed now."

"I'm kind of tired, too. Get the TV turned on in the bedroom, and I'll be right up." Joe wanted to run down to his office to give Hannah a small booster shot, but she was still unconscious. He gave the needle to Amanda and said, "You saw how I did it. Just stick it in and push in the plunger if she comes to if you want her out again. You can do whatever you want to her. I'll be back as soon as I can."

Joe headed upstairs to go to bed with Lisa. "Did you take your sleeping pill yet?"

"No, I was thinking about not taking one tonight. I'm so tired I don't think I need it."

Not tonight of all nights, Joe thought. The basement was soundproof, but it would make him feel better if he knew Lisa was truly out while he had a victim there.

"What will happen is you'll fall asleep quickly, but then you'll probably wake up and not be able to get back to sleep." *Take that fucking pill,* he thought.

"You're right, Joey." Joe got up and got her a sleeping pill.

Lisa took the pill and said, "Thank you. Goodnight and sweet dreams, Joey. I love you."

"Goodnight, baby. I love you." Joe gave her a kiss and sighed with relief. Once he was sure Lisa was sound asleep, he headed down to the basement.

"Joey, if Lisa wasn't in the picture anymore, we could do this whenever we wanted."

"We'll see. Like you said, who knows what the future holds." Joe got out a couple of bottles of industrial-strength superglue. He unchained Hannah's leg from the beam, took the cap off the superglue, and turned the bottle upside down over her mouth. He laid a bead of glue across her lips, from one corner to the other.

"Did you give her that shot?"

"No. I had fun with her the way she was. She never woke up."

Amanda sat there and watched him. "Two more things for now."

He squirted superglue up one of her nostrils and pinched it shut. He flipped her on her stomach, cut the zip-ties off her wrists, and pulled both of her arms up behind her.

"Wait, Joey. What if you superglue her arms in front?"

"How do you mean?"

"Turn her back over. I'll show you." Joe turned her over. Amanda took Hannah's right hand and put it on her left breast, her left hand on her right breast. "Glue them like that."

"That's awesome. We do make a great team. Pick up the right one."

She picked up Hannah's hand. Starting on a new bottle of superglue, he covered her left breast. Amanda put Hannah's hand back on her breast and pressed it down, making sure her nipple stuck out between her fingers. She picked up Hannah's left hand so Joe could put glue on her right breast. Amanda pressed her hand back down on her breast, again leaving her nipple sticking out between her fingers.

Joe patted Hannah's face, then broke open a vial of smelling salts and waved it under her nose. She shook her head and coughed.

"This is something I've fantasized about doing for a long time," he said. She just stared, unable to say anything. "You probably have lots of questions. I'm Pastor Joe. The drug is still working well, so you're still not sure if this is a dream. It's not. They were too late getting those security cameras hooked up. I picked you because you were an easy target. You also looked like a hot chick I'd love to fuck."

His words made her squirm. She tried to move her hands off her breasts but couldn't.

"Your family is probably going crazy looking for you. What turns me on more is my wife and kids are upstairs asleep. I write my sermons down here in the basement. Kind of ironic, don't you think? Mandy, would you like to squirt some superglue into each of her eyes? Taking away most of your senses will make the things you feel more intense."

As Joe sat up, Amanda grabbed him by the back of his head and pulled him in close for a deep kiss.

She took the glue and said, "It would be my pleasure." Joe held Hannah's head still.

A muffled scream escaped from Hannah.

Amanda put the tip of the bottle right into her left eye and squeezed it. She did the same thing to her right. "That was fun."

Hannah struggled to no avail. She was now totally blind and couldn't speak. She had to be in extreme pain as the superglue burned her eyes. Amanda held Hannah's face to the side and squirted a gob of superglue into her right ear. Hannah kicked her feet and tried to scream.

"Look at you take charge," Joe said with a huge smile.

Amanda turned Hannah's head the other way. Hannah fought her. Joe helped hold her head in place. Amanda squirted superglue into her left ear while she made out with Joe. Now Hannah was deaf, too.

Joe put some lube on himself and sank between Hannah's legs. He decided not to use a condom. It was too late to avoid leaving evidence. He would have to figure out a good way to get rid of her body and any evidence.

As Joe raped her, he thought about his family upstairs and Amanda there with him. It was all so kinky. He could tell Hannah was crying, but no tears got through the super glue. All she could do was breathe through one nostril. She felt the pain as Amanda slapped her face and pinched her nipples while she continued to make out with Joe.

"Oh my God, it feels so good. Mandy, get on your hands and knees over Hannah's body. Lay down on top of her."

She straddled Hannah's body. He screwed Amanda on top of Hannah.

"Oh God, you're so kinky." Amanda kissed and licked Hannah's face while Joe screwed her. After several minutes, Amanda got off Hannah, and Joe raped her again.

"God, I'm so horny," Amanda said as she masturbated.

Joe was so turned on that he couldn't hold back. As orgasm approached, he grabbed the superglue and handed it to Amanda.

"She just has one nostril to breathe through."

Amanda squirted superglue up her other nostril and pinched it closed. After she dropped the tube of superglue, Amanda's hand found its way back to her own wet hole. Hannah was like a bucking bronco. Amanda had an incredible orgasm watching her.

Once Joe got off Hannah, she bucked and flopped around a little more. Her movements slowed down, and soon they stopped completely.

"That was intense. I didn't think I would ever stop cumming. Thank you, Joey. I love you. Wouldn't I be the perfect wife for you?"

"You're welcome, Mandy. I love you. It turned me on much more that you enjoyed it so much. You'd make an awesome wife for me, but I'm married."

"For now," Amanda smiled coyly.

"One last thing to do." He handed her a knife and said, "Stick her a few times."

"Isn't she dead already?"

"I plan to throw her body in the river. As her body decomposes, it will bloat with gases that can cause her body to float if she were to come loose from the chains I'm going to wrap around her. This will help those gases escape, so her body is less likely to surface."

"I didn't know that," she said, taking the knife from him. She raised it up high and came down hard in the middle of Hannah's chest, then her belly. "That was fun."

He wrapped Hannah in the tarps she laid on, and Amanda helped carry her body out through the tunnel to the bed of his pickup. He wrapped a heavy chain around her and several times around her neck and secured it with padlocks.

Amanda kissed him and said, "Good luck, Joey."

He walked her back to her room and locked her in.

Joe left in his truck and parked on the side of the road by one of the bridges that crossed the largest river around the city, but a car would drive by every minute or two. He was surprised at how many people drove by in the middle of the night.

This isn't good, he thought. He'd left too much evidence to dump her body in the woods.

Joe drove several miles down the road and found a more remote bridge. There was no one in sight in either direction. He quickly pulled over in the middle of the bridge and got out. Looking both ways again, he decided to risk it and rolled the tarp and chain-clad body out to the end of the bed of his truck. He struggled to get it high enough to throw it over the railing. All the chains made her quite heavy.

He was able to lift her head and neck just enough to get it over the railing. Her head hung over, and her shoulders were near the top. He lifted her shoulders onto the railing. He grabbed the chains around her chest and pulled. Her body slid several inches with each tug. On the third tug, her body fell headfirst into the river.

He watched it quickly sink. He looked around and felt satisfied nobody had seen him. He got back in his truck and started to drive as a car came up behind him. On his way home, he thought, *Maybe I need to get rid of Amanda. I've taken too many risks because of her.*

Joe was still turned on from his latest conquest. Lisa was asleep already, and she'd been asking too many questions lately. He went to Amanda's room. After over a half hour of rough, kinky sex, they collapsed beside each other on the futon and held hands.

After resting a while, Amanda asked, "Have you ever killed someone by hanging them?"

"I haven't done that. I'll think about it." *Maybe I could hang you,* he thought.

TWENTY-THREE

HANGING AROUND

The following day, Lisa asked, "What would you like for lunch?"

"I'm not feeling hungry yet. I'll be in my office."

"What are you hiding down there, Joey?"

"What are you talking about?"

"You spend more time down there than up here."

"I work when I'm down there. You want to come down and look around?"

"Sure. I haven't been in the basement since we moved here two years ago."

Joe felt a little nervous. *Did I leave anything out she shouldn't see?* he wondered.

Lisa followed him down and looked around. Everything looked normal. She looked at the computer on his desk. Luckily, he had a sermon he was working on pulled up on the screen. She even looked in the bathroom.

"What do you think?"

"You have a nice office, Joey." She gave him a kiss and went back upstairs.

He locked the doors and then stopped in to see Amanda. "Maybe I can try hanging someone today. If I do, I'll let you know how it goes."

He loaded up his black bag with anything he thought he might need. He put it and a long piece of rope on the floorboard of his truck. He threw a stepladder in the bed. He drove around for a while. It was well after lunchtime, and he got hungry.

He pulled into a bar and grill for a burger and beer. The bartender slid Joe's hamburger and fries in front of him. He was over halfway finished when a lady moved from where she was and sat down on the barstool beside him.

"Hi, my name is Stephanie. Would you like to buy a lady a drink?"

"Isn't it a little early to be drinking?"

"Hmm...is it? Looks like you are," she said, gesturing to his beer. "Besides, I've already had a couple."

"Ok, you got me, Stephanie. Bartender, bring this lady a drink and put it on my tab."

"Thank you. Would you like to go out sometime?" She tried to get a better look at him. He was still wearing his hood over his head. "You look familiar. Have I seen you before?"

"I usually try to disguise myself when I'm out in public. They call me Pastor Joe." He pulled his hood back.

"Oh my God, you are. I can't believe I was hitting on you. Please forgive me. I just thought you looked like a nice guy."

"I guess I can't blame you for having good taste," Joe laughed. "You look pretty nice yourself."

The bartender brought her the drink, and she took several gulps. The glass was already over half empty. "How old are you, Stephanie?"

"I'm thirty. Pastor, would you mind watching my drink while I use the restroom?"

"Sure thing," Joe said. As soon as she walked away, he pulled a vial out of his pocket and looked around. The bartender was on the other side of the bar looking the other way. He quickly poured it into what was left of her drink and stirred it with a straw. Joe devoured the rest of his burger.

By the time Stephanie returned, he had finished his lunch and was drinking his beer. She took a sip of her drink. After several minutes Joe could tell the drug was already kicking in. She was acting quite drunk and drugged. He stood up.

"Want to go for a ride?"

Stephanie took the last sip of her drink. "Sure. If I can't trust Pastor Joe, I couldn't trust anyone. Where are we going?"

Joe downed the last of his beer and left cash on the bar for the bill. "I'll show you a cool place I found a while back in the woods." The place he had in mind wasn't easy to get to. The ground was very rocky, and there was no road. They headed down the road. His four-wheel-drive truck helped as Joe turned off the main road into the woods.

"What a ride," Stephanie said, lying slumped over. "I love this." Between the drink she downed and the tranquilizer, she was very mellow. They stopped in a small open field past the rocky area with a few scattered trees. Joe got out of the truck, his black bag in hand. He set the bag on the ground, opened the passenger door, and helped Stephanie get out. She couldn't stand well on her own. Joe thought, *She almost got enough of the drug.* The ground was covered with soft grass.

Joe grabbed her and pulled her in for a hug. Before they knew it, their hands were all over each other, tongues dancing in and out of each other's mouths.

She pulled back and said, "I'm sorry. What would your wife say?"

"I don't plan on telling her. Do you?" Joe asked as he unbuttoned her blouse.

"Mmm, you're almost hard already. Your dick is huge!" Pretty soon, they were both naked. They rubbed their bodies together. "I'm not usually like this," she said. "I'm not a slut, but I want you so bad. I only had three drinks, but I feel so fucked up."

"I want you, too," he said as he lay on the grass.

Stephanie climbed on top of him and rubbed her crotch on him for a few minutes while he laid back with his eyes closed. She bent over and gave him a passionate kiss. She rolled off and lay beside him on the grass.

Joe rolled over on top of her and kissed her, their tongues once again dancing in and out of each other's mouths. This didn't feel the same, either. He just met her, but he already felt a connection with her. He rolled over and pulled her back on top of him.

She lifted up and guided him into her wet hole. She slowly sat down on top of his massive pole. It took several times of going up and down. She slowly let it go a little further inside with each stroke until she was wet enough and stretched out enough that she could speed up a little. "Damn, pastor, God sure blessed you." She rode him fast and hard. When she slowed down a little, Joe picked her up and laid her on her back.

Before climbing on top of her, he made a pit stop between her legs. He licked and sucked on her clit as she screamed with pleasure. He reached into his bag and pulled out a bottle of water with a spout top. He squirted cold water on her crotch. She probably thought this was part of kinky sex. In reality, he was trying to wash away his salvia.

He put on a condom. He never had a chance at the beginning because of how fast things moved. The details of his plan had definitely changed, and he enjoyed the hell out of it. He pushed his penis inside her and screwed her for several minutes.

"Get up," Stephanie said. She stood up and faced the tree right beside them. She leaned forward, held herself up with her hands against the tree, her legs spread and her butt sticking out. "Come and get it, pastor!" Joe came up behind and slipped into her.

"This feels so naughty. I'm doing it outside during the day with a married preacher."

After a while, Joe pulled out, leaned up against the tree, and pulled her close. He stuck his tongue in her mouth. This was the best outdoor sex he could remember. Was it just sex? It felt more like making love. He lifted her right leg and slid his cock back inside her.

"Get down on your hands and knees."

Stephanie got on all fours. Joe got on his knees and entered her from behind. The strokes of his penis got harder. Stephanie came very loudly. Joe was so turned on that he came, too. The two of them laid back on the grass. Once they recovered, Stephanie said, "That was awesome."

"That was. I love you." Joe was shocked. Why did he say that? "Oh shit, that just slipped out. We don't even know each other, but I feel a connection with you."

"I feel the same way. I wish you weren't married. I'd grab you up in a heartbeat."

"See what you get when you hit on a married preacher?"

"I'm sure glad I did. Do you have any more water in that bag? I'm thirsty."

"Actually, I do." He got out another bottle. "I want to ask you something personal. Be honest. Did your dad ever abuse you, Stephanie?"

"Not exactly," she said. "It was my uncle. I was thirteen. He forced himself on me. I actually enjoyed it at first. I went back for more. Then I realized how wrong it was and told him I didn't want to do that anymore.

He wouldn't take no for an answer. He raped me every time he got the chance after that. I finally got the nerve to threaten him that I would tell my mom. He didn't like it, but he was scared of getting arrested. He tried to talk me into having sex with him again for a while whenever he saw me. I kept telling him no. He finally stopped asking."

"I have a sense about that kind of thing."

After resting a while longer, Stephanie said, "I feel refreshed. How about you?"

Joe pushed her on her back, knelt between her legs, and kissed her breasts. He put on a new condom and slammed his rod inside her with one hard thrust. She let out a shriek.

"I love fucking you. Do you want to get kinky?"

"What do you think?"

"Lay on your stomach," Joe said. He reached into his bag and pulled out a couple of zip-ties. He put one around her wrist and one around the other wrist, through the first zip-tie behind her back.

"Bondage, cool." She rolled over on her back. "Are you going to fuck me now, pastor?

"You bet." He grabbed her by her shoulders and pulled her up onto her feet. He bent her over and entered her from behind again. Grabbing her hair, he pulled her to him. He stood still, pulling her back and forth by her hair. He held her hair in one hand and slapped her ass with the other.

"You're so kinky! I love it." He screwed her from behind like this for several minutes.

He pulled out and said, "Honey, the best is yet to come. Give me a minute. First, I have something for you to wear." She sat down. He reached into his bag, pulled a blindfold, and put it over her eyes. He walked over to his truck and got the stepladder and the rope out. He saw the perfect tree to use. He climbed up to the top of the stepladder.

"Pastor? Are you still here?"

"Yes. I'm just getting the next part ready. I think you'll like this."

He took the rope and threw it over the lowest sturdy limb. He tied it off so it would hang at the correct length. He tied a slipknot on the end that hung down.

He grabbed Stephanie by her shoulders and helped her up. "Walk over here with me. Step up onto this stepladder. It's right in front of you." She felt around with her foot and found the bottom step. "It's four steps up. The fourth one is a platform."

He held onto her and helped her to the top. He climbed up and joined her on top. He caressed her and slid his hand between her legs. She squirmed nervously when he slipped the rope around her neck. "You're in good hands. Trust me." He pulled her hair out of the loop and pulled the knot snugly to her neck. He let her flowing hair fall back over the rope. "Give me half a minute, and I'll be right back," he said. He went to get a bottle of water.

He climbed back up on the stepladder and squirted water over her chest to try to wash his saliva away. She squealed. He entered her from behind. While he fucked her, he pulled on the rope for about twenty seconds at a time. After a little while, he turned her around, lifted her leg, and stuck his cock back inside. He pulled the blindfold off.

She looked around as Joe was still sliding in and out of her.

"Could this be any more perfect, pastor? We're fucking in the middle of a field in the middle of the day up on a ladder. Damn, I love your kinkiness! Oh God, I'm cumming!"

"You ain't seen nothing yet, baby." He quickly climbed down.

"Where are you going?" Joe masturbated while he watched her. He kicked the stepladder. It slid a little bit. "I'm cumming, pastor!"

He kicked the stepladder out from under her. "You wanted kinky." She fell low enough that the tips of her toes almost touched the ground. Joe's orgasm came instantly. Stephanie was still alive. She kicked and struggled for her life. She looked at Joe. He set the stepladder back up and helped her back onto it.

Gasping for air, she said, "I thought you were going to kill me. That turned out great."

"I love you, Stephanie. Did you really believe I would kill you?"

"I did. I was scared."

"I have an eighteen-year-old sex slave locked in my basement. This was Amanda's fantasy. I wish I didn't have to kill you." He pulled the stepladder out from under her again. "Too bad I'm happily married and have a sex slave already," he said as she struggled and kicked her feet, gasping for air. He shot a video of her hanging with his cell phone until she was dead. He headed out of the woods and left Stephanie hanging there.

Another woman Joe told he loved. He had never told anyone that other than Lisa. Then Amanda came along. This one had been abused, too. Could he actually tell, or was it a coincidence? *Maybe I should ask my victims I don't feel a connection with if they were abused.*

Joe got home before Lisa and the children. The first thing he did was to go down to check on Amanda. She was lying down watching TV. "Hi Mandy, I have a little something to show you." He pulled out his phone. "Check this out, baby." He showed her the video of Stephanie dying as she hung from the tree.

"Holy shit, Joey! You did it!" Amanda said excitedly. "Thank you so much. You better delete that video before anyone else sees it."

"I will. I hung her for you. I just wanted to share it with you. How are you feeling?"

"Yucky. I hate having periods. Thanks for caring."

"I can't help but care. I love you."

"It's okay, Joey. It'll all be good in the end."

"It would destroy Lisa if she ever found out about you. She's been acting suspicious lately. My kids would hate me, too, and I wouldn't blame them. I don't ever want to hurt them. At least you already know all my secrets. You're the only one in the world who does."

"If it's okay with you, I'd like to nap now. The Midol you got me helped a lot."

Joe showered and changed his clothes. When he was finished, he went downstairs to find that no one was home yet. He decided to cook dinner to surprise Lisa again. This way, he could also make sure there were plenty of leftovers for Amanda. By the time Alexa and Scotty got home, the house already smelled good. Lisa got home a half hour later.

"It smells great in here. I should get home late more often. Thank you, Joey. This was a nice surprise. How come you made so much? It's for your midnight snacking, isn't it? I have noticed you've lost weight. I'm proud of you."

"Thank you, baby. I've lost fifteen pounds so far. I'm about halfway to my goal."

After dinner, Scotty went to play video games. Alexa went to call Kevin.

"Want to watch a movie tonight?" Lisa asked.

"Sounds good. You choose the movie, and I'll make us some Mai-Tai's."

"And maybe a bag of microwave popcorn before you make the drinks?"

"Sure thing. Any other snacks you want to nibble on during the movie?"

"Just you, Joey. I'm not sure what to watch. What are you in the mood for?"

"There's a new movie about a serial killer. I hear it's based on a true story."

"Sounds interesting. I've always been fascinated by serial killers. I find them interesting. I like seeing how they screw up and get themselves caught. It's always something stupid. Why are serial killers so stupid? I guess they have fucked up brains. That's why they're serial killers in the first place, right Joey?"

"There might be other reasons, too," Joe grunted angrily. He felt insulted. "Maybe they were abused when they were kids. I think it's only the dumb ones we hear about, and the smart ones never get caught."

"That's true, Joey. Maybe what they went through screwed them up. I guess it's not all their fault they turned out the way they did if that's the case."

TWENTY-FOUR
THUGS

I
t was finally Friday, the last day of school for the week. That was the first thing Joe thought about when he woke up. He knew where he wanted to go.

"Good morning, Joey."

"Good morning. Got any plans for today?"

"Oh, Joey, I'm sorry I forgot to tell you I'm volunteering at the church again. I'll be gone all day."

"I have some running around to do anyway."

After breakfast, Joe went down to his office to prepare for the day. He spent some time with Amanda.

"Good morning, Mandy. How'd you sleep?"

"I slept good. How about you?"

"I had a pretty good night."

"You weren't feeling so hot last night, so I didn't go into detail. I hope you enjoyed the video. I liked doing it so much because I was thinking about you. That's why I made it."

"Did you delete it yet?"

"Not yet. I want to show it to you again while I tell you the story. Are you up to it now?"

"Yes. Tell me."

"I wish you could have been there. It was awesome." He told her the whole story. Amanda got turned on. They watched the video again before Joe deleted it.

AT THE MORNING BRIEFING, Stone said, "We have a total of ten **DARK** murders that we know of, not counting the homeless couple.

We have a missing eighteen-year-old girl who disappeared from the grocery store parking lot where she was rounding up carts. We have a half dozen people we've identified as shoppers from the security cameras inside the store around the time of her disappearance. I will talk to everyone who was shopping there around that time.

Our new tip line has received a couple of dozen calls daily. We've been chasing down every possible lead, but nothing solid on the serial killings so far."

"Any tire tracks near that hanging, Stone?" Captain Connors asked.

"No, sir. The ground there is pretty much nothing but rocks. We had to walk in. I don't know if a four-wheel drive truck could make it there."

"Well, something must have made it there. We got some unknown male DNA from her body, but there is no match yet."

"We got a tip from a bartender that she was there early afternoon. She left with a short, older man. He said she had a habit of picking up older men. The guy wore a hoodie the whole time he was there. He didn't get a good look at his face. We're still interviewing the victims' family, friends, and neighbors," Stone said.

Officer Kent walked into the room, holding a report. "We traced that stolen .38 caliber revolver to the East End gang. We have officers questioning some of them right now. They've narrowed it down to three possible suspects."

"Get the three of them in here. Keep them separated," Stone said. "Bring them in three different cars and put them in three different interview rooms. We'll interview them separately and then compare notes. Let's see if we can get one to roll over on the others."

"One small problem. We only have two interview rooms," Officer Kent reminded him.

"Put one of them in my office and have someone stay in there to keep an eye on him and all my stuff," Captain Connors said.

"Yes, sir," Officer Kent replied.

The three suspects were transported to the station in three separate cars so that they couldn't get their stories straight with each other. Carlos Rodrigues and Jesus Fernandez were put in the two interview rooms while Damien Gonzalez was put in Captain Connors's office. After about thirty minutes of the interview, the three interrogators gathered to compare notes. They got three different stories from the three suspects. They returned to their interview rooms and told their suspect that the other two had confessed and that they knew about their involvement.

They asked each one if they'd take a lie detector test. Rodrigues and Fernandez both refused. Damien Gonzalez said he would. They told him they would let him know if they decided to give him the test, but he insisted he wanted to.

"If this can prove I didn't have anything to do with it, I want to take the test. I didn't know anything about it. Give me the fucking test so I can go home."

After hours of questioning and re-questioning the suspects, the details of both Carlos' and Jesus' stories kept changing. Damien insisted he told the truth, and his story stayed the same. He insisted he had nothing to do with either of the crimes, but he heard about the robbery and murder after it happened.

"I can't tell you if it was those two, or I may be the next one shot in the head. I heard about it on the news. There was talk after that, but like I said, I can't tell you who said what. I want to live, you know. These guys will kill a snitch. I won't admit to a crime that I didn't do.

I have a family. I've been working on trying to get out of this gang alive."

Jesus finally confessed to the robbery but insisted he knew nothing about the murder.

"Carlos and I were the only ones there. After I got the money from the old guy, I walked out and got back in the car. I wondered what was taking Carlos so long. Then I heard two gunshots. Carlos got in the car and drove off. I asked him what the fuck was that back there. He told me he fired a couple of rounds into the ceiling to scare them so they wouldn't call the cops. He said he told them if they called the cops, they were dead."

"But he already shot them, right?" Stone asked.

"Yeah, I guess. But I didn't know that until I saw the news the next day. I was too scared to say anything. He bragged it was him who killed them, but no one ever said anything about rape and murder of some bitch with a kid. Hell, I was with him when he ditched the gun."

Stone joined Detective Scott. Together, they wore Carlos down, and he confessed that he and Jesus robbed and killed the old couple.

"Which one of you had the gun?" Stone asked.

"I had the fucking gun, alright? But I don't know anything about no raping shit. I ditched the gun after we robbed them. There were only two shots fired."

"How do you explain that we found the gun with three spent rounds?" Stone asked.

"I don't know, man. Maybe someone found it and shot it. All I know is that rape shit wasn't me," Carlos said. "I'd never kill a kid. I swear, man. That's some sick shit. Hell, I admitted to shooting the old couple. That's all."

Detectives Scott and Stone and Officer Kent got back together to compare notes again. They all agreed they believed Damien Gonzalez had nothing to do with this incident.

"He's your guy," Stone told Officer Kent. "Get him home. We're going to arrest the other two for armed robbery and two counts of capital murder committed during a robbery."

"Damien, your buddies confessed to the robbery and murders," Captain Connors said. "We'll get you a ride home. Our undercover officer'll drive you in an old, beat-up family sedan. No police car, okay?"

"Thanks a lot, man. You know they watch for shit like that."

"Good luck. If there's anything we can do to help you get out of the gang, let me know, and we'll do whatever we can. Gang banging ain't the life. Your family needs you."

JOE SAT in his easy chair watching television. Shortly after sitting down, the door opened. "Hi, dad!" Scotty waved to him on his way to his bedroom.

"Hello, Daddy," Alexa said.

The front door opened again. "Hi, Mom," Alexa said, heading to her room to call Kevin.

"Hi, Alexa. Hello, Joey."

"Hello baby, have a good day?"

"Long but good."

Joe ordered pizza for dinner. Several minutes later, the doorbell rang. Joe opened the door to a tall man in a brown suit. "Hello, pastor, I'm Detective Ronald Stone," he said, flashing his badge.

"Hello, detective. What can I do for you?" Joe didn't expect this. He had to appear calm.

"Have you seen this girl?" He showed Joe a picture of Hannah.

Joe thought for a minute. "I've seen her a few times at the grocery store."

"She disappeared from the parking lot. I saw you shopping there on video from inside the store around the time we believe she disappeared."

"I haven't seen her in a while. What about the cameras in the parking lot?"

"They weren't hooked up yet. Did you notice anything unusual when you were there?"

"No. I didn't see anyone when I put my groceries in the car. I hope you find her soon."

"Me too. Did you see anyone in the parking lot?"

"I saw Mrs. Corinth get out of her car when I got there. No one was in the lot when I left."

"Did you see a string of grocery carts in the middle of the parking lot?"

Joe thought for a minute and said, "No, the only carts I saw were random ones people left here and there."

"If you think of anything, give me a call," Stone said, handing him a business card.

Joe closed the door and sighed. "Son-of-a-bitch," he said under his breath.

The next time the doorbell rang, it was the pizza Joe ordered. After stuffing themselves while watching a movie, everyone went to bed and fell asleep quickly. Joe was glad that Lisa was too tired to want sex. He was also too tired.

After everyone was asleep, Joe's overfullness was gone. He went down to his office. He brought Amanda some more food and drinks, including a couple of leftover slices of pizza.

"I'm going out tonight for a while. I was too tired to do anything but go to bed, but I got my second wind."

"Before you leave, could we have a quickie?" she asked. Joe took his clothes off, then he took her clothes off with her help.

"Will you rip my panties off me like you do with the **DARK** victims? Will it hurt?"

Joe didn't answer. He kissed her and licked his way down to her neck. His hand found its way to the crotch of her panties. He grabbed them tightly and ripped them off. Amanda let out a shriek. He rubbed her clit and then let two fingers slide inside her. He worked them in and out of her while he sucked on her nipples. He lifted her legs and shoved his cock into her. She let out a scream of pleasure.

"You make me feel so good," she panted. "I'm already about to cum. Fuck the shit out of my little pussy." Amanda tensed up as she came with several loud moans. Joe didn't slow down. He kept screwing her. "Cum inside my little pussy, master. Fuck me hard. Oh God, I'm going to cum again."

That was all Joe needed. He came with a loud grunt.

This caused Amanda to cum again very loudly. They both lay there for several minutes. Finally, Amanda said, "Thank you, Joey. That was awesome."

"Yes, it was, baby," he said, kissing her. "I guess I will have to buy you more panties soon. Did you like that?"

"What do you think? I came twice in less than ten minutes. I loved it. Maybe you should stock up on a bunch of cheap pairs," she said.

They lay there for thirty minutes talking. Joe got up, cleaned up, and dressed to go out. He didn't have any plans other than looking around. He had been so tired earlier, but now he couldn't imagine going to sleep. He grabbed his black bag. He drove his truck, parked downtown, and walked around.

It was 11:30 p.m., and Joe hid in an alley, waiting for prospective victims to walk by. A male voice behind him said, "Give us that bag and your wallet." Joe turned around and saw two shirtless young men, both pointing guns at him. He recognized their gang tattoos on their chests. While he slowly handed them the bag with his left hand, his right made its way into his back pocket. They opened the bag and looked inside.

"Holy shit, man! This guy is some kind of sicko."

While they both stared into the bag, Joe pulled a razor-sharp knife out of his back pocket and opened it. As they looked back up, he quickly sliced all the way across both their throats simultaneously.

They froze in place, dropped their guns and Joe's bag, and put their hands up to their necks. They both hit the ground one after the other.

"Son-of-a-bitch, you fucking assholes got blood on my bag. I hope you didn't get any inside."

Joe knelt as they writhed in pain, gurgling sounds coming out of them, and stabbed each of them through the heart. He carved the symbol of their rival gang into their chests. He cleaned the blood off it with one of their pant legs. He hoped everyone would think this was a gang hit. He wiped down his bag with the other pant leg as best as possible and called it a night. The murders were in self-defense, but it was good enough to satisfy him for now. At least he got two thugs off the streets.

When Joe got home, the first thing he did was put his leather bag in the shower in his office. He got some old rags, took everything out, one thing at a time, and wiped each down. When he was finished cleaning the contents of the bag, he wiped out the inside and then grabbed a jug of bleach.

He began all over again. He wiped everything down with the bleach, including the inside and outside of the bag. After everything had been wiped down with bleach and dried, he loaded the items back into his bag and stashed them in the tunnel. He put the rags, gloves, and hoodie in the fireplace and burned them to get rid of any evidence.

He got undressed and fell into bed upstairs in his bedroom, glad Lisa didn't wake up. He got along much better with Amanda now.

In the morning, Joe woke up before Lisa and the kids. He made breakfast. The smell woke them, and they headed downstairs.

After breakfast, Joe asked, "Does anyone have anything they want to do today?"

"Can I go to the mall in Phoenix?" Alexa asked. "Some of my friends are getting together there today."

"Can I go, too?" Scotty asked.

"Me too," Lisa said with a smile.

Joe cleaned up the kitchen while the rest of the family went upstairs to get ready. He quickly ran a plate of bacon and eggs down to Amanda.

When they arrived at the mall, he stopped at the south entrance to drop them off. "We'll all meet here at five," Lisa said.

"Don't buy more than we can fit in the car."

"We can always come back tomorrow for the kids," Lisa laughed.

After dropping them off, Joe drove away, not knowing where he was headed yet. He drove less than a mile up Peoria Avenue when he saw a young lady in a crop top, a short denim skirt, and cowboy boots hitchhiking. He was ready to pull over to pick her up when the car in front of him stopped, and she got in.

He decided to drive over to the mission and hang out with Mark for the afternoon. He couldn't concentrate on a murder. All he could think about was Amanda and the detective.

Joe parked in the back and saw Mark taking some trash to the dumpster. "What are you doing here today?" Mark asked. "You get lost?"

"Yeah, I dropped the wife and kids off at the mall. They took my credit cards and told me to get lost," Joe laughed. "Anything you need some help with here today?"

"If you could give me a hand folding the legs and moving some of these tables against the wall, that would be a huge help. I could do it myself, but it sure goes quicker and easier with two people. You'll be blessed for all your help."

"I'm already blessed. Speaking of which, let's move those tables so I can pick up my blessings from the mall." They both laughed.

"During Thanksgiving and Christmas, people are more giving," Mark said as they worked. "Most people don't think about the homeless the rest of the year. You need to eat every day to stay alive. You should bring that up in one of your sermons."

"I will. That sounds like a great idea. People need to eat and drink. On that note, do you have a cold bottle of beer hiding in here?"

"I may have a couple." Joe followed him into the walk-in refrigerator.

"Those are giant drink coolers. I've never seen one that huge before," Joe said, pointing to one of the larger ones. They were oval with two spigots, one on each side, so two people could get a drink simultaneously.

"We have two more in the back of the fridge. These are new. We used to spend more time refilling the old, smaller ones than anything. The larger ones hold fifty gallons of fruit punch, and the smaller ones hold twenty-five gallons of baby formula." Each cart had a large cooler and a small cooler.

"I never noticed before. I don't know how I could have possibly missed seeing them."

"I do. All you ever have here is beer," Mark laughed. "Every weekend that we serve food, we'll set out the four carts. Some people bring extra baby bottles, and some bring jars to fill. All eight of those are completely emptied during one meal. After that, they have water to drink. Some people come by just to get baby formula."

"That's a lot of gallons going out," Joe said, developing a plan.

"Yeah, it is. It's a custom setup, including the heavy-duty rolling carts. With both coolers full, cart and all, each is a thousand pounds. Even then, they still roll easily."

Mark got them both a beer. They sat at one of the tables and drank.

"I need to take a leak."

While Joe was in the back, he snooped around to see what might be there that he could use. He wanted to lower the number of homeless people on the streets. Just because they were homeless didn't keep them from having babies. Something he saw gave him an idea.

"Ok, man, last swig of beer, and I'm off to pick up my credit cards and family."

"Thanks for stopping by. It's always good to see you, Joe. And thanks for your help."

When Joe arrived at the mall, he drove by the entrance before looking for a parking space. As he did, he saw Lisa, Alexa, and Scotty walk out the door together. They approached the car, their hands filled with shopping bags. Joe popped the trunk. The three of them worked at getting it all in.

TWENTY-FIVE
CAMPING

That evening in bed, Lisa said, "I'm tired from all the shopping today. Goodnight, Joey."

It was 11:30 pm. Joe wanted to get laid badly. He also felt like he needed to kill someone. This past year, his urge to kill had become stronger and more frequent. He knew the more often he killed, the greater the chance he would get caught. Having a detective show up at his home didn't help his confidence. He made sure Lisa was asleep and decided to check out another local bar.

He got up and headed down to his office. He looked in Amanda's room and found she, too, was asleep. He got dressed in his killing disguise and headed to his truck.

He drove to the aptly named bar, The Happy Place, and parked around the back. Joe walked in through the back door and looked around.

Looks like there are some pretty drunk ladies here. This should be like fishing with dynamite, he thought. He saw a young lady sitting at the bar. She swayed while she drank. He sat down beside her.

"That seat is taken," she said. "My friend went to the bathroom. I'm supposed to save the seat."

"I'll move as soon as he comes back, okay?" Joe said.

"When *she* comes back," she said. "I guess that's okay for now."

"I'm Joe. What's your name?"

"Ashley. Are you new around here? I don't remember seeing you here before."

"No, I don't go to bars too often. What are you drinking?" He looked at her drink, which was almost half gone. "That looks delicious."

"It's called Liquid Marijuana. It *is* delicious. It's one of those dangerous drinks. You don't taste the alcohol but feel it when you stand up. Wanna taste?"

"Sure, thanks." He took a little sip with a straw. "That's quite flavorful. I'll have to get me one. How old are you, Ashley, if I may ask?"

"I'm twenty-four. How old are you, Joe?"

"I'm double that, but I feel more like I'm twenty-four than forty-nine. Where's your friend?"

"She went to the bathroom a while ago. Oh man, she's over there making out with some guy. I bet she's gonna want to leave soon."

In a few minutes, her friend came over. Joe looked away. "Hey girl, this guy wants to party. Do you want to come with us?"

"No, I don't want to leave with some strange guy from a bar in the middle of the night. You better be careful, Kim. Besides, you're my ride."

"Come on, I want to party with that hunk over there. Maybe we can have a threesome. We've never done that," Kim said, kissing Ashley on the cheek.

"No, thank you. You go be a whore if you want. I don't do threesomes. Even if I did, I wouldn't want to have sex with my best friend. That's fucked up, girl. I'll get a Lyft. I don't think I'd want to ride with you anyway. You're too damned drunk."

"Your loss. It would be awesome." Kim left with the guy.

"Stupid bitch will wind up dead one of these nights."

The bartender came over just as Ashley finished her drink. "Two liquid marijuana, please," Joe said.

The bartender set the drinks down and said, "That'll be fifteen dollars."

Joe threw a twenty-dollar bill on the bar. "Keep the change."

"Thank you, Joe. That was nice. I didn't even ask." Joe and Ashley drank and chatted, although she was pretty drunk. Halfway through her drink, Ashley said, "I have to pee. I'll be right back." She stood up and almost fell, but Joe caught her. She giggled and said, "I'm alright. I can make it."

"Are you sure? Can you make it back?

"I guess we'll see," Ashley laughed. "Come pick me up if you see me on the floor."

She headed to the bathroom. As soon as the door closed behind her, Joe looked around to make sure no one saw. He palmed a small vial and covertly poured its contents into Ashley's drink.

When she got back, she said, "See, I told you I could make it." She sat down, picked up her drink, and sucked the rest of it down at once.

"Damn girl, you can drink!" Joe exclaimed.

"Thank you. It was nice meeting you, Joe," she said, pulling her cell phone out to order a ride home.

"Wait, Ashley. I just had one drink. I can drive you home."

"Sorry, sweetie, but I don't take rides from strangers in bars, even when drunk. I'm not like my stupid friend."

"If I tell you a secret, will you promise not to tell? It's no big deal. I just like my privacy."

"Sure Joe, what's your secret?"

He pulled his hoodie back just enough for her to see. "I'm Pastor Joe."

"Sorry, pastor. I didn't know. What are you doing in a dive bar in the middle of the night? Are you living a secret life?"

"Yes, I'm on a mission to save you from the drunks. That's why I'm driving you home."

"I can get my own ride. But thank you." She stood up and fell back onto the stool, dropping her phone on the floor. "Woo, I guess I may need a little help getting to the door without hitting the floor," she laughed loudly. "Hey, that rhymes. I should write that down. Getting to the floor before hitting...wait a minute. Screw it," she laughed.

The drug was distorting her thinking. "What was I doing?"

Joe said, "I'm driving you home, remember?"

"I thought I was getting a ride-share."

"You are. I'm here to take you home. I'm parked right out back."

He stood up, took Ashley by the arm, and helped her to the back door, leaving her phone. He helped her into the front seat and put her seatbelt on. By the time he got in, she was unconscious. He drove up an old mountain road until he got to a local campground back in the woods closed for the season. The trailer the campground hosts lived in was empty. They were on vacation. The locked trailer door was easy for Joe to break into.

He went back to his truck to get Ashley. He unbuckled her seatbelt and carried her into the trailer. He laid her down on the bed and took her clothes off. Once completely naked except for her sheer pink panties, he rolled her over and zip-tied her arms behind her back. He rolled her on her back and spread her legs.

When he rubbed the crotch of her panties, she squirmed. He grabbed the crotch of her panties with one hand and the waistband with the other and yanked hard. They ripped off. He smacked her gently in the face, back and forth, as he raped her.

"Wake up, Ashley. Come on, baby. Wake up." She came to, opening her eyes. "Mmm...yes. Oh...that's so good," she mumbled. She got a confused look on her face. "Where are we? How did we get here?"

"We're camping."

"We're camping? Wait, why are you fucking me? Was I so drunk that I let you? You need to stop now, pastor. Seriously, I mean it."

"We are in a trailer at the closed campground. I brought you here to this trailer that I broke into to rape you."

"What the fuck! Get off me, dammit! Pastor, stop!"

"You think your friend is okay?"

She was confused and disoriented. She had trouble thinking straight about what was happening. The alcohol and the tranquilizer mixture clouded her thinking.

"Why would anyone suspect Pastor Joe of being a serial killer?"

"Why are you doing this?"

"It's all part of God's plan to save humanity. I don't know if you heard, but I'm God."

"You're not God, you're just a pastor."

"I'm not a pastor. That pastor gig is just to make me a shit load of money."

"Get off me," she said as she struggled.

"I guess you should have gone with your drunken friend and her new lover and had a threesome. You could be eating Kimberly's hot snatch right now while her new friend fucked you. One question, Ashley, were you abused as a child?"

"Hell no, my dad was great. Nobody ever abused me before."

After Joe had an orgasm, he rolled over and lay beside her, resting for a few minutes until he regained his strength. He sat up and looked at her. She looked at him with fear in her eyes, but she was too drunk and drugged even to sit up.

"I have something I invented to try on you. It's the first time I've tried it. We'll get to see how good it works," he said as he pulled his contraption out of his bag.

"What the hell is that?" she slurred. "Pastor, what are you going to do with that?"

"This oxygen mask is screwed onto this little propane bottle from my camp stove. I think breathing in propane instead of oxygen might kill you. I wonder how long it will take you to die."

"No, please don't kill me. I'll do anything," she begged. Tears poured down her face. "Don't do this, pastor. I swear I'll never tell anyone. Oh God," she cried.

He turned on the propane and put the mask over Ashley's mouth and nose. She coughed and turned her head side-to-side to try to get it off. Joe lifted the mask. She choked and gasped for air. As soon as she could breathe again, she begged, "Please don't kill..." He put the mask back over her face.

"Looks like this works really good." He pulled the mask off again. "This is turning me on. It's working well, don't you think, Ashley?"

She choked and gasped. Once she could breathe, she said, "No. It's bad. Please don..." Joe put the mask back over her mouth and nose. This time, he left it a little shorter time. When she finally breathed again, she begged, "Please don't kill me."

Joe smiled down at her. He kissed her on the lips. He could taste the propane. Then he put the mask over her face one last time and held it there.

She struggled as hard as she could to get the mask off her face. She tried to roll away. Her legs kicked wildly. After a short time, she slowed down until she stopped moving. He held it there a little longer. When he took it off, she was no longer breathing and had no heartbeat. He turned off the gas. He wasn't crazy about the smell but loved how good it worked. He licked his lips. He tasted the propane from when he kissed her.

He loved to watch his victims suffer like he suffered when he was young. He felt that he had to get it out of his head. He would always feel better after passing the nightmare to someone else. Once he felt it come back, he had to kill again.

A Ranger checked on the campground at least once a week. Joe left the door to the trailer open so whoever came by first would see the open door, check inside, and find her dead body. He hung her ripped-up panties on the trailer's doorknob.

He got back in his truck and drove home. He was back in his office around two. Amanda was still asleep. He gave her a kiss on the top of her head. He got cleaned up and was back in his bed before 2:30 a.m.

TWENTY-SIX

REALTOR

Lisa and Joey woke up together. "Good morning, Joey."

"Good morning," Joe said. "How about I make breakfast for everyone this morning? I'll take a quick shower, then go downstairs to start. You can take a long, relaxing shower while I cook. Breakfast should be ready when you're done."

"That's sweet," Lisa said. She gave him a kiss.

He got in the shower for five minutes and then headed downstairs.

When Lisa came down a little while later, Joe put breakfast on the table. "Perfect timing."

Joe had made bacon, scrambled eggs, and hash browns. He made an extra-large helping of everything, hoping to have some leftovers for Amanda.

A little while after they finished breakfast and everyone else had left the kitchen, Joe grabbed some leftovers and went to his office. He entered Amanda's room. "Good morning, Mandy. I brought you some bacon, eggs, toast, and orange juice for breakfast." He set the food down on her tray table and kissed her.

"Good morning. It smells awesome. Thank you."

"You're welcome, baby. It's not always easy to sneak all this food down to you without getting caught. Lisa knows I bring food down here, but not usually right after I just ate."

"Did Lisa make breakfast for me?"

"No, I made breakfast this morning."

"A good man who can cook. I do love you, baby," she said as she took a bite. "I love you, and I love your cooking."

"I love you. Can I get you anything else to eat or drink while I'm up there? Maybe some jam for your toast? I see you've already made yourself coffee."

"This is plenty for me, honey. This is more than I need. I can't believe how good you take care of me. No one ever did anything special for me, even when I was little. I've never been this happy before."

"I've never been so happy before, either. I'm glad you want to be with me, and you're not just here because I kidnapped you." Joe said as he pulled her close for a long kiss while he pictured Lisa upstairs waiting for him to return. He drank a quick cup of coffee with Amanda. He kissed her again, then walked away. He looked back and said, "I'll see you soon, Mandy. I love you."

"I love you, too. You'd make me an awesome husband, Joey."

"Tell that to Lisa. She's pissed at me, and I'm getting tired of her shit." Joe locked the door and headed back upstairs. *Maybe I should kill Lisa,* he thought.

"There you are," Lisa said. "What were you doing in your office?"

"I straightened up. It was getting messy."

"If you'd leave the door unlocked, I could help you keep it cleaned up. Why do you need to keep the door locked all the time?"

"It's my man cave."

"Are you hiding something down there, Joey?"

Joe thought for a minute. The secret door to the tunnel was closed and locked. Amanda was locked in her room. "What would I hide down there? Come take a look if you want."

Joe and Lisa headed down to the basement. Lisa looked all around again. She didn't see anything unusual.

That evening, Joe didn't feel like going anywhere. He went to bed with Lisa and slept.

After he recorded several sermons that the network approved, Joe convinced them to let him preach a live sermon with the teleprompter. Pastor Joe's sermon was on the subject of "Love Thy Neighbor." Lisa wasn't feeling well, so she stayed home and watched Joe on television.

From the TV, Lisa heard Joe say, "We all need to be there for one another and help watch out for each other. There are some sick people out there taking the lives of innocent victims, but our God is a strong, merciful God who watches over his flock as long as you do your part. There are also many hungry people out there. We need to consider them all year round, not just during the holidays. Just like you and me, these people need to be able to have healthy food and drink every day.

This ministry donates a lot of money to the Charity Mission here in Phoenix. The need is great all over this country and all over the world. If God blessed you, share a little of your blessings all the time. Hunger is not a seasonal problem."

Towards the end of his sermon, Pastor Joe adlibbed a bit off the script on the teleprompter. "God Almighty sent me here to do his work. He put me in charge to lead all of you down the correct path. He gave me this power for you. I am an extension of God; thus, I am God. My words are God's words. I will lead you as he tells me to. I'm now asking all of you at home to reach deep into your pockets to help God's end-time work. I ask every person listening to send at least twice as much as usual to this ministry if you've never given before, I ask you to please help now.

I need your money for God's work. I'm here to save mankind. Satan is trying to destroy God's plan, but we must stay strong and vigilant against his evil forces. He's trying to shut down this ministry. He wants Pastor Joe off the air. We can't let Satan win. We need to stop having babies to save mankind from extinction. Once again, Satan would win. This is my command. This is the command of God Almighty!"

As soon as his sermon was over, Joe headed back home.

Joe arrived home and shouted, "Lisa, daddy's home," as he climbed the stairs to the master bedroom. "Hi, babe. How are you feeling?"

"I feel a tiny bit better. I slept a lot." She stared at him with a pissed-off look. "What's wrong with you, Joey? Why the hell did you basically say that you're God again?"

"In a way, I am. He sent me here to save mankind."

"Save mankind from what?" she asked.

"From itself. From extinction!" Joe exclaimed emphatically.

"Joey, are you on drugs? This shit sounds like something I'd expect to hear from a crackhead."

"No, I'm not on drugs. Dammit, woman, I know what I'm talking about. You know I'm not a druggie."

The phone rang late that evening, and Joe answered it in bed.

"Mr. Bain, I..."

"Yeah, but I was..."

"Can't we talk about this?" Joe slammed the phone down. "Fucking Bain!"

The sound of the slamming phone woke Lisa. "What's wrong?" Lisa asked, looking a little concerned. "What did he say?"

"The fucking network pulled my show because I didn't follow the fucking script."

Lisa just shook her head at him, turned over, and went back to sleep.

That evening and all day Monday, the end of Pastor Joe's sermon made international news. "Pastor Joseph Romano, known to his followers as Pastor Joe, claimed that he is God and was sent here to save mankind. Some are asking if he is the second coming of the Messiah, and others are wondering if he lost his mind. He begged everyone to send him more money for God's end-time work." They played a clip of the end of his sermon. "The network has pulled Pastor Joe's sermons off the air."

For several weeks, Joe hadn't felt like making love with Lisa. He didn't feel like he needed her for sex. He had Amanda for that. She loved who he really was.

It was finally October 31^{st,} and the temperature outside got pretty chilly in the evenings. It would be a cold night for the trick-or-treaters. Lisa always handed out the candy to the little witches and demons.

Joe left Lisa to deal with the trick-or-treaters and went down to his office. He pulled out a burner phone and called a realtor he saw a picture of on the sign in front of a house for sale. In his fake voice, he said, "Hello, Jackie Garcia, I got your number off the realty sign in front of the house at 3750 East 2nd Street. My name is John Peterson. My wife, Julie, and I are looking to move there from Flagstaff, and I'm interested in seeing this house. It looked like no one was living there when I drove by."

"The house is currently empty," Jackie said.

"Would it be possible to see it in the evening?"

"I can show it to you at whatever time is convenient for you, John."

"Is the electricity on? We can't get down there before it's dark."

"The electricity is on. What time could you get there?"

"Does 7:30 tomorrow night work for you?" he asked.

"It does. I'll see you and your wife tomorrow night."

After dinner on November 1^{st,} Joe went to his office to work on a sermon. He still occasionally preached at a local church. Lisa didn't give him a hard time because she knew he was depressed about his show being canceled. He was actually going to meet the realtor.

He snuck out the usual way, and when he arrived in the neighborhood, he parked one street over, walked around the corner, and waited. He didn't want her to see him walk to the house or want his truck seen parked right outside. Once she entered, Joe approached the front door with his black bag in hand and rang the doorbell.

Jackie answered the door, and Joe held out his gloved hand to shake hers. "Hello, I'm John Peterson." She was a young, petite lady with average-sized breasts for her small frame. She had long, dark brown hair. She was dressed nicely in a white button-down blouse and a somewhat conservative skirt that fell to about three inches above her knees.

She smiled, shook his hand, and said, "Hi, I'm Jackie Garcia. Come in, John, and I'll show you around. Is your wife, Julie, here?"

"No, she couldn't make it tonight."

Joe closed and quietly locked the door as she walked into the living room. He walked up behind her, put his arm around her neck, and choked her as she struggled to escape. His other hand held a chloroform-soaked rag over her face.

She struggled hard but was no match for him. She kicked his shins and flailed her arms around to hit him. She grabbed his wrist that held the rag with both hands, but she couldn't pull it away. During the struggle, A lamp crashed to the floor from an end table. After several minutes, she was unconscious. He laid her down on the living room floor. He reached into his bag, pulled out a syringe, and injected her with a tranquilizer.

Joe searched through her purse and found her cell phone and car keys. He left the phone there in her purse. He found the door that led out to the garage. He opened the garage door and looked around. He didn't see anyone outside. He walked out, got into her SUV, and drove it into the garage. Back in the house, he picked up Jackie's body and laid her down in the back seat. Then he drove her to a secluded area in the woods ten miles away.

He was glad she drove an SUV with a roomy backseat. He climbed in the back with her, taking all her clothes off except her blue panties. After zip-tying her arms behind her back, he did his signature move. He ripped her panties from her caramel brown flesh.

He put a condom on and entered her. Jackie came to but was still groggy and disorientated. "What's happening? Where am I?" Jackie slurred. "John?"

She struggled to get away but was too drugged up to fight back. "I'm Pastor Joe, and it's about time for you to die, bitch."

"Huh? Pastor? Uh..." She seemed unsure if this was really happening. "Stop! Wake up, Jackie. I have to wake up now. This is just a bad dream. This isn't happening."

"Baby, this is real, and it is happening. The news calls me **DARK**." He slapped her face and punched her chest. "Does that feel real?"

"Get off me." Joe ignored her. "My company knows I came here to meet you. They have your name and phone number. You better stop."

"They don't have my name. They have John Peterson's name, whoever the hell that is. My name is Joseph Romano. The number is for a burner phone I got rid of. They have no idea where we are. We're not anywhere near that house." He smacked her hard again.

He reached into his bag, pulled out a large, heavy-duty zip tie, and looped it around her neck. He snugged it up and pulled her hair out from under it. When he felt close to orgasm, he pulled the zip tie as tightly as possible. She struggled and gasped for air as her body lurched beneath him. Joe had a massive orgasm. Her movements slowed down as life left her.

He drove Jackie's SUV back to the edge of the woods. He hung her ripped-up panties on the gearshift knob. Joe looked around. It was after 10:00 p.m., and no one was around. There wasn't a house in sight. He grabbed his bag and walked the rest of the way back to his truck. He left Jackie naked and dead in the back seat of her SUV. He took the long way out of the neighborhood so he wouldn't have to drive past the house he abducted her from.

The next couple of days were uneventful for the most part. Joe and Lisa were barely talking to each other now.

After breakfast, Joe said Friday morning, "I have some running around to do today. I'm going to drive my old truck. Is there anything you need from me?"

"No, I've got my own running around to do," Lisa said.

He went down to his office and saw Amanda for a little while.

"How are you feeling today?" Joe asked.

"I feel a lot better."

"Good. I'm going out this morning. Hopefully, I'll have an exciting story for you later."

"Have fun and be careful."

He grabbed his black bag, hoodie, and gloves and stashed them in his truck. Then he went back upstairs to say goodbye to Lisa.

He walked out the front door and across the yard to the detached garage. He headed back to the neighborhood where he'd seen the girl's parents leave for work before she left for school. He had waited to get around to this one for a while. He didn't see anyone outside, so he parked down the street and waited.

He didn't have to wait long. He watched her parents leave. He waited a few minutes, then got out of his truck. Someone tapped him on the shoulder from behind before he could grab his black bag off the seat. He turned around and asked, "Yes?" It was a lady he recognized. He didn't know her, but he'd seen her around town several times, even in attendance for his sermons.

"Can I help you?" she asked. "Do you belong in this neighborhood?"

Ten seconds later, she would have caught him going into that girl's house with his leather bag. He pulled the hoodie off his head and said, "Hi, how are you today?"

"Oh, Pastor Joe. What are you doing out here this morning? I didn't recognize you under that hoodie. I'm Robin Hall."

"Hi Robin, it's nice to meet you," he said as he shook her hand. "I'm just trying to help keep an eye out for the killer. My schedule constantly changes, so I didn't sign up for a time or place. I just try to keep an eye out whenever and wherever I can."

"I have to tell you, pastor, I was so scared. I thought I was going to come face-to-face with the serial killer. Thank God it was only you. Thanks for your help."

"It's the least I could do. We need to catch this SOB as soon as we can." *If she only knew,* he thought. *I'm the SOB they're all looking for.*

"I better get back on my watch. Once again, it was nice to meet you," Robin said.

"Same here. Good luck." *Good luck, you fucking bitch.* As she walked away, he thought, *I better be careful. At least she didn't follow the rules and just call the police like she was supposed to. I'm lucky she didn't do the right thing.*

He wished he could kill her, but that wouldn't be wise. It would be too much of an increased risk. Still, it made him feel better to fantasize about doing it. Joe decided to call it a day and headed home. When he arrived, he told Amanda about how he almost got busted.

"Holy shit, Joey. You better be more careful. I love you," she said.

"You're right. I've really pushed my luck lately. Did you know that in the late nineties, long before you were born, The Roadside Strangler killed twelve prostitutes in the Dallas, Texas area? Their prime suspect was a trucker who killed himself.

I killed the prostitutes and the trucker, too. I made the trucker's death look like a suicide so they would blame the murders on him. I saved the panties from the last prostitute I killed and put them in the trucker's pants pocket after I killed him. The other eleven pairs of panties I stashed in the sleeper compartment of his truck. I've been different serial killers through the years in different parts of the country."

TWENTY-SEVEN
THANKSGIVING

It was finally the day before Thanksgiving.

"The house looks nice, and what you're cooking for tomorrow's meal smells great."

"It's been a productive day," Lisa said. "The kids were helpful. I worked them hard."

"You guys are a great couple of kids," Joe said. "Come here, family hug time." They all gathered in a circle and had a long, warm embrace.

"By the way, guys, we have a surprise for you. We're having company for Thanksgiving," Joe said.

"Is it Kevin?" Alexa asked excitedly.

"No, it's Jerry, Vicky, and Makayla," Joe chuckled. Alexa gave him an angry look. "We told them to leave Kevin home."

"That's not funny, Dad. He's one of the main things I'm thankful for."

Joe laughed. "We'll just have to wait and see how many of them show up."

"The Newharts are coming up tomorrow? Awesome!" Scotty exclaimed.

"We need to get to bed soon so we can get up early enough to stuff that turkey and get it in the oven," Joe reminded Lisa.

"I sure hope that's not the only thing you want to stuff," Lisa whispered. Joe had sex with Lisa that night, though he hadn't felt close to her for a while. He kind of felt like he was cheating on Amanda.

In the morning, the smell of turkey filled the air when Alexa and Scotty woke up.

"It smells good in here," Scotty said. "How long until we eat?"

"I'm making omelets and turkey sausage for breakfast," Mom said. "Go wash up, guys. It'll be ready in a jiffy."

"And hot chocolate?" Scotty asked. "That might hold me over until turkey time."

"Sure thing, Scotty. It's a special day."

"I'm going to start a fire and keep it burning all day," Joe said.

Around 11:00 a.m., the Newharts arrived. Alexa and Scotty ran out ahead of their parents. Alexa opened the back door. "I missed you, Kevin!" she exclaimed.

Kevin exited the car and said, "I missed you, too." They hugged and kissed.

"Alexa, look who else is here," Lisa said. "Kevin brought his family."

"Sorry, Mr. and Mrs. Newhart. It's great to see you again. I've missed you too, Micki. You have suitcases. Are you staying for the weekend?"

"Yes, we are," Vicky said. "We're leaving Sunday morning so we can get some of our Christmas decorations up before we go back to work."

"I missed you, Micki," Scotty said. They hugged and kissed.

"Come inside," Lisa said. "We'll have some special milkshakes later that Joe likes to make on Thanksgiving."

"Everyone sit and relax," Joe said.

"Nice fire," Jerry said. "Good thing the kids split lots of wood."

"Yeah, we have plenty for a while. I like to have a roaring fire all day whenever the weather gets cool enough."

"So, tell me about these special milkshakes Lisa mentioned."

"I put mint chocolate chip ice cream in the blender. I add some Crème de Cacao and Southern Comfort and blend it. I call it my adult chocolate chip milkshake."

"Damn, that sounds good."

"We usually have them as dessert. They're very filling."

Dinner was finally ready and set out on the table. There was a twenty-eight-pound turkey, homemade stuffing, and all the sides, including Lisa's homemade rolls.

"One of my favorite parts of Thanksgiving is all the leftovers," Joe said. "I'm sure the Newharts wouldn't mind having some leftovers to take home with them."

After everyone ate, Lisa said, "For dessert, we have pumpkin pie, whipped cream apple pie, ice cream, and Joey's milkshakes. We'll have that a little later."

"This weekend is when we'll be getting a Christmas tree and decorating it," Joe reminded everybody. "We need to get the outside Christmas decorations up. The Newharts offered to help."

Everyone sat around and chatted. Joe excused himself. "Nature calls." He picked up a magazine off the coffee table to have something to read while he was in the bathroom.

He quickly made a plate of food for Amanda and ran it down to her. "I brought you more than you can probably eat so that you can have some leftovers down here. I'll bring you some dessert later."

"I'm glad I have extra time to eat all this food. It smells fantastic. Thank you. Happy Thanksgiving, Joey."

"You're welcome, Mandy. Happy Thanksgiving. I'll bring you some containers for your leftovers the next time I come down." Joe gave her another kiss, then headed back upstairs. He walked quickly into the bathroom.

WHILE JOE WAS out of the room, Vicky took Lisa aside to talk privately.

"How are things with you and Joe?"

"Not great. We don't talk much lately, and I'm not sure what he's up to. I think he might be cheating on me."

"Oh no. I hope you're wrong," Vicky said, hugging Lisa.

"We hardly ever have sex anymore. It feels like we're just going through the motions when we do. He used to always be horny."

"Maybe he's just depressed over losing the show. Does he still talk about being God?"

"No, he doesn't talk much about religion anymore, except he goes down to his office to work on sermons. I really don't know what he's doing down there."

"Maybe he's watching porn on his computer."

"I wish. Then at least he'd probably come back up horny."

"I know he loves you. You guys will figure it out."

"I hope it's soon. I've tried to talk to him about it. He says nothing's wrong. I'm sure he's hiding something."

"I'm always here for you. Maybe Jerry can talk with him. See what he can find out."

JOE WALKED out of the bathroom. Lisa said, "There you are."

Lisa put away all the leftovers and straightened up the kitchen with Alexa and Vicky's help. They sat down for some pumpkin, apple pie, and Joe's milkshakes. When they were finished with dessert, they sat in the living room together to watch their first Christmas movie of the year, as was their tradition every Thanksgiving night. Alexa, Scotty, and Makayla were so full they fell asleep before it was over. Kevin sat and stroked Alexa's hair as she laid her head on his chest, sleeping.

After everyone was in bed and asleep for the night, Joe headed back down with a slice of apple pie and one of his adult milkshakes.

He also brought Amanda several containers. She filled them with leftovers, including the apple pie, and put it in her fridge.

"Thank you, Joey. The milkshake was awesome, but now I feel like the turkey. I'm stuffed. I hope you don't mind, but I just want to sleep."

"I'm glad you liked it." He laid down with Amanda until she fell asleep, then headed back upstairs to sleep in his own bed with Lisa. He was full, too. He fell asleep quickly.

In the morning, Joe woke to a very quiet house. It was peaceful. He walked down the hall and looked in Scotty's room. It was empty. Then he looked in Alexa's room. She was still half asleep. She looked up with squinty eyes and said, "Mornin' dad."

"Good morning, Alexa. I know Mom is probably Black Friday shopping. Do you know where Scotty and the Newharts are?"

"Yeah, they all went shopping with mom. I told them I wanted to stay home and sleep. She said she will shop, then drop the boys and Micki off at Chet's house."

"Do you mind if we talk?"

"I don't mind. I love being a daddy's girl." Joe sat on the edge of her bed.

"I love that too. I know this is a very personal question you probably don't want to talk about with your dad." Joe paused for several seconds, then asked, "Are you still a virgin?"

"Why would you ask that? Of course I am. I'm only fourteen. I haven't even had a real boyfriend yet, and I'm not in any rush."

"What about Kevin?"

Alexa looked away and giggled. "I like him a lot, but he lives like a million miles away. We've never even gone on an actual date. I would love to have him as a boyfriend, but I still think I'm too young to have sex."

"In the future, whenever you do, way in the future," Joe laughed nervously, "please be careful and use birth control. Your mom got pregnant right after we started having sex. Before raising a family, I want you to have lots of fun. No more than two kids, I hope."

"I agree. No more than two kids."

When everyone got home from shopping, Joe and Alexa were sitting at the kitchen table eating turkey sandwiches.

"No one is allowed to look in my car," Lisa said. "I have presents I still need to wrap, so I can get them under the tree once it's up."

"Where are the boys and Makayla?" Joe asked.

"Spending the day at Chet's house and having dinner there. They'll call when we need to pick them up. Alexa, they would like you to join them. I'll drive you if you want."

"OK, Mom, as soon as I finish my sandwich."

"Ok, but we'll have to use Dad's car if he'll let me drive it. Jerry and Vicky went shopping alone after we got home."

"Have fun, and don't wreck it," Joe said as he tossed Lisa the keys to his Ferrari. After they left, he went down to his office.

He walked into Amanda's room. "I love you, Mandy. I brought you a turkey sandwich."

"I love you too. Thank you. Set it on the tray table, and I'll eat it in a little while."

"Do you want to play some cards, or would you like to fuck me?"

"How about I fuck you first, then we play some cards?"

Amanda's face lit up. "That sounds perfect." She took off her t-shirt and tossed it on the floor. She reached out and opened Joe's pants and pulled his cock out. She licked her lips and said, "I don't think I could ever be with another guy. Your huge cock has me spoiled."

She sat on his lap and slid her pussy back and forth on his staff. After a few minutes, she lifted, grabbed his hard-on, and guided it inside her. She rode him like this until they both reached orgasm.

After sex, they sat there naked, playing cards for a while. "Joey, you better get back upstairs," Amanda said.

"Okay, baby, I'll be back tonight with some more leftovers."

When the kids returned that evening, Jerry asked, "Did you have fun with Chet today?"

"Yeah, we had a great time. We played video games most of the day," Scotty said.

"I'm glad I could join you," Alexa told Kevin.

"You guys should go on a date," Joe said. He winked at Alexa.

She gave him a dirty look and said, "Dad!" Joe laughed, and then Alexa laughed, too.

They got the house decorated for Christmas inside and out on Friday and Saturday. Once they got the tree set up, the guys moved to the outside while the ladies decorated it.

They set up a life-sized manger scene on the front lawn. Jerry and Kevin's help made it so much quicker. After the manger was up, Jerry and Kevin went back inside to warm up.

"I have a surprise this year," Joe told Scotty. "We are only putting up a few lights out here this morning. I have a crew coming to set up a killer light show where all the different decorations light up to the sound of music. They'll be here early afternoon. Don't tell anyone. They'll find out after dark when we turn them on. They don't need to know ahead of time. Just you and me, son." Joe put his arm around Scotty's shoulder.

"Yeah, Dad, just you and me," Scotty smiled. Scotty removed the strings of Christmas lights and ensured they weren't tangled.

"All we need from those lights are the blue icicles that go across the front," Joe said. "Those will stay on. The rest will be the show."

After sundown, Joe called everyone to come out front to see the decorations. "I have them set up to be turned on and off with a remote app." Joe hit a button on his phone, and the Christmas tree lit up in the front window. He hit another button and then recorded a video of the house. The music played, and a few lights lit up first on one side of the yard and then on the other. Soon, the music got louder, and the entire front yard was alive with a fantastic light show that danced all over the house and lawn in time to Christmas music.

"Wow, did you guys do this all yourselves?" Lisa asked.

"This is awesome, Joe," Vicky said.

"Jerry, Kevin, Scotty, and I did the decorations, but I hired a company to come out and set up the music and the light show," Joe said. "Pretty cool, eh?"

"Very cool, Joey. It's beautiful. I love it." Lisa looked at Vicky and said, "I wish you didn't have to go home tomorrow. On Monday I'll be on the computer all day anyway, spending money. I can't wait until Christmas. You'll be here, right?"

Vicky walked over to Lisa, hugged her, and said, "We wouldn't miss sharing it with you guys for anything." She gave Lisa a friendly kiss on the lips.

Sunday morning, Lisa made a good breakfast to send the Newharts down the road. She also made up a package of leftovers for them to take home.

"Scotty, we probably won't be here for your birthday in a few weeks. We wanted to give you a little something," Jerry said, holding out a wrapped present.

"You didn't need to do that, but thank you." Scotty took the present and asked, "Can I open it now while they're still here?"

"I guess that would be okay," Lisa said.

He ripped the wrapping paper off. "It's a drone! Thank you, guys. This is awesome." He hugged Jerry and Vicky. He had a fist bump with Kevin and then a kiss and a long hug with Micki. "I love you," he whispered in her ear.

"Me too," Micki said.

"I wish you didn't have to leave this morning," Alexa told Kevin.

"I wish we could be together every day."

"I'll miss you, Kevin," she said as she hugged him. "I wish you all could stay up here. You already feel like part of our family. I wish we all lived in the same town."

"I know, sweetie. We wish that, too," Joe said.

"I don't have any good friends here. You are my best friend," Lisa told Vicky. A tear rolled down her face.

Joe shook Jerry's hand and said, "I'll miss you too, but I won't cry. I promise. Come here. Italians don't just shake hands, we hug," Joe said. He really did love having the Newharts around as much as the rest of the family did.

Scotty hugged Makayla and said, "I'm going to miss you, Micki."

"I'm going to miss you, Scotty," Makayla said as she hugged him and then shyly ran to the car.

As the Newharts drove away, Kevin yelled out of the window, "I love you, Alexa."

Alexa yelled back, "I love you, Kevin."

"First love is so sweet and can also be so painful sometimes," Lisa said.

Joe put his arm around Alexa. "It'll be alright, sugar. Go to your room and text him."

"Thank you, daddy." She walked inside and then ran up to her room.

"You know Joey, she's got a good head on her shoulders. I'll be happy as long as she doesn't get pregnant. We should probably talk to her now. Let her know how to avoid it besides abstinence. That doesn't work with most teens. As a teenager, I fell in love with this man, and we had sex almost immediately. I don't think they've done that yet."

"I talked with her about that Friday morning while you were shopping. She says that she's still a virgin, and she doesn't feel ready not to be. I told her to be sure she used birth control whenever that changes."

"I bet she loved having that conversation with her dad. Was she embarrassed?"

"Actually, she was very mature about it, considering she was talking about it with her dad. It feels good they can be comfortable talking with us instead of it being such a taboo subject."

TWENTY-EIGHT

CAVE-IN

I t was Cyber Monday, another day for Lisa to shop, this time online. After lunch, Joe said he had to get out of the house. Lisa knew he liked to shop for Christmas early to avoid the mayhem of the packed stores.

Joe had something else in mind other than gifts. He had purchased most of his Christmas presents before Thanksgiving. He drove around different neighborhood streets to look for another victim. He had a plan that he came up with weeks ago. This one wasn't going to be one of his DARK victims. He saw a young cutie walk down the street. He slowed down and pulled up beside her. He pulled the hood off his head and said, "Hi, I'm Pastor Joe. Would you like a ride?"

"Hi, pastor. I'm Kathy," she said. "No thanks. I don't have far to go."

Joe heard someone call out to him from across the street. "Hello, pastor. Nice to see you other than at church services."

It was a lady he knew well. "Hello, Mrs. Duncan. It's nice to see you, too. I'm keeping an eye on the young ladies out here."

"That's good, pastor. I am, too. We'll keep this street safe, at least.

Our family takes shifts. We watch this street twenty-four hours a day. It's terrible, these murders and all."

"Yes, it is. Thank you so much for your family's help. You have a great day." He turned to Kathy. "Are you sure you want to walk the rest of the way?"

"I guess I could use a break. It's a bit cold out." Joe drove her the rest of the way home and told her, "You be safe now, and don't trust anyone."

He drove to a different neighborhood. He saw a pretty black lady walking down the street. He took his hood off and pulled up beside her. She recognized him immediately.

"Pastor Joe. It's nice to meet you. I'm Melissa. I heard you lived here. I didn't think I'd ever meet you in person."

"It's nice to meet you too, Melissa. Where are you heading?"

"I'm going to do some shopping. My car's in the shop."

"Honey, it's too cold for you to walk out here. Hop in. I'll give you a ride."

Melissa sat down in the passenger seat, and he drove down the road. "It's so warm in here, pastor. Thank you."

"You're welcome. Is it okay if I take you someplace special before you go shopping?"

"Sure, I'm not in a rush now. This must be my luckiest day ever."

"I guarantee you'll never have a luckier day the rest of your life. How old are you?"

"I'm twenty. I can't wait until I'm twenty-one."

"So you can drink and party in the bars?"

"Well, that's part of it. That's not what a pastor wants to hear from a young lady, right?"

"Hey, we all look forward to having a good time. I drink in the bar sometimes, myself. People look forward to becoming adults so they can do things they weren't allowed to do before. I was young once. Twenty-one was party time."

As they chatted, Joe drove down a deserted dirt road.

"Where are we going?" she asked. "I don't think this road goes through."

"You'll see. It's a special place, I know." They got to a dead end and stopped. Joe pulled a stun gun from the glove box, put it against Melissa's neck, and pulled the trigger. Her whole body quivered uncontrollably, and her eyes rolled back in her head. He held it there until he was sure she was completely incapacitated. He reached into the back seat and pulled a syringe from his bag. Melissa was still conscious but couldn't move except for involuntary twitching. Joe grabbed her arm, tied a quick tunicate, and injected the drug into her vein.

"Wha...what are y...you doing, pa...pastor?"

"You're going to sleep for a little while. God, you're beautiful."

Melissa was soon unconscious. Joe pulled up to an abandoned horizontal mineshaft at the end of the road that went down into the side of a mountain. It had been shut down for safety concerns years ago. There had been several small cave-ins. After three miners died down there, they shut it down for good.

Joe parked his car near the entrance of the mine. He exited and moved the barrier that blocked the entrance enough to squeeze by. He walked back to the passenger side of his car, pulled Melissa out of the seat, and picked her up while holding his black bag. He wore an LED light on his head so he could see as he carried her deep into the shaft.

He laid her down on the ground and took her clothes off. Then he took his clothes off. With his plan, no one should ever find her body—no need to worry about evidence.

"I haven't been with a beautiful black lady in a long time." He got down between her legs and raped her.

Melissa came to. "Pastor Joe? Where are we? Oh my God. What are you doing? Get off me." She seemed groggy and disoriented from the drug, and it was too dark to see. Joe had turned off his headlamp before she came to.

"I have a question. Were you ever abused as a little girl?"

"What? No! This is the only time anyone has ever abused me."

"That's what I thought."

"Leave me alone, you pervert," she said. "Take me home now."

Joe turned on his light. "Not yet, baby." He sat down beside her and turned it off again. Melissa tried to sit up, but Joe pushed her back down. She just laid there in the darkness.

He climbed on top of her and raped her again. The harder he raped her, the more dirt fell on and around them. Her screams caused more dirt to come loose from above. Joe felt an orgasm build up. Every time he was about to cum, he would stop.

He wanted to make it last as long as he could. The whole mine shaft could collapse and kill them both at any second. That added to the intensity he felt. Finally, he couldn't hold back anymore. He groaned very loudly as he came. More and more dirt fell from above.

She begged again, "Please let me go home."

"You *are* home, baby," Joe said. "This old mine shaft is about to collapse. You'll have your very own tomb, just like my son, Jesus."

"What the fuck? I don't want a tomb. Your son is Jesus?"

"Yes, and I'm your God. You'll have no more pain or sadness ever. You'll never get sick again. This is my gift to you." Joe got dressed, turned on his headlamp, and quickly headed towards the entrance.

Something half-buried caught his attention. He dug it out with his hands. It was an old forgotten stick of dynamite. He headed toward the mouth of the mineshaft. He heard Melissa cry out for help. He looked back and saw her try to crawl.

Once he was out, he put a condom over the dynamite and put it in his bag. He put the bag in his trunk and grabbed a sledgehammer. He walked over and hit the beams several times. The entrance collapsed, blocking the way out with tons of dirt and rocks. There was no way to know how deep into the cave-in went. If the cave-in didn't bury her, she would die of dehydration and starvation, if not of asphyxiation.

"Her body will never be found," Joe said, marveling at his latest accomplishment. "She's buried forever." He brushed the dirt off the best he could.

He put the sledgehammer back in his trunk. As he got into his car, he saw a forest ranger pull up. He parked and walked up to Joe's car as he rolled down the window.

"Pastor Joe, what are you doing out here?" Ranger Kelly asked.

"I was checking out where this road went. I didn't know it was a dead end."

"Yeah, it is. The only thing here is that old mine." He looked over at it. The dust had already settled. "You best keep away from it. It's not safe. It looks like the entrance recently collapsed."

"I will. I saw you on the news. That serial killer killed your wife. My sincere condolences, ranger."

"Thank you."

Joe watched Ranger Kelly walk over to check out the mine as he drove away.

Joe drove through a carwash before heading home. He had a few presents he had already wrapped in the trunk.

On his way home, he stopped and picked up a dozen roses each for Lisa and Amanda. When Joe got home, he went through the tunnel to clean up. He dropped off the roses for Amanda in his office. Then he parked in the garage, carried the gifts into the house, and put them under the tree.

"Lisa, I got you a little something to say I love you." He handed her the roses.

"Oh, Joey, that's sweet! I love you, too," Lisa smiled. "I have a little something for you, baby." She pulled him in for a warm hug and kiss. "Would you mind if we invited the Newharts over for dinner next weekend? They're both off work the following Monday. I was thinking after dinner we could play cards."

"Sounds like Lisa's missing the Newharts, too. Let me know what they say when you invite them. I will be driving around Wednesday to deliver some holiday care packages. Then I'm going to one of the homeless shelters with Mark to help."

"Scotty will be fourteen this week. Can you believe it?"

"It sure goes by fast."

"This Saturday afternoon, we'll help serve a hot meal to people at the Charity Mission in Phoenix. Maybe the Newharts could come up and help," Lisa suggested.

"Afterwards, they can drive to Canyon City with us."

"I'll call them as soon as I put these beautiful roses in a vase."

"I don't think the kids will complain. Mark and Anita would appreciate the help."

Lisa called Vicky. They talked for over an hour. Joe overheard Lisa tell Vicky about the roses. She said she wasn't sure if they were a loving thing or a guilty thing.

Joe headed downstairs to give Amanda the roses. Her roses were already in a vase.

Amanda was thrilled. "Red roses. Joey, they're beautiful! I love them. This is the first time anyone has ever bought me flowers."

"I'm glad I could be your first."

"I have to give you a proper thank you, Joey." She took off her shirt, reached out, and opened his pants. She slid her hand into his underwear. "It's soft." She quickly pulled his pants down and dropped to her knees. She took it all in her mouth. Once it was hard, she pushed him down on the futon and climbed on top of him. She felt him fill her.

"I'm still always surprised every time we have sex, just how tremendous your cock is. It feels so fucking good."

"We need to make it quick. Lisa's expecting me to be right back up." Joe moaned in ecstasy. "This is so awesome. I love you so much, baby." She rode him faster and harder. Amanda moaned loudly. "I wish we had more time, my little sex slave."

"Take all the time you need, Joey. I'll always treat you better than Lisa will," she said as she moaned. "God, I want you to cum inside of me. Fill me up with your cum, Joey."

"You're an awesome lover," Joe said between moans. "You always make me feel so good. I'm so close, baby." When she heard that, it didn't take Amanda long to reach a powerful orgasm that caused Joe to shoot his load inside of her with a loud grunt.

They kissed, then Amanda got off him and said, "Go back up to your old wife, you naughty preacher man."

Joe went to the bathroom to clean up before he got dressed. He quickly told her about Melissa in the mineshaft and the stick of dynamite he found.

"I love you, Joey. Please be careful. I need you."

"It should be stable. It was cool and dry in the mine. I'll keep it refrigerated."

Joe headed back upstairs.

"The Newharts will be there Saturday," Lisa said. "They're looking forward to it. We'll meet up with them at the Charity Mission."

TWENTY-NINE

SCOTTY'S BIRTHDAY

Tuesday was Scotty's fourteenth birthday. After breakfast, Joe and Lisa called Scotty into the living room.

"I know your birthday party isn't until this evening," Mom said. "Dad and I wanted to give you your birthday present this morning in case you want to start using it."

"Happy birthday, son." Dad handed him a wrapped box.

As Scotty took it, he heard a phone ring. He looked around to see whose phone it was. "No way," he said as he put the box up to his ear. He ripped the paper off and opened the box. It was a cell phone. The call was from Alexa.

Alexa walked around the corner with her cell phone in her hand. "Surprise."

"You guys are awesome!" Scotty exclaimed excitedly.

"We already programmed some phone numbers for you. Obviously, there's Alexa's number. Mine, Mom's, Kevin's, and Vicky's numbers are also in there. Vicky lets Makayla use her phone sometimes since she doesn't have her own cell phone yet," Joe said.

"We thought you might like to call Micki before your party since she can't make it," Lisa said.

Scotty was so happy he smiled from ear to ear. "Can I go now? I have a phone call to make."

"Before you ask, you can stay home from school today. I already arranged with your teachers to have your catch-up work ready for you," Lisa said.

"Thank you so much, mom and dad." He hugged them both. "Thank you, Alexa, for being my first call. I love you guys. I don't want to stay home from school. Is it okay if I go?"

"You *want* to go to school today?" Mom asked.

"That way, I can get all my friend's phone numbers, and I won't have any makeup work."

"Okay, you can go to school," Lisa said.

"Thank you." Scotty ran up to his room to call Micki before he had to leave.

That evening, they had Scotty's birthday cake. He received a few more gifts from his family and friends. Scotty declared it his best birthday ever.

"They grow up so fast. Before we know it, they won't be teenagers anymore," Lisa said.

"Enjoy it while you can," Joe replied.

After Scotty's party was over, it seemed like a good time to start work on another sermon, or so he told Lisa.

"Joey, you don't have to stay up with me if you have work to do. I'll just be going to sleep anyway."

"You fall asleep before me anyway. I'll go work on it then."

After Lisa was asleep, Joe went down to the basement. He walked into Amanda's room and lay down with her. They had a pleasurable quickie and then fell asleep. He spent most of the night with her. It was close to morning when he woke up. He hadn't set his alarm. He kissed Amanda and said, "I love you, baby."

"I love you too, Joey. I wish you could just stay with me."

"That would be nice." Joe headed to bed upstairs.

In the morning, Lisa was happy to wake up beside Joe.

Opening his eyes, he said, "Good morning, love."

"Good morning to you," Lisa replied. "You have anything you need to do today?"

"Actually, I'll be running around a bit this afternoon."

"Great, that means I can take the kids Christmas shopping. I hate waiting until the last minute. The stores are so crowded, and all the good stuff is gone."

"You have fun doing that. I wish I could join you," Joe said sarcastically.

"Nothing like going shopping with two teenagers."

After lunch, Lisa took the kids and went shopping.

Joe headed down to his office to prepare for the day he had planned. He grabbed Amanda's dirty clothes, took them upstairs, and put them in the washing machine. He spent time with her until he needed to move them from the washer to the dryer, and then he brought the clean, dry clothes down to her.

"I'll fold them and put them away. Thank you for washing them for me," Amanda said. "You have a great day. I'll be waiting to hear all about it."

"You're the best girlfriend any guy could ask for. Thank you, Mandy. You have a great day, too."

Joe left to help at the local food bank. When he arrived home, Lisa was already home, watching TV while dinner simmered in the kitchen. With nothing more to do, Joe spent some time with Lisa.

"Joey, I didn't expect to see you tonight," Lisa said as she stood and hugged him.

"I missed you." He sat down on the couch with her. Lisa leaned up against him, and they watched TV and cuddled up.

That evening, Lisa went to the bathroom once everyone was in bed. Joe lay there naked and watched TV. Lisa came out of the bathroom wearing only her sheer pink panties. Joe's head turned instantly.

"I bet I can guess what you want tonight."

Lisa climbed on top of him and said, "Yes, you can. It needs to be a quickie, Joey. I need to get up early tomorrow." She kissed him passionately.

"Why do you need to get up early?"

"Remember that church thing I volunteered for again a while back? It's tomorrow. I'll be gone from 8:00 a.m. until 7:00 p.m."

"Well, let's get this show on the road." He thought it was great she'd be gone all day.

Lisa climbed off him and licked his penis. She got back on top of him and sucked his cock as she straddled Joe's head. This was his cue to lick her. After a few minutes, she got off him and sat on him again, easing his penis inside her. They screwed hard and fast. It was another ten minutes before Lisa came. Her orgasm excited Joe so much that he came fairly quickly.

"That's what I call a great quickie. Fifteen minutes of sex, and we both had orgasms," Joe said.

He felt distant from her emotionally, but he still enjoyed the sex. They fell asleep quickly. Joe woke to an empty house. He got up, put on his boxers, and walked downstairs to grab a quick bite. There was half a coffee cake left. There was still some hot coffee.

Joe stood at the counter and drank coffee and ate coffee cake. He felt better with something in his stomach. He went to lie down with Amanda. As he cuddled up to her, she woke up.

"Good morning, Joey. I love you." She gave him a kiss.

"Good morning, baby. I love you." They cuddled, and both fell back asleep. Joe woke up an hour later. He kissed Amanda on the cheek. She opened her eyes and smiled at him.

"How about some breakfast?"

"Sure, Joey. What are we having?"

"Would you like some bacon and eggs?"

"Sounds good."

"There's some coffee cake to hold you over on the counter. Do you want to come upstairs and help me make it?" Joe asked as he watched the expression on her face.

She sat up, and her face lit up. "Are you serious? I would love that, but is it safe?"

"The kids are in school, and Lisa won't be home until tonight. I'm nervous, but I'm excited, too."

They went upstairs together. Amanda was in awe as she looked around the house. "This is the most beautiful home I've ever seen."

They made breakfast together, ate, and cleaned up the kitchen.

"Would you like to see the rest of the house?" he asked.

"Sure, master," she smiled.

Joe showed her around downstairs, then took her upstairs and showed her the bedrooms, saving the master bedroom for last. She sat down on the bed and bounced on it.

"This is a comfortable bed. You sleep with Lisa here."

"Yeah, I wish I could sleep with you here."

He sat beside her, pulled her close, and kissed her. They made out like teenagers. He pushed Amanda back on the bed.

"Joey, wait. Do you think we should do this here?"

"I want to so badly. It would be so naughty. We can make it quick if you want. I think about you every time I have sex with Lisa."

Joe stood up and took his boxers off. Amanda stripped quickly. Joe climbed on the bed and helped her. They rolled around the bed together as they kissed passionately. Joe slid his hand between Amanda's legs to find her already wet. She pushed him down on his back and took his rod in her mouth. Then she climbed on top of him and sat on his hard cock.

"I can't believe I'm fucking you in your bed while your wife's at church. This is so fucking naughty. I'm already about to cum."

Joe rolled her over. He wanted to be on top of her when he came inside her.

"Am I lying on Lisa's pillow?"

"Yes, you are." He pounded her hard. The naughtiness of it excited them both.

She tried to hold back, but she was too excited. She had an

incredible orgasm. Joe tried to keep going until she had another orgasm.

After he came, he said, "This was so kinky, I couldn't hold back anymore."

"My naughty master, I almost came as soon as you said I was lying on Lisa's pillow."

They lay there together and hugged and kissed for several minutes. They got up and took a shower together. They soaped each other up and rubbed their soapy bodies against each other.

"Joey, this was an awesome morning."

"Yes, it was, baby! I wish I could leave you up here. I need to go out after we eat lunch."

"It's okay, I love my room. Maybe one day this one will be mine." They went downstairs and ate lunch together. "Thank you for such a special morning. I never expected anything like this. It was so much fun. Now get going."

"You make it hard for me to leave." Joe walked with her down to her room and hung out with her for a little while before leaving.

Joe stopped by the house of an older couple who couldn't attend church services because of health problems. He dropped off a casserole Lisa made for them. Afterward, he went shopping before heading home.

It was a peaceful afternoon. Lisa wouldn't be home early enough to cook, so Joe made dinner. He wanted it to be ready when she got home after a day of volunteering. He also made sure there were plenty of leftovers. He got out six pork chops.

The kids should be home soon. After school, Alexa had dance class, and Scotty stayed with her and watched the class so they could walk home together. He figured he had enough time to watch one show before he had to start dinner. Just as the show ended, Alexa and Scotty walked through the front door.

"Hi, Daddy. How was your day?" Alexa asked.

"Peaceful and relaxing."

"May I go to my room and play video games?" Scotty asked.

Do you have any homework?

"Do you have any homework? That comes before games, you know."

"I know. I didn't have much. I finished it at Alexa's dance class," Scotty said. "I'll call Micki first."

"Go ahead and play. I'm going to start dinner. Mom won't be home until around seven."

Scotty ran up to his room.

Joe made his own version of Alfredo sauce. While the sauce simmered, he made small meatballs. Then he set up the large pot with water and heated it. He got a loaf of seasoned buttered garlic bread from the freezer and pre-heated the oven.

By the time Lisa got home, the house smelled great. She walked up to Joe and gave him a hug and kiss. "I sure didn't expect this, Joey. Thank you. You are the best husband a woman could ask for."

Joe thought, *if she only knew the truth about me, I bet she'd change her mind.*

"I love helping out. You had a long day." Joe poured her a glass of wine and told her, "Go sit down and relax. The kids are in their rooms. Dinner will be ready in five minutes. You can say hi to the kids when they come down to eat."

Joe and Lisa went to bed before Alexa and Scotty. Lisa fell asleep right away, but Joe wasn't tired. He lay there and thought about the day. He had sex with Amanda right there where Lisa slept. He felt horny thinking about it.

Joe headed down to Amanda's room. Her face lit up when she saw him.

"You want to tear up my little pussy?"

"How could I say no to that? Come here, you sexy little piece of ass." Joe grabbed her by the button-down blouse she wore and ripped it open, buttons flying across the room. He pushed her down onto the futon, grabbed her feet, and pulled off her sandals. He opened her pants, grabbed the bottom of the legs, and jerked them off her. That pulled her off the futon onto the floor. Joe ripped her panties off and dove face-first into her crotch on the floor. She let out a scream of pleasure as he sucked and nibbled on her clit.

After a few minutes, she begged, "Fuck me, Joey. I want to feel your cock inside me."

Joe got up and picked her up. He threw her back up onto the futon and shoved his hard member into her wet hole.

"Oh God, Joey. I love your big, fat dick! Fuck me hard. You make me feel so good."

"I love fucking that hot, little pussy of yours," Joe said as he slammed into her hard.

"Joey, fuck me like a dog. Fuck me like a dirty fucking dog!" He turned her over onto her knees and entered her from behind.

After a while, Amanda said, "Master, fuck me hard and rough. Pretend I'm one of your victims. Smack me around and call me nasty things."

He smacked her hard in the face. "Shut the fuck up, you fucking little bitch. Don't tell me what to do." He grabbed her right nipple and squeezed and twisted it hard. "I bet you love this, you fucking little whore. Honey, I'm going to rip your little cunt apart," he said as he slammed his cock into her as hard as he could.

She screamed the whole time, a mixture of pain and pleasure. Joe put both of his hands around her neck and strangled her. He could tell that Amanda was about to cum. He let go of her neck and pulled his dick out.

He grabbed her around the waist, picked her up, and flipped her over. He threw her hard onto the futon. He grabbed her ankles and pulled her towards him. She was now on her knees, bent over. As he entered her from behind and said, "Don't think I'm gonna stop just because you have an orgasm, you fucking slut." He smacked her ass hard, and she moaned loudly. He smacked one cheek and then the other.

Amanda tensed up as Joe felt wave after wave of orgasm flow through her.

He bent over her and choked her again. Her intense orgasm

helped trigger Joe to shoot his load inside her. After they rested several minutes, Joe said, "Damn girl, you might actually be as kinky as me. That's saying something."

"Only with you, Joey. I never was kinky before I met you. Not that I had all that many sexual experiences before we met, not counting the crap my parents put me through."

"I couldn't imagine Lisa ever being this kinky." He cuddled with her. They both drifted off to sleep, totally drained and happy. In the middle of the night, Joe woke up and headed upstairs to slip into bed with Lisa.

In the morning, Joe got up and made breakfast. Lisa woke up and rolled over to see Joe was already up. In the bathroom, she noticed what looked like a purple hair stuck on her face. She pulled it off and looked at it. It looked like a blonde hair that had been dyed purple. She looked over the bed and found another blonde and purple hair on her pillow.

She headed downstairs. "Good morning, Joey."

"Good morning. Breakfast is almost ready. Sleep well?"

"Yeah, I slept fine. Has anyone else been in our bed?"

"No, why would anyone else be in our bed?"

"I found some purple hairs on my pillow."

Joe thought for a moment. "Oh, I bet I know what happened. I was in town, and a family said hi to me. This one teenage girl kept hugging me. I think she had purple hair. I must have got some on me. Sorry, baby."

"Do you have a girlfriend, Joey?"

"No, I have a beautiful wife."

Lisa dropped the subject but still seemed suspicious.

THIRTY
NUMBER THIRTEEN

E arly Saturday afternoon, the Romanos drove down to Phoenix to help serve the homeless a hot meal. The Newharts drove up from Tucson to help as they had arranged. While they cooked everything and ready to serve, Lisa asked Vicky, "Are you guys coming to our place tonight?"

"Yeah, that sounds like a good plan. We'll leave early on Monday. That way, we don't run into too much rush hour traffic. How are things with Joe?" she whispered.

"I thought they were getting better, but then I found some hairs on my pillow. He came up with an excuse. I don't know what to believe."

"If you ever need a place to stay, let me know."

After everyone finished eating and the mission cleared out for the night, all the volunteers worked quickly to clean the place up.

"The next meal we have planned is the Christmas meal," Mark said. "We'll also be handing out food boxes to families. Thanks to you, Joe, we've had so much food donated by local grocery stores."

"Glad that I could help out, buddy. I just told them I'm God, and they must obey my command to give you lots of food," he joked.

"Hey, whatever it takes," Mark laughed. "You know, Jerry drove up here a couple of days ago to help me with some financial paperwork."

"Yeah, I told him I'd do it for free. He insisted I take the money. He told me it wasn't his money. Pastor Joe was paying me, so I took it," Jerry said.

"Thanks for all your help, Romanos and Newharts. Now get out of here. I know you have a long drive home. Drive safely."

"We will, Mark. See you soon," Joe said. The two families headed out. Scotty and Makayla rode together in the Newhart's car. Alexa and Kevin rode with the Romanos.

When they arrived, the four kids went upstairs. Joe built a fire in the fireplace, and the adults sat in the living room and drank wine and beer. It wasn't long before everyone was ready for bed after the long day.

Lisa made everyone omelets for breakfast, along with sausage links and English muffins. After breakfast, Scotty and Kevin split more firewood while the girls watched. Right after they finished, it began to snow. It was the first snow of the season. They sat by the fireplace with their parents and watched it snow through the front window.

The weekend passed too quickly. The Newharts left for home after lunch. Lisa went to boot up her computer. Joe went down to his office to get some of his own supplies for his day. He used his tunnel to load supplies in the bed of his truck. He spent some time with Amanda before going out. The two of them sat in the chairs behind the detached garage. This was the first time they sat out there in the morning.

"There's this hot redheaded bartender I plan on abducting as my last DARK victim. I've wanted her so bad since I first saw her. Even if I weren't going to kill her, I'd still want to get some of that. She's so fucking hot, baby. I have the best plan for her."

"Hotter than me?" Amanda pouted.

"Nothing personal, but she's the hottest woman I've ever seen. I wish I could bring her home and keep her."

"What about me? Do you want to replace me with this bitch?"

"Don't worry, Mandy, I could never replace you."

"I hope not. I love you." A tear rolled down her face.

Joe realized Amanda was upset. "Don't be jealous. She'll be dead soon."

"You promise?"

"I promise. You're still my girl. I love you. I don't love her." They sat and talked for a while, and then they walked back to Amanda's room so he could lock her in.

Joe went back upstairs to tell Lisa he was leaving. "Have a great day. I'll see you later." He drove the car over to the detached garage to get his supplies out of the back of his truck.

Joe first went to the abandoned warehouse where he killed Sarah Kelly earlier in the year. He opened the rollup door, drove in, and closed it behind him. Opening the trunk, he pulled out a roll of masking tape, a paint pan, a paint roller, and a can of flat black, quick-drying paint. He found a spot between the shelves that had the room he needed. He made a large square with masking tape on the floor, in the middle of the aisle, and painted the inside of the square with the flat black paint.

After he left the warehouse, Joe drove down to Phoenix and bought some supplies for the weekend. He drove around to grocery stores to talk with the managers. He looked for commitments to help sponsor the mission's hot meal events all year. The managers of the stores all promised to support the mission by donating food. He quickly checked in at the Charity Mission and then returned to the warehouse.

He parked inside again and pulled out a two-inch-wide paint roller and a can of fluorescent red paint that he picked up while he was in Phoenix. He pulled up the masking tape and painted a large red circle in the middle of the black square. Then, he painted a pentagram inside the circle and added the number thirteen with a stencil in each space between the points of the pentagram.

This would be the thirteenth and final victim of his DARK persona.

He pulled out two battery-powered black lights and four leather bondage restraints. He tied the restraints to the bottom of four shelves by the outside points of the pentagram. He mounted the two black lights at the top of the shelves, one on each side of the aisle facing down. Joe then drove home to spend some time with his family before dinner.

"You get everything taken care of down in the valley today, Joey?" Lisa asked.

"Yep, it's all done until Saturday. Do we have any money left in the bank?" Joe asked. "Or should I ask if they had to close down the internet to restock it?"

"Of course we have money in the bank. Everything I ordered online is on a credit card," she laughed. "I'd have to buy the whole internet to spend it all, Joey."

"That's what I was afraid you were doing."

When they went to bed, Joe set a vibrating alarm on his phone for midnight. When his alarm went off, he went down to Amanda's room and told her he was leaving. She wished him luck, even though she still seemed jealous. He needed to get to the bar in Skull Valley before it closed at one.

Holly O'Reilly was a spunky, flaming red redhead. She always wore her hair in long, braided pigtails. Joe put on his DARK outfit and left in his truck. He pulled into the bar's parking lot, parked back in a dark corner and waited for Holly. She was the last one to leave the bar, locking it up before heading to her car. They were the only ones left in the deserted parking lot. When he saw her, he pulled his truck into the space adjacent to hers. He took his hood off and rolled down his window.

"Hi, I'm Pastor Joe."

"Hi, pastor. What are you doing here in the middle of the night? Looking for the devil?"

"Yes, I am. How'd you know?" he laughed. "I just want to talk for a little bit. Do you have a few minutes?"

"Sure. I'm Holly. It's nice to meet you."

Joe got out of his truck and walked up to Holly, holding out his hand to shake hers. "Please, call me Joe. That pastor stuff is my work. It's nice to meet you, Holly. How old are you, if I may ask?"

"I'm twenty-six."

"Twenty-six is double thirteen. People are superstitious about that number."

"Yeah, I don't know why. Hotels don't even admit to having a thirteenth floor. They go from twelve to fourteen. Like people don't know that's really the thirteenth floor."

Joe moved closer to her. She was stuck between her car and Joe's truck, with Joe blocking her escape route. On the other side of her was the wall of another business.

"Have a seat. I want to take you someplace to show you something special. It will only take a few minutes."

"Um...I don't know. I need to get home to my boyfriend."

Joe grabbed her and stuck a needle in her thigh. Holly screamed, "What the hell are you doing?"

Joe opened the passenger door of his truck and pushed her in. Holly tried to fight him off. She kicked and screamed. He held her down with his body. He held both her wrists with one hand while his other hand covered her mouth. She tried to bite him through his leather glove. He punched her in the face. Then, he put his hand back over her mouth. After several minutes, her struggle slowed down and then stopped.

Once Holly was unconscious, he closed the truck door and drove to the warehouse.

Parked inside the warehouse, Joe pulled Holly out of his truck. He left his headlights on so he could see. She started to move a little. He quickly carried her body to the aisle with the pentagram. He stripped her naked except for her bright red satin panties. He laid her down, secured her wrists and ankles with restraints, and then turned on the black lights. It was almost 2:00 a.m.

The fluorescent red paint, her flaming red hair, her red fingernails, and her red satin panties all glowed like they were on fire under the black lights. He walked back to his truck and turned the headlights off. The sky outside was dark and overcast. The only light in the warehouse now came from the black lights. He wrote 666 on her forehead with a fluorescent red marker.

Her head was at the bottom point of the pentagram, and her arms and legs were spread out in the other four points. He knelt down behind her head and lightly smacked her face. "Wake up, bitch." She was very disoriented. "God says you must pay for your sins."

"Uh...where are we, pastor?"

"You asked me if I was looking for the devil because you knew I was. You'll never repent. You must be punished. You in your flaming red panties covering that evil hole that gives you power over men."

"Power? What power? What's the hell's wrong with you?"

"You're the final one. You're number thirteen of the DARK murders. Look at the word devil. It's evil with a 'd' added on to disguise it."

Holly came around more. "Help! Help me!" she screamed as she struggled to get loose.

Joe smacked her face hard and reached into his bag for a roll of duct tape. He put a strip over her mouth and then stepped over her to grab his bag. He turned around and knelt between her milky white thighs. He grabbed her panties with both hands and pulled them as hard as possible. They easily ripped off, exposing her glowing red pubic hair.

Joe raped her. Holly screamed in pain through the duct tape. Joe reached orgasm after only several minutes.

He reached up and turned off both black lights. It was completely dark. Holly struggled and screamed. Joe quietly stepped back and leaned against the front fender of his truck, resting for ten minutes in the darkness. Once Joe recovered from round one, he quietly felt his way along the shelf the black light was attached to.

He reached across the aisle, grabbed the other black light, and turned them on simultaneously. After ten minutes in total darkness, the lights temporarily blinded her. It was too bright for her to see anything but purple light. He pulled the tape off her mouth.

"Pastor, I swear to God, if you let me go, I'll never tell anyone. Please pastor, I'm scared. Where are you?" He stayed silent. "Joe? Are you here?"

"Bride of Satan, you underestimate me. I know all your tricks. I'm here to make sure you get what's coming to you: eternal damnation."

He laid on top of her quivering body to rape her again. After he finished, he stepped over her and knelt behind her head. He grabbed her pigtails and crisscrossed them under her neck. They were long enough that he crisscrossed them again across the front of her throat and laid the extra length of hair out to the sides.

"What do you want from me?" Holly cried. "I want to go home to my boyfriend. I'll never say anything to anyone, I swear."

He grabbed the hair wrapped around her neck and pulled.

"Please don't kill me, pastor," she sobbed.

He increased the pressure. He strangled her with her own hair until she was unconscious. He let go and took out three plastic squeeze bottles filled with nitric acid.

Joe put them on the floor, put rubber gloves over his leather ones, and put on a gas mask. He took the cap off and replaced it with the nozzle it came with. He began between her legs. He stuck the nozzle up inside her and squeezed the bottle hard. The intense pain woke her. She screamed louder than ever as the acid burned her from inside.

He watched her writhe in pain, then filled up her belly button with acid to watch it bubble up as it ate away her flesh. He squirted acid on her nipples, then in her eye sockets, being careful not to get any on her forehead so the number 666 he'd written there would be preserved. Holly screamed in agony as the acid burned her everywhere.

He used two bottles and half of the last one, squirting acid all over her arms, legs, and body. He saved the last ounces to shoot down her throat. She screamed as he stuck the nozzle into her mouth and emptied it into her throat.

Her body involuntarily convulsed and jerked as the acid ate away her insides, her arms and legs still restrained. Joe walked over to his truck, took the gas mask off, laid on the back seat, and napped. When he woke up, he checked on Holly. She was probably dead before he even got back to his truck.

Her skin was extremely burnt and bubbled. The acid had burned all the way through her flesh in many spots. He left the black lights on. He knew it wouldn't be long before her body was found. He drove out of the warehouse. He went back and closed the roll-up door and locked it. When the police arrived, they'd have to use the side door. They'd see the complete impact of his work under the black lights.

THIRTY-ONE

KINKY SEX

The next night in bed, Lisa said, "I'm sorry for how things have been between us, Joey. I love you and want to be there for you. Can we work on being happy together again?"

"I would like that. I've missed feeling close to you, Lisa." They kissed and went to sleep.

The following day, the Romanos drove down to Phoenix. When they arrived at the mission, they saw Mark out front. Joe got out and yelled to Mark, "Hey there, stranger."

"Welcome. It's always nice to see you guys. Come on inside and have a drink."

They went inside and sat at a table. "Here's the check for the roof repairs that I promised you, Mark," Joe said, handing him one.

"Thank you very much, Joe. Who needs a drink?"

"What do you have?" Scotty asked.

"Well, I have Anita's homemade eggnog and..."

Scotty interrupted him, "Eggnog." Everyone agreed that sounded good.

"Eggnog all around," Mark said.

Anita came out of the kitchen carrying a tray of drinks. "I have some adult eggnog, too. There's a little something extra in them."

"I didn't even know you were here. It's nice to see you, Anita," Lisa said, standing up to hug her. "What extra do we get in ours?"

"Southern Comfort."

"Sounds good," Joe said.

Lisa took a drink. "This is yummy."

"Ours is too, Mom," Alexa said. "Can I have a little taste of yours?"

"Ok, but just a little taste."

"Dad, can I have a little taste of yours?" Scotty asked.

"When I'm almost finished. I remember you not wanting to give me my beer back."

"What's this? Scotty drank your beer, Joey?" Lisa asked.

"Oops," Joe laughed. "I let him have a taste one day."

"Just a taste? I guess that's okay."

After a while, Scotty finally got a taste of Joe's eggnog.

"Mark, we need to hit the road soon. We should all hit the head before we leave. Ladies and children can go first. I'm going to be a little longer than the rest of you."

After Lisa, Alexa, and Scotty finished using the restroom Joe got up and headed that way. "I'll try not to take too long, but I'll probably be a while."

"We know what that means," Lisa said.

"See you in an hour," Mark laughed.

He had seen pallets stacked up with five-gallon buckets of antifreeze in the workshop area the last time he was there. He pulled his leather gloves out of his pocket and put them on. He picked up two five-gallon buckets of antifreeze, took them into the walk-in refrigerator, and set them down. He went back for four more buckets, brought them into the refrigerator, and closed the door.

The first thing Joe did was to empty five gallons of the fruit punch into an empty five-gallon bucket and dump it down the sink, just outside the refrigerator. He did this with each of the four fruit punch dispensers. Opening the lids on all four of the larger drink dispensers, he poured five gallons of antifreeze into each fruit punch dispenser.

He did the same thing with the four smaller drink coolers, pouring two and a half gallons of the antifreeze into each of the twenty-five gallons of the baby formula, pouring the extra formula down the kitchen sink, and rinsing out the bucket. He picked up a wooden paddle they used to stir large pots of soup. He used the paddle to mix up the fruit punch, then rinsed it off and stirred up the baby formula. He rinsed the paddle off again and put it back where he found it.

He put the lids back on all eight drink dispensers and stashed the six empty antifreeze containers behind some of the full ones. *There should be a lot of people drinking punch with their Christmas meal. At least hundreds of babies will be drinking the baby formula,* he thought. One hundred gallons of baby formula and two hundred gallons of fruit punch were poisoned with antifreeze. *If this plan works, there should be so many less hungry mouths to feed and so many less homeless people on the streets.*

The downside was that Joe knew Mark and Anita might drink some punch. He wished he had a way of knowing how many people would die from the punch and baby formula. Joe finished using the restroom and came back out. All he needed to do was pee, but he let them think he took a dump.

"Boy, I was getting ready to send a rescue crew in there to dig you out," Mark laughed. "I guess it's a good thing you went before you left."

"You know what they say, when you gotta go, you gotta go," Joe said, shaking Mark's hand. "Best of luck, Mark. We'll see you soon. It's almost time for the Christmas meal."

"Yep, we'll be serving it on Christmas Eve. We're going to have a Santa here this year giving out gifts to the little ones under twelve," Mark said. "It should be a good year if we don't run out of gifts too soon."

After visiting with Mark and Anita, the family headed home.

The next morning, Lisa woke up with Joe cuddled up to her. "Good morning, love."

"Good morning. Have you been awake long?" she asked.

"Just a couple of minutes. I couldn't resist holding you close."

"Oh, Joey, you're so sweet. I love you," she said.

"I love you."

"I better get up and get the children off to school. You just stay here and relax while I take care of them. I plan on taking care of you when they're gone," she said.

Joe smiled, "I've tried harder to keep my grumpiness to myself."

"Why don't we work on that grumpiness together so we'll both be happier?"

"Get out of here. The sooner the kids are off to school, the sooner we'll be back together. Send them in here before they leave so I can hug them."

Joe laid back on the bed and thought about how special Lisa was to him. He felt like he was falling in love with her all over again but on a higher level.

What would happen to her and the kid's lives if they ever found out who I truly am? he wondered. He wondered if he was becoming what society would call normal, or at least closer to it than he'd ever been, except for having a sex slave in the basement.

But I'm in love with her, too, he thought. *I was supposed to kill her. Have I changed?*

Alexa and Scotty walked into the master bedroom. "Dad, I've never seen you just lay around in bed in the morning," Alexa said. "You deserve a break."

"I agree. You're always working on something." Joe sat up in the bed with a pillow on his lap and hugged Scotty. He didn't want either of the kids to see he was pitching a tent waiting for Lisa. "Have a great day at school, son. Behave yourself and stay out of trouble."

"I always do," Scotty smiled.

"Come here, Alexa." Joe gave her a hug and a kiss on the cheek.

"You have a great day at school, too. Get going, guys. You don't want to miss the bus."

"Okay, Daddy, I'll see you this afternoon if you're home," Alexa said.

"Yeah, Dad, see you later, alligator," Scotty said.

"After a while, crocodile," Joe responded.

When the kids left, Lisa ran up the stairs and jumped on the bed. "I feel so much closer to you than I have in a long time, Joey." She took her robe off and threw it on the floor.

"Same here, baby." He grabbed her and gave her a passionate kiss and hug. He let go, and Lisa immediately took off her top. Joe pulled her close for another hug. Her naked breasts felt good against his chest. While they were still hugging, he felt Lisa reach down and grab his cock. He reached down and repaid the favor by rubbing the crotch of her panties. He thought about what Amanda said about Lisa not being kinky. "Lisa, would you like to try a little kinky sex?"

"I guess if you want. You can play it by ear and do whatever you want." Lisa grabbed his cock and begged him to put it inside of her.

"I want kinky." He reached down between her legs, grabbed her panties, and ripped them off with one hard tug. Lisa gasped. "Stand up and bend over the bed." She did as he requested. She was already quite wet. He entered her from behind, slamming it hard on the first thrust. She screamed in pain and pleasure. He fucked her hard and fast for several minutes before slowing down a little. He took one of his hands off her thigh and smacked her ass hard, then slowly worked his finger an inch into her asshole.

"Joey!" she protested at first. He screwed her while he fingered her asshole. After the initial shock, she seemed to forget about what was where. He felt her about to have an orgasm when he stopped and pulled his finger and his penis out of her.

"Why did you stop, Joey? I was about to cum."

"I'm giving you kinky. Turn around and suck my cock." She did as he requested. Joe grabbed her by the back of the head and shoved his cock down her throat as far as she could take it and held it there for about ten seconds, then he pulled it out. Holding her head, he pushed it back into her mouth and slid it in and out.

"I love to fuck your face."

Every once in a while, he would push it all the way in as far as he could and hold it there for fifteen seconds at a time. After a while, he pulled his cock out of her mouth.

"Oh God, Joey! That was intense! I wasn't sure that I'd like it at first."

"Stand up and lean against the front window." The curtains were open, but the sheers were still over the glass.

"No, Joey, everyone will see."

"They won't know what they're seeing through the sheers if they even look up this way, but we'll be able to see them just fine because we'll be close to them looking down."

She shrugged and walked over to the window. "Put your hands up against it and spread your legs." As she spread her legs, Joe entered her from behind. They could see school kids walking by, the younger ones with their parents. These were their neighbors. The naughtiness seemed to turn her on even more. She had an intense orgasm within minutes. He fucked her as she had wave after wave of mini orgasms, one after another. Another fifteen minutes passed, and Joe ordered her to lay down on the bed, which she did. He climbed on top and directed his cock back inside her without using his hands.

As he moved in and out, he put his hands around her neck and squeezed just a little while he kissed her. He shoved his tongue deep into her mouth. As he pounded her harder, he squeezed her neck harder. She grabbed his wrists and tried to pull them away, but this only made him squeeze tighter. After a short time, he eased up.

"I'm cumming!" she screamed.

He squeezed hard again and grunted, "Me too!"

They both reached a tremendous orgasm together. Joe rolled off her, and they both just lay there for several minutes. They were both covered with sweat. Lisa broke the silence.

"Boy, Joey, I guess you do know kinky. I was scared whenever you came up with something different, but it all turned out to be awesome! I thought you were going to kill me towards the end."

"Lisa, I would never do anything to hurt you unless I just made it hurt so good."

"I trust you, Joey. I just got scared because we never did anything like this before. I'm okay now. It turns out that Mama likes kinky. That was awesome!"

"It sure was. Maybe it'll be your turn to come up with kinky things to do next time."

"I guess I better study up. I'm sure there are plenty of ideas online. I'm not sure if we can make love again today. You wore me out."

"No worries, baby. I'm worn out, too." Joe looked at the clock. "It's almost lunch time already. We've been in here longer than I thought."

"Any requests for dinner tonight, Joey?"

"How about spaghetti and meatballs with your cheesy garlic bread?"

"Sounds good. While you're out, could you pick up a couple of things?"

"Sure, baby. Make me a list."

"I planned on it. I know you never remember everything when you go without a list. I love you, but you can be a little forgetful sometimes, Joey."

"Yeah, getting older doesn't help my memory either." *Having so many murders to plan and taking care of my sex slave doesn't help my memory either,* he thought. "That's why I have you, to keep me straight. You kept me straight this morning. I think we both need a shower. What do you think?"

"Yeah, Joey, I know what you mean, but I think we better go solo. You take a shower while I fix us some lunch. Then I'll take mine. Is a salmon salad wrap good for you?"

"Perfect. Don't you go peeking in the shower at me," Joe laughed. He turned the shower on, and Lisa stayed in the bedroom. Once he got in, she peeked around the corner. Joe saw her and laughed. "Where's my wrap?"

"I'm on it," she laughed and walked out.

Joe finished his shower, dressed, and headed to the kitchen. He walked up behind Lisa and hugged her. She enjoyed the hug from behind, then turned around and kissed him.

"Your turn to get cleaned up, you dirty girl."

THIRTY-TWO
DYNAMITE

Once Lisa was asleep for the night, Joe went down to spend some time with Amanda.

"Do you still have that dynamite?" she asked.

"Yeah, I don't know what I'm going to do with it. I got ahold of a remote blasting cap. One of these days, I want to see if it's still good."

"I have an idea for it. Can I see it?"

Joe went to get it. He showed her the dynamite. It still had a condom over it.

"That looks like it would make a perfect dildo to rape someone with, then blow her up."

"Damn, what a great idea. I know a lady we can use it on. Want to go for a walk?"

"Now? Sure," she smiled.

"Not yet. I want to wait until the middle of the night, so hopefully, nobody will be out."

Amanda pulled Joe close to make out with him.

After midnight, Joe said, "Dress in a dark skirt and top."

"I'll be ready to go soon," she said excitedly. "I'll wear black stockings and shoes but no panties."

While Amanda changed her clothes, Joe dressed for the evening. While they got ready, Joe told her what he did to the drinks at the mission. The thought of possibly killing a lot of people at once seemed to turn her on.

"Tina lives one block over. She's going through a divorce."

Joe put the dynamite in his black bag. It now had two condoms covering it. They walked together hand-in-hand.

"It feels so good outside tonight. It's so quiet and peaceful. The air is fresh and cool," Amanda said.

When they arrived at Tina's house, Joe approached the front door. He had his lock picks, but he hoped to find an easier way in. He looked under the doormat. Nothing was there. There were several medium-sized rocks close to the door. He looked under the rocks. He found a spare key under the last one. He opened the door, set his bag down, and closed and locked the door behind them.

They heard a voice from the bedroom. "Hello, is somebody out there?"

Joe looked at Amanda and put his finger up to his lips. He crouched in the corner of the dark living room, waiting for Tina to come out. Amanda crouched down behind him. He had a chloroform-soaked rag ready. He threw Tina's house key across the room.

Tina came out to investigate the noise and walked right past him. He sprung up, grabbed her from behind, and held the rag over her mouth and nose. Amanda helped him hold onto her by grabbing Tina's legs. She struggled to get away for several minutes until she faded out. Joe carried her into her bedroom and set her down on the bed.

"Amanda, would you please strip her naked? I'll get my bag."

He came back and pulled out leather bondage restraints. Amanda attached the straps to her wrists and ankles as Joe attached them to the bed.

"Girl, this is your lucky night. I will be with you for the rest of your life," Joe said. "I'm even sharing my beautiful young girlfriend with you."

Amanda smiled. "I like you calling me your girlfriend." Joe gave Amanda a hug and kiss.

When Joe was completely naked, he climbed on top of Tina. He felt her naked body against his. Tina slowly regained consciousness. Reality slowly returned.

"Wha...what are you doing? Who are you?"

"Hi Tina, I'm Pastor Joe."

"What? Why are you..." Amanda quickly put her hand over Tina's mouth.

"Hold on, honey. I'll get you some duct tape," Joe said as he reached down and pulled the roll out of his bag. He put a piece of tape over Tina's mouth. Joe raped Tina as she struggled to get loose. Amanda played with herself while she watched. She took the bondage cuff off Tina's left wrist and rubbed Tina's hand between her legs.

Muffled screams filled the air. Amanda sucked on Joe's nipples as he reached orgasm. It all ended with Joe's most intense and longest orgasm he could remember in a long time. Between the skin-to-skin contact with a beautiful young lady and being able to rape her without a condom, as Amanda watched and helped him, it couldn't get any better.

Amanda put the bondage restraint back on Tina's wrist.

"We need to get home," Joe said. He took the condom-clad dynamite out of his bag.

Amanda took the dynamite from him and rubbed it on her crotch. Joe handed her a tube of lubricant. She put some on the end and slid it into her soaking wet pussy. She worked it in and out. Joe pulled it out of her. "Turn around and bend over, Mandy." He fucked her with it from behind until she was about to cum. Tina just stared at Amanda bent over her as Joe fucked her with the dynamite.

"Bite her neck, baby," Joe said. Tina cried hysterically.

"Yes, master," Amanda said, biting down on Tina's neck until she bled while Joe continued screwing Amanda with the dynamite. Amanda had a huge orgasm. "That was awesome, Joey! Thank you for sharing this with me." Amanda's face was covered in Tina's blood.

"You got it, my little sex slave. Get off her and wipe yourself off on the sheet really good. Make sure that you don't leave any of her blood on you."

"Yes, master." She licked her lips, tasting Tina's blood, then wiped her face on the sheet. Tina lay there with a look of terror on her face.

Amanda took the stick of dynamite, shoved it inside of Tina, and masturbated her with it. Joe pulled the duct tape off Tina's mouth.

"Please help me. My neck is bleeding. I'm so dizzy."

"You're dizzy from losing all that blood."

Joe got up and got dressed. While he was dressing, Amanda screwed Tina with the dynamite. She worked it in and out of her like it was a dildo. When she was finished playing with the dynamite, she left it deep inside her.

In the meantime, Joe was in the kitchen unscrewing the natural gas line to the stove. When he returned to Tina's bedroom, the smell of natural gas filled the air. He pushed the blasting cap into the end of the dynamite.

"No, no, no. God, please, don't! Help me! Oh God! No!"

Joe and Amanda left and quickly walked home together. They arrived back inside the Amanda's room. Joe pulled up an app on his phone and handed it to Amanda.

"Push this button to blow her up."

Amanda took the phone with a big smile on her face. "I get to do it? Thank you, baby!" She pushed the button on the screen.

Nothing happened for several seconds. Amanda looked at Joe with a questioning look on her face. Suddenly, a large explosion rocked the neighborhood.

"That was the most intense thing ever! Thank you. I'm a serial killer too now," Amanda said, sounding proud.

"You're welcome, baby. You may need to stay in your room for a while and be quiet if you hear anyone searching down here. I think this may have been a mistake, but it was fun. If law enforcement ever finds you, I want you to blame everything on me. Tell them I kidnapped you, and you're a victim. I won't be any worse off. I'll already be screwed. There's no sense in both of us going down. I've earned whatever I get. Just know, no matter what happens, I will always love you, sweetheart, forever!"

Joe headed upstairs to see if the blast woke Lisa up. They met in the kitchen. "Did you hear that explosion, Joey? What in the world was that?" Jerry, Vicky, and all four kids joined them in the kitchen.

"I don't know, baby. I was in the basement. I drifted off to sleep. That woke me up, and I ran up here to check on you," he said as he hugged her. "I guess we'll probably find out on the news tomorrow." After a while, they all went back to bed.

WITHIN SEVERAL MINUTES, there were sirens and flashing lights in Tina's neighborhood. There were four fire trucks, a paramedic ambulance, six police cars, and TV news trucks. Even Homeland Security and the FBI arrived on the scene pretty quickly. When the dynamite exploded, it ignited the natural gas filling the house. The explosion started a fire. What was left of the house was fully engulfed in flames.

All her neighbors were now outside. They watched the firefighters work to extinguish the fire and discussed what may have caused the explosion and fire. By the following day, the fire was out.

With the fire extinguished, the investigation began. They never found Tina's body. It had been splattered all over the room and burned away into the ashes.

A cell phone rang while the detectives were looking around the crime scene.

"Stone here."

"This is Ranger Kelly. I don't know if this is important, but I saw

Pastor Joe near that old condemned mine the same day that twenty-year-old girl disappeared. The mouth was completely caved in. I noticed fresh hammer marks on the beams. I think someone did this on purpose."

"Pastor Joe lives a block over from a crime scene we're working on right now. This information should give us enough to get a search warrant."

"Do you think Pastor Joe is responsible?"

"You never know. We have DNA from the hanging lady to try to match."

THIRTY-THREE

SEARCH WARRANT

T he next morning, after breakfast, Joe and Lisa sat in the living room by the fireplace with the Newharts. After lunch, they sat outside on the back patio, drinking wine coolers in front of a fire in the fire pit.

"Hey, do you guys want to play cards?" Lisa asked.

"Sure, do you play poker?" Vicky asked. "We like to play for money to make it more interesting if you guys are up to it."

Everyone agreed. The Romanos conspired to lose on purpose because they knew the Newharts could use the money. By the time they were finished playing cards, the Newharts had won $680 from the Romanos. They tried not to make it obvious that they lost on purpose, or else the Newharts would have won well over a thousand dollars.

At 6:00 p.m., the doorbell rang. When Joe answered the door, he was served with a search warrant by Detective Stone. Officer Kent and lab assistant Cindy Williams accompanied him.

"Why are they searching our house?" Lisa asked. "Do you think it has something to do with that explosion last night?"

"I don't know, baby."

"We checked just about everywhere," Detective Stone said. "We have one more place to look. What's behind this door, and where's the key?"

Alexa piped up, "That's the door to Daddy's basement office."

Joe gave Alexa a dirty look. For the first time, he was truly scared. Not for himself, but he didn't want his family and friends there in the middle of anything bad as it went down. He knew he had to do something fast to try to get them out of the house.

"Who has the key to the basement?" Officer Kent asked.

Joe thought hard but couldn't find any excuse to keep them from searching the basement.

"I do," Joe said.

He handed the key to Officer Kent, who unlocked both locks on the basement door. Detective Stone and Cindy followed Kent down the stairs with Joe a little way behind them. When they reached the bottom, they were surprised to find another door with two locks.

Detective Stone turned and saw Joe behind him. "Pastor, we need you to wait upstairs."

Joe turned and walked back upstairs. He felt like screaming but knew he had to keep his cool.

After searching the basement, the police left with Pastor Joe's desktop and laptop computers, several black hoodies, black leather gloves, boots and shoes, and a bag of scraps from the fireplace. They also took the clothes hamper from the house.

They never found his secret tunnel with the hidden wall safe, leather bag, and Amanda. The safe was where the most damning evidence was, like the sedatives and earrings from his victims. Amanda didn't even know about the safe.

"Before we go, we would like to get a DNA swab from each adult here," Cindy told them. She swabbed Jerry, Vicky, Lisa, and finally Joe. His was the main one they were interested in.

Back at the police station, they went through everything they confiscated from Joe's house and basement.

"Nicole, Caroline, check this out. Can you believe this?" Cindy asked.

"Oh my God!" Nicole and Caroline both gasped. "There's blood on this piece of leather we got out of the fireplace. Let's see what else we can find."

"We need to get a DNA profile from that blood," Caroline said.

"I'll get the piece of leather sent to the lab for DNA testing," Cindy said. "It already tested positive as human blood. Now we just need to find out who's blood it is. I'll make sure I get it there before I leave. Don't forget, I'll fly out tonight to see my mom for Christmas. I had a two-week vacation planned. I changed my plans because I know I'm needed here, so I'll be back in four days."

"We also sorted out all his dirty clothes from the hamper and sent them out for DNA testing. Hopefully, we can find some DNA on his pants or underwear that match even one of the victims," Nicole said.

"This may be bigger than we could have imagined," Nicole said fearfully. "We've had a number of young ladies disappear lately that haven't been found."

"Good work," Stone said. "Let me know what else you find. Shit, you never know what anyone is capable of."

"Gather any other information you come up with, and we'll head out to the Romanos tomorrow morning to bring Joe in for some formal questioning," Captain Connors said. "Get some rest tonight. We've all been working over sixteen hours today. The day after tomorrow is Christmas Eve. In the meantime, let's see what else we can find before talking to him. Put a rush on that DNA. Once we have that, we hopefully have the smoking gun we need for a good arrest. Rushed, the DNA results could still take weeks."

Detective Scott tapped Detective Stone on the shoulder, "Our IT guy, Jeff, has been going through Pastor Joe's computer. There are hundreds of porno movies. Most of them are rape and snuff movies. A lot of them start off with the woman being drugged."

"Shit!" Stone exclaimed. "What kind of pastor is this son-of-a-bitch?"

"That's not the only thing he found. This is a partial list of things he ordered online: twelve black hoodies, twelve pairs of black leather gloves, four rolls of duct tape, two quarts of chloroform, two battery-powered black lights, and the list goes on. There are searches on different ways to kill people. Jeff said if the letter postmarked from Alaska was typed on one of his computers, he could probably retrieve a copy on the drive even if he didn't save it. That could be another smoking gun."

"We'll go first thing in the morning to bring him in for questioning. We need to get warrants to tow his vehicles so we can search them while he's here. We'll hold off on arresting him until we get the DNA results unless he gives us something good in the interview. We need to find everything we can on this SOB before we arrest him to lock up this case. We need to make sure we dot every 'i' and cross every 't,'" Connors said.

"This will be a very high-profile case if we arrest the pastor. For now, we'll keep a stake out on him. This news will go international. We don't want to look like fools if anything is overlooked. We need to ensure it's an airtight case before spilling the beans. As far as we tell the media, Pastor Joe is a person of interest for now."

THIRTY-FOUR
ON THE RUN

Joe knew this was a big mistake. As soon as the police left, he got online on a burner phone and ordered two plane tickets to Atlanta, Georgia, for that evening. He just wanted to get the hell out of there before the police picked him up.

"Lisa, I have to fly to Los Angeles tonight for a very important conference," Joe informed her.

"What the hell? You're just telling me now? We have company. The day after tomorrow is Christmas Eve, Joey. Why do you have to go now?"

"I just found out about it a few minutes ago, honey. I feel bad leaving right now. I'll be back tomorrow. You think you can live without me that long?"

"You better be back before Christmas. This can't wait a couple of days?"

"No, it can't. I'll be back tomorrow, I promise."

"This is bullshit, Joey. You'd better be back tomorrow."

"I need to run down to my office for a minute. I'll be right back."

Joe ran down to tell Amanda what was happening. "I should've taken the time to think this out. I need to get the hell out of here, and

I'd like to take you with me if you want to come. If you don't, I'll just let you out."

"I want to be with you."

"Ok, get this suitcase packed with what you need, as long as it fits in this one suitcase." He handed her a small suitcase. I have to get back upstairs. I'll be back soon to get you. I love you, Mandy."

Unbeknownst to her, this suitcase had ten thousand dollars in hundred-dollar bills hidden in the liner. Joe also had a secret Swiss bank account with over six hundred million dollars that Lisa didn't know about.

The suitcase was just small enough that it could be a carry-on. Amanda packed some clothes. She smashed her favorite stuffed animal in the suitcase, making it fit. It was a small, pink teddy bear that she named Snuggles. She had Snuggles ever since she could remember.

Joe went upstairs to the master bedroom to get things prepared. He set out four juice glasses and four shot glasses. He filled the eight glasses with wine cooler.

He went back downstairs. "I want to explain why the police were searching our house. So, let's have a family and friend meeting upstairs in my bedroom," Joe said. "That means all the Romanos and the Newharts all need to come upstairs to my bedroom."

"Can't we talk in the living room?" Lisa asked.

"I have a little treat planned for everyone upstairs."

Everyone headed upstairs.

"First, we toast. Shot glasses for the kids and juice glasses for the adults."

Everyone picked up a glass. "When we toast, we drink it all down simultaneously." Joe held his glass up high. "Romanos and Newharts, best family and friends forever!"

Everyone held their glasses up and said, "Best family and friends forever!" They clinked their glasses together and drank the drinks straight down.

"That tasted good," Kevin said. "Can we have more sometime, dad?"

"We'll see, son," Jerry replied. "It was good."

"I want you all to sit on the bed so we can pray."

"So, what's up, honey?" Lisa asked. "Why were the police searching our house? Is something wrong?"

"No baby, nothing's wrong," Joe reassured her. "I just want to tell you all how special you all are and how much I love each and every one of you."

"I love you too, Daddy," Alexa smiled.

"We all love you dad," Scotty added.

"We love you guys, too," Vicky said.

Alexa and Kevin sat there looking into each other's eyes. Kevin had his arm around her.

"You know I love you, Joey. We all do." Lisa said. "Is something going to happen?"

"Thank you all for understanding that I have to leave town tonight. I want everyone to hold hands and bow their heads in silent prayer for a minute."

After a minute of silently praying, Makayla said, "I feel weird."

Jerry tried to stand up and fell back down on the bed. Vicky shook nervously for a few seconds, then calmed down as she slumped on the bed.

"No worries. You're just going to sleep for a while."

"Joey, did you drug them?" Lisa asked. "Did you drug us?"

Joe walked over and sat down on the bed beside her. "I'm only trying to help, baby."

"Trying to help with what, Joey?" Lisa started to sway.

Joe threw his arms around her and hugged her tightly. She hugged him back.

"I love you, Joey." Lisa kissed him. "I'll always love you, no matter what. I promise. I don't care what the police say."

Alexa said, "I feel kind of weird, too. Daddy, what's happen...ing? I'm dizzy." Alexa had trouble keeping her eyes open. "Daddy, was there something in that dri... drink you gave us? We didn't start to fe... feel weird until we...drank it."

"Me too," Scotty said, swaying on the bed. "I feel...uh..." Scotty fell over onto the bed.

"You're just going to sleep for a while," Joe said.

Lisa looked at him and asked, "What the hell did you d...do, Joey?" Lisa leaned over, not being able to hold herself upright. She slipped out of Joe's grasp as he hugged her.

"You guys just relax and sleep. We're all going to be together forever."

Joe leaned over and gave Lisa a long kiss. "Just sleep, my love, sleep in peace," Joe said as Lisa's eyes closed. Everyone was out cold. He kissed Scotty on the forehead. Then he kissed Alexa. "Sleep well, my little Lexi," he said, thinking about his nine-year-old cousin that began his lifetime killing spree.

"Maybe I'll see you all in heaven if there is such a place and if I could sneak in." Joe took Kevin's hand and put it in Alexa's hand. He did the same with Makayla and Scotty's hands and with Jerry and Vicky's hands.

He walked back around to the other side of the bed again. He sat Lisa up on the bed and hugged her. He didn't want to let go.

"I love you so much, my baby. You deserved so much better than me. If you only knew, Lisa. If you only knew."

He gave her another long kiss, then gently laid her down with all the rest of her family and friends. "Together forever," he whispered. He took Lisa's hand and put it in Vicky's other hand. "I don't want you to be all alone, baby," he said, knowing she couldn't hear him.

Joe headed downstairs. On his way down, he pulled out his cell phone and ordered fast food for him and Amanda and had it delivered. He grabbed a pre-packed suitcase he had stashed in the tunnel just in case of such an emergency. His suitcase had another ten thousand dollars in cash hidden in the liner, along with different IDs, passports, and Social Security cards.

He had two thousand dollars in cash in his pants pocket in case he needed money for anything right away. He couldn't use anything that could be traced, like a credit card. He would need to change his name and looks to start life in another part of the country.

He checked on Amanda. "Joey, you have to get rid of your family for your own good now. You can't leave witnesses." Joe hesitated, and then he headed back upstairs.

The now bone-dry Christmas tree had its lights plugged into a WIFI switch that Joe could turn on and off with an app on his cell phone from anywhere he had a signal. Joe stripped the rubber casing off the wires near the bottom and draped some tinsel over them. He had experimented with this idea a while back, down in the basement. He never envisioned using this on his own family. When he turned the power on, there were more than enough sparks to ignite a fire.

He looked at his phone and saw that his food was just down the street. He stuck his phone in his pocket and headed out front to wait on the porch. The driver pulled up, looked at Joe, and smiled.

"Hi, I'm Danielle, you ordered food from Arby's, right? You're Pastor Joe."

"Yes, I did, and yes, I am," Joe smiled back. "Nice to meet you, Danielle."

"Nice to meet you, pastor. Everybody calls me Dani."

"I have a deal for you if you want to make a lot of money tonight. I need a ride, but I don't want anyone to know I'm leaving or where I'm going. Of course, you're getting paid for the food delivery and a tip through the app. I don't know if you've heard, but I've had a lot of death threats lately. Don't look now, but did you see the car parked across the street when you drove up?"

"Yeah, that black car with dark tinted windows. How long has it been sitting there?" Dani asked. Joe knew it was an undercover cop staking out his house.

"Yes, that car. He's been parked there for hours. Don't look, but about fifty yards behind you is an old, detached garage. That car is facing the opposite direction from that garage. Log out of your app as if you're done working for the evening. Leave here like you normally would after making a delivery. Then turn around, come back, and pick me up on the other side of that detached garage. I'll pay you well in cash to give me a ride. Please don't tell anyone, okay?"

"Okay, pastor, I'll meet you there in a few minutes. Just because they disagree with what you preach is no reason for someone to kill you. I also drive for Lyft, so I'll log out of that app, too."

"Thanks a whole lot, Dani," Joe said.

Joe walked back inside with the bag of food and headed down to his office so he could use the tunnel to get to the garage. He headed out through the tunnel with Amanda in tow. He gave Amanda half of the money in his pocket to hold onto, so they each had a thousand dollars cash. When they got to the other side of the garage, they only had to wait about a minute before Dani pulled up with her headlights off.

The two of them sat in the backseat with the fast food, two extra-large sodas, and their suitcases. Joe told her to drive out of his neighborhood and would tell her his plan. Once they were out of sight of the stakeout, he had her pull into a parking lot to see if she would help.

"What I need is a ride for me and my daughter, Mandy, to Sky Harbor Airport in Phoenix. I need to get there quickly and incognito. I have to do something about the people who want to kill me. I'll give you a thousand dollars cash. Would you be willing to do this for me? If you don't feel comfortable, I understand."

"You want me to drive you down to Phoenix for a thousand dollars? That's a lot of money, pastor. Are you sure? It's only a two-hour drive round trip."

"I'll give you the cash up front if you'd like," he said. He pulled the cash out of his pocket and showed it to her. "I have to catch a plane for a crucial meeting."

"Ok, pastor, I'd be happy to drive the two of you there. A thousand dollars is way too much, though, pastor. I don't want to take advantage."

"Dani, I have more money than I could ever spend. I love sharing when I can." After a couple of minutes, he asked her, "How old are you?"

"I'm twenty-three, pastor. I'm doing this to save up. I'm getting married soon, and we'll need lots of money, especially if we want to start a family."

"Here's the thousand dollars I promised. That should help a little. Please call me Joe."

"Just hang onto the money until we get there."

Joe put the cash back in his pocket. He handed a turkey sandwich to Amanda from the bag. He ate his sandwich and curly fries while Dani drove. He had ordered two extra-large fries so they could share them with Dani, too. He also shared his drink with her after she ate some fries. They chatted most of the way there.

They talked mostly about sports. When they got to the airport, Joe told her to stop in the cell phone lot. A large digital board showed the status of all the flights and the gate where they would arrive.

As Dani parked her car, Joe looked at the board. "Looks like my flight has arrived already. They'll probably start boarding soon."

Joe grabbed Dani's arm and gave her a shot of succinylcholine.

"Pretty much instantly, you can't move, including the muscles your body uses to breathe. You can't even blink, though you can see. You're completely paralyzed, even though you can still hear me as you die of affixation. Too bad I don't have more time. I would have loved to fuck you. I had to make sure you never told anyone you drove me here, and you never have any babies."

Joe unbuckled Dani's seatbelt and pulled her over the seat into the back. He got out, tossed Amanda a hoodie, and sat in the driver's seat. Amanda put it on and sat in the passenger seat. Joe drove Dani's car to the long-term parking lot.

As he exited the car, he heard a lady say, "Is that you, Pastor Joe? Where do you think you're going?" He turned around to see Cindy Williams, the lab assistant who came to his home with the officers. She was right behind him. She was on her way to catch her flight to visit her mother. "You can't leave town now."

He grabbed her, spun her around, and put his hand over her mouth. She struggled and kicked him in the shin as he pushed her to the ground between the parked cars. She tried to fight him off. Amanda jumped on top of her legs as Joe held her body down.

He grabbed her neck and strangled her, digging his thumbs deep into her windpipe. While strangling her, he banged her head against the pavement several times. Soon, her eyes stopped moving. She stopped trying to fight him off. Her body went limp. He slid Cindy's dead body under Dani's car.

Looking around, he was satisfied no one saw or heard the struggle. They grabbed their luggage and walked to the terminal.

Joe went into the men's room and locked the door in a stall. While he was peeing, he opened the app on his phone and turned on the Christmas tree lights at home. He deleted the app and turned his cell phone off. He took the SIM card out. When he washed his hands, he also cleaned the phone. He left the back off so it would be full of water, ruining it. He wiped it down to get any fingerprints off it and threw it in the garbage. He left the burner phone in Dani's car.

Joe dropped the SIM card in a garbage can in the lobby, and they headed for check-in. He gave Amanda an extra hundred and twenty dollars, so they didn't both have the exact same amount of cash.

Soon, Joe and Amanda boarded the plane.

"As far as the police knew, I'm still at home," Joe whispered.

THIRTY-FIVE

CRASH LANDING

Once the plane leveled off, Joe and Amanda put headphones on to listen to music. They held hands, sat back, and closed their eyes for a relaxing flight.

I wonder if my family woke up in time to make it out before the house burned down, Joe thought as he drifted off to sleep and dreamt.

Joe was in bed with Lisa. It was very early Christmas morning. All four of the Newharts were on the bed, unconscious. Joe was wide awake. He sat up and looked around the dark room. He looked at the clock on the nightstand. It was 2:22 a.m. He shook Lisa. "Baby, it's 2:22. Wake up, Lisa. It's 2:22."

"Is that why you woke me up, Joey?" she asked, annoyed. "What does 2:22 have to do with anything?"

Joe stared at her. Suddenly, he blurted out, "It's 2:22 BITCH!" He lunged at Lisa with both hands around her throat. She struggled to no avail. Once she was unconscious, he let go of her neck. He ripped her panties off and raped her.

When she regained consciousness, she asked, "Joey, what are you doing?"

"Shut up!" he screamed. He choked her again until she was dead as he reached climax. He sat up and realized he had a gun in his hand. He had forgotten about the Newharts. Now, the Newharts sat on the bed and stared at him. He shot Jerry, Vicky, Kevin, and Makayla as they screamed, one bullet in the head for each. He looked at their dead bodies, then looked at his hand again. It was empty.

He looked around the room again. He realized he was no longer in his bedroom. He was in Scotty's room. He had both his hands around Scotty's neck. Scotty kicked and hit him. Joe squeezed harder. He pushed his thumbs into his son's windpipe. He let go and looked down. Scotty was dead.

He closed his eyes and shook his head. *What did I do?*

He opened his eyes. Everything was fuzzy. He rubbed his eyes. He saw he was in Alexa's room. He looked at his girl peacefully asleep. He said, "We all have to go." He leaned over, grabbed Alexa by the neck, pulled her up, and choked her until she was dead.

He opened his hands, and she fell back onto her bed. Her wide, open, dead eyes stared up at him. But it was no longer Alexa's eyes. It was his nine-year-old cousin, Lexi, staring up at him. Her eyes felt like they burned holes through him like lasers. He felt his head get hot from her stare. She screamed at him, "Why did you kill me? Why?"

He closed his eyes and screamed, "No!"

Over an hour into the flight. Joe woke up to his own scream. "Oh my God! It was a dream," he said. "That scared the hell out of me." He couldn't get how disturbing that dream was out of his mind. "What did I do to my family?" He put his hands over his face and shook his head.

"Are you okay, Joey?" Amanda asked. "What's wrong?"

The flight attendant rushed over. "What's the problem, sir?"

"Sorry, I just had a horrible dream. I'm alright."

Joe looked at Amanda and said quietly, "It was the worst dream I ever had. I killed all my family and friends."

"You still have me, Joey." She held his hand and kissed him. "Everything's going to be alright. It was just a dream."

The italic portion is internal thoughts.

"You're all I need," he said. "I love you, Mandy."

"I love you, too. I'll be back. I need to use the restroom." She got up and walked away.

Did the tree catch fire? Did they make it out in time? If they didn't make it out, were they still unconscious? The smoke would surely kill them upstairs before the fire could burn them up. Then we can be together forever because I'm their God, and I sent them to heaven. He shook his head, trying to clear his confusion. *I hope they made it out. I shouldn't have done anything that might harm them. It's too late now.*

These thoughts played over and over in his mind. He closed his eyes and slumped down in his seat. He quietly said, "I wonder if there is a God, a heaven and hell. If there is, I'm sure to go to hell. Or am I God? Am I his messenger, and I've really been doing his work? I must be God. God can't die." Joe's delusions were getting worse by the minute now.

Suddenly, the plane shook and bounced like it hit some extreme turbulence that lasted over two minutes. The lights went out several times. The turbulence stopped. Joe sat up. He felt the plane roll back and forth as they lost altitude.

A soothing voice came over the intercom, "This is your captain. Please remain calm. Stay seated and fasten your seatbelts. We'll be making an emergency landing. The flight attendants will help once we're safely on the ground. Brace for impact."

The two flight attendants went down both sides of the aisle to ensure everyone was prepared for a crash landing, with seatbelts buckled and their heads on their laps.

The plane vibrated hard. Joe looked out the window. He saw smoke coming out of the left engine, bursting into flames. People screamed. The fire disappeared. He looked out the window again. The left engine was gone. All he could hear over the passengers' screams was the right engine sputtering. Joe looked for Amanda. She hadn't come back from the restroom. Joe and Amanda's suitcases were at his feet. He didn't want to put them in the overhead with all that money in them. Joe held onto the handles.

The plane flipped to the left. One of the flight attendants landed hard on top of Joe. Then, the plane lurched to the right. The tip of the right wing hit a tree. The flight attendant flew off him. He watched her hit the luggage compartment so hard that it cracked her head open. Blood went everywhere, from her and several people, including the other flight attendant, who got banged around hard.

Most of the overhead compartments opened, and luggage flew all over. Out of the right-side window, he could see that the right wing had snapped off. The plane was down to one wing and no engines.

Joe saw the ground. There were rows of what little was left of old corn stalks as far as he could see, except for groves of fruit trees in the distance.

The plane touched down hard and bounced. When it hit again, there was the loud sound of metal cracking. People prayed out loud. It bounced a third time. This time, Joe saw a noticeable crack around the middle of the fuselage.

The fourth time, it hit extra hard. The plane broke in half, the front end spun off to the right and exploded in the grove of trees. The tail section slid straight ahead to a hard stop in the middle of the field over a thousand yards past where the cockpit burned. The huge opening was packed with pieces of old corn stalks.

Some of the passengers in the front part of the back half of the plane who were still alive as they touched down were smothered by thousands of remnants of old corn stalks jammed in their faces.

Once the fuselage stopped, passengers pushed through the pieces of old stalks and streamed out of the opening. They ran through a growing fire as fast as they could. People stepped on and over bodies in front of them. Most people in the tail section were still alive, except for those at the front of the opening and the flight attendants. A huge explosion sounded. Not everyone in the tail section that was still alive made it far enough away before the plane exploded.

Within twenty minutes, rescue choppers arrived. A total of one hundred eighty-seven people, including passengers and crew, had been on the plane. The FAA investigation lasted several weeks in the field and several months in the hangar. Their findings showed that the crash was caused by mechanical failure due to a lack of proper maintenance combined with extreme turbulence.

The maintenance records showed the planes hadn't received the federally mandated maintenance that they should have. The FAA shut down the entire airline. They ordered that each of the company's planes have a thorough inspection monitored by federal aviation agents before they were allowed to fly again.

One hundred thirty-three people were confirmed dead in the crash. Thirteen people were seriously injured, including a few who lost limbs. Thirty-seven lucky people made it out without any life-threatening injuries.

EPILOGUE

Amanda Barns woke up. A nurse stood over her as she opened her eyes.

"What happened? Where am I?"

"You're in the hospital. You were in a plane crash last week," the nurse said. "You got a nasty concussion, but the doctor thinks you'll be all right. Your leg got pretty banged up."

"Did anyone else survive?"

"Over thirty people survived. You were lucky to be in the rear restroom. It was just about the only thing they found somewhat intact. Is there family we can call for you?"

"No. I don't have anybody." Amanda lay there wondering if Joe had survived the crash. She was afraid to ask. She noticed her left ankle and foot were in a cast. Her head ached. She drifted back to sleep.

She had only been in the ICU for four days before they moved her to a private room. They kept her in the hospital for a few months for physical therapy and observation. They ran many tests to ensure no serious internal injuries or complications from the concussion.

She still wondered where Joe was. *Did they find him and arrest him? Was he dead?* She wondered. She wished he was there.

When she was released from the hospital, the airline flew her back to Phoenix. She was extremely nervous about flying again, especially by herself. At least she was unconscious during the crash. She had been knocked out when the turbulence began. All she knew was she missed Joey. The airline got her a ride from Phoenix to Canyon City so she could move back into her old house.

She asked the driver to drive by where she had left her aunt's car many months ago. It still sat there with the keys in the ignition. She got in and tried to start it, but the battery was completely dead. The driver gave her a jump. The car started right up. She drove herself the rest of the way home.

She had a place to live, a car, and eleven hundred-twenty dollars cash in her pocket. It wasn't too long after she arrived home that the airline settled out of court with her for $500,000.00 for her pain and suffering and her lost luggage. They also paid all her medical bills.

The Canyon City Police Department never investigated Amanda Barns. A mistake on the manifest showed her sitting in a different seat. The woman that the manifest showed sitting in her seat was found dead. The investigators assumed she was Joe's companion. They ran her DNA. It didn't match any DNA in CODIS.

When all the bodies and body parts were identified, there were one hundred and eighty-three people accounted for out of the one hundred and eighty-seven registered passengers and crew. Some only had a piece of their body found in the wreckage that had to be identified through DNA. No trace was ever found of four people. They were assumed to have been at the point of the explosion.

One of those four was a passenger registered as Anthony Marino. This was the same alias he had been known to use several times to book flights and hotel rooms. His friends, family, and the rest of the world knew him as Pastor Joseph Romano.

THE END?

(Schrödinger's Cat)

ABOUT THE AUTHOR

Louie Nunziato graduated from writing songs and short stories to writing his first novel during the Covid-19 crisis. From the lockdown in his home in Phoenix, Arizona, he embarked on this new phase of writing thanks to the help and guidance of his editor and mentor, Troy Lambert. When he's not writing, you can find him in his recording studio with a band or playing one of his many guitars. With five kids and eight grandkids, it can sometimes be hard to find the time for much more.

If you enjoyed this book, you should read the sequel Dark Murders 2 / Creeper. It will answer the question of what really happened to Paster Joe.

www.ingramcontent.com/pod-product-compliance
Lightning Source LLC
Chambersburg PA
CBHW052022020726
47501CB00004B/1196